PUFFIN BOOKS

BBC CHILDREN'S BOOKS

UK | USA | Canada | Ireland | Australia
India | New Zealand | South Africa

BBC Children's Books are published by Puffin Books, part of the Penguin Random House group of companies whose addresses can be found at global.penguinrandomhouse.com.

www.penguin.co.uk www.puffin.co.uk www.ladybird.co.uk

First published 2024
001

Written by Tim Dedopulos and Dave Knowles
Puzzles set by Roland Hall
Illustrations by David Moreno Buisán

Printed and bound in Great Britain by Clays Ltd, Elcograf S.p.A
The authorized representative in the EEA is Penguin Random House Ireland, Morrison Chambers, 32 Nassau Street, Dublin, D02 YH68

A CIP catalogue record for this book is available from the British Library

ISBN: 978–1–405–97184–3

All correspondence to:
BBC Children's Books
Penguin Random House Children's UK
One Embassy Gardens, 8 Viaduct Gardens
London SW11 7BW

Penguin Random House is committed to a sustainable future for our business, our readers and our planet. This book is made from Forest Stewardship Council® certified paper.

BY TIM DEDOPULOS, ROLAND HALL AND DAVE KNOWLES

PUFFIN

Contents

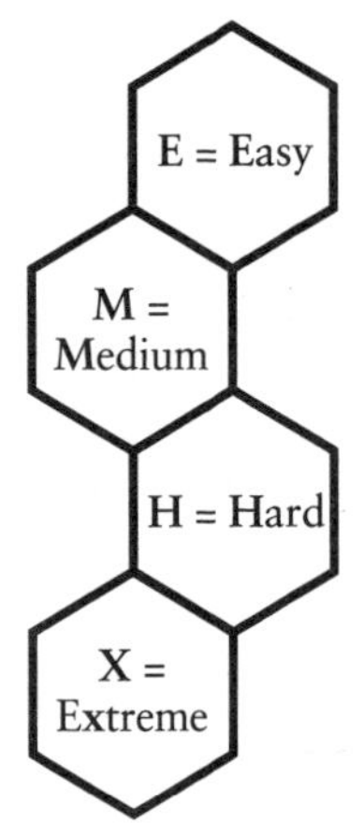

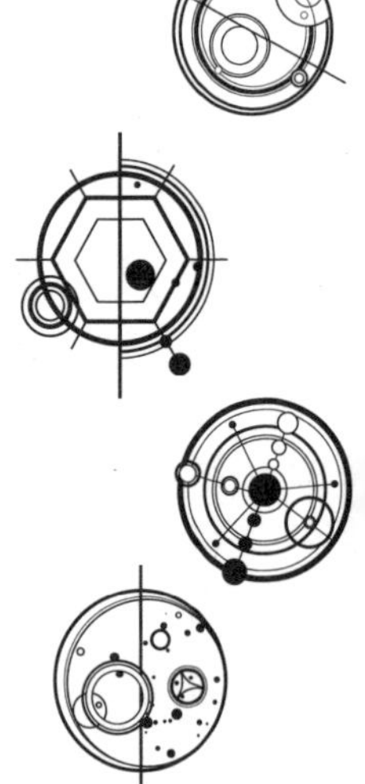

Contents

Introduction

One of Britain's great contributions to science fiction, *Doctor Who* is a part of global culture. It has given us instantly recognisable images such as the Daleks and the TARDIS, and almost every sci-fi fan knows that the Doctor is a mysterious alien who travels through time and space protecting the good and the innocent.

Fittingly, the origins of *Doctor Who* are almost as mysterious as the Doctor's own history. We do know that legendary Canadian producer Sydney Newman came up with the basic elements of the show, including the Doctor and the TARDIS. But many others were critical to the Doctor's true birth – Donald Wilson, CE Webber, Verity Lambert, David Whitaker, Terry Nation, Ron Grainer and Delia Derbyshire, to name a few.

Over the course of this book, you'll be taken on a whistle-stop tour of the Doctor's history and companions. There are puzzles in here representing a wide selection of the Doctor's notable adventures, and including all of their incarnations.

While the puzzles are all inspired by specific story lines, it's best if you think of them as taking place in a parallel dimension one jump over. There's lots of reasons why we have to deviate a little from canon, ranging from making the answers too obvious through to the mechanical demands of crafting a fun puzzle to solve. We have kept as true to established facts as possible though, so please forgive us our little liberties.

If you're not familiar with solving logic-grid puzzles, the next few pages will explain the principles – refer back to it any time you need to.

Most importantly though, have fun!

– The authors.

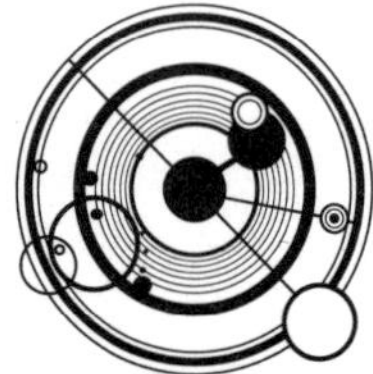
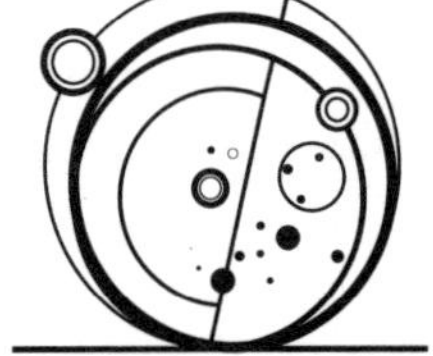

How to Solve

A logic-grid puzzle presents you with several lists of similar things – people, places, times, concepts, colours and more. Each of these lists has the same number of pieces, which, for people, could be the Doctor, Ruby and Rose, as in the example below.

The puzzle is to sort all the different pieces into groups. Each group is made up of exactly one piece from each list – for example, the Doctor, the TARDIS and the sonic screwdriver. No piece is used twice, so you end up with the same number of groups as the number of pieces in one list.

To help you figure out which pieces from the different lists go together in correct groups, you have clues and a grid. The grid is always arranged in blocks, so that every piece in each list can be compared against every piece in every other list. This lets you record the information in the clues, and quickly see, for example, which person is in which place.

	The Doctor	Ruby	Rose	TARDIS	UNIT HQ	Big Ben
Sonic screwdriver						
Psychic earring						
Time window						
TARDIS						
UNIT HQ						
Big Ben						

In the grid above, you can see that the puzzle it is for has three lists: people, places and tools. The blocks are set up as 3x3 squares, and so one block compares people with places, one compares people with tools and one compares places with tools.

Typically, when you know that two pieces go together in the same group, you find the box where those two pieces intersect, and put a tick in it. Similarly, when you know that two pieces do not go together, you find the box where they intersect and put a cross in it.

So if the clues tell you that the Doctor and the TARDIS go together, but Rose and the psychic earring do not, your grid would look like this:

	The Doctor	Ruby	Rose	TARDIS	UNIT HQ	Big Ben
Sonic screwdriver						
Psychic earring			✗			
Time window	✓					
TARDIS						
UNIT HQ						
Big Ben						

One important thing to remember is that each group has just one piece from each of the category lists. So if the Doctor is in the TARDIS, that means that Rose and Ruby are not in the TARDIS, and also that the Doctor is not at UNIT HQ or Big Ben. So each time two pieces definitely go together, you also find out where pieces cannot.

	The Doctor	Ruby	Rose	TARDIS	UNIT HQ	Big Ben
Sonic screwdriver						
Psychic earring			✗			
Time window						
TARDIS	✓	✗	✗			
UNIT HQ	✗					
Big Ben	✗					

These two types of information can work together to show you when two other pieces have to be linked. For example, in the grid above, you can see that Rose is not using the psychic earring. So let's say that you then learn that the Doctor is using the sonic screwdriver, and mark that in along with the options it rules out.

	The Doctor	Ruby	Rose	TARDIS	UNIT HQ	Big Ben
Sonic screwdriver	✓	✗	✗			
Psychic earring	✗		✗			
Time window	✗					
TARDIS	✓	✗	✗			
UNIT HQ	✗					
Big Ben	✗					

Now when you look at the grid on the previous page, you'll see that Rose is not using the sonic screwdriver, but she is also not using the psychic earring. That means she has to be using the time window, and that only leaves the psychic earring for Ruby to be using. So although no clue has told you anything about Ruby's tool, you know which one it has to be. You can use all the information to complete the grid, and then fill in the answer diagram, as below. Each puzzle has a main question to answer, so indicate that by drawing round the correct shape too.

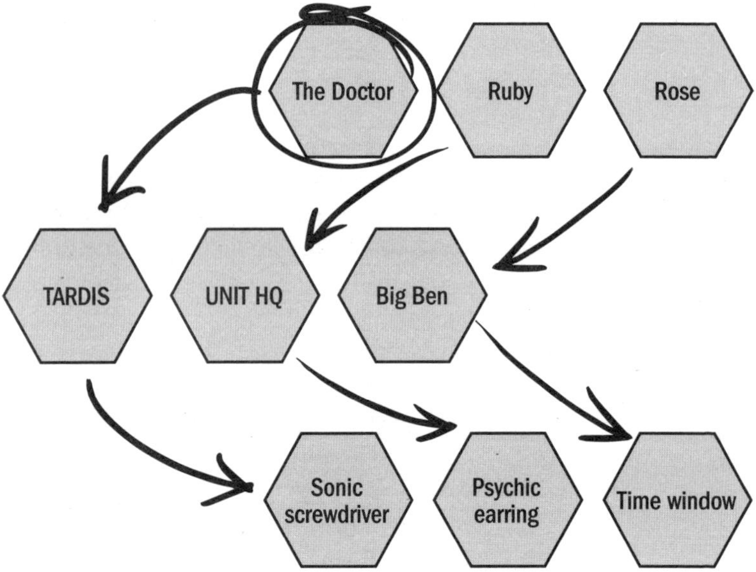

The Doctor
Ruby
Rose

TARDIS
UNIT HQ
Big Ben

Sonic screwdriver
Psychic earring
Time window

And that really is all you need to know in order to solve logic-grid puzzles in general, and the ones in this book in particular.

The puzzles herein are split between easy (three lists of three pieces), medium (three lists of four pieces), hard (four lists of four pieces) and extreme (five lists of five pieces). The extreme grids will look daunting at first, but don't be put off – they work using the same principles as in this example. It just takes more blocks (of 5x5) to make sure each piece can be compared to each other.

Each puzzle in this book contains information about the puzzle's setting and a question; a correctly labelled logic grid of the right size; facts about each piece in each list; details that tell you how certain pieces do or do not fit together; and a block of hexagons – one for each piece – that you can use to track your final answer by drawing links.

Although the details are definitely the primary clues, you are going to need to refer to the facts given in the puzzle as well. For example, a clue might mention the heaviest object, so you'd need to refer to the facts about the list of objects to see which one that is.

You'll also need to link information together in the more complex puzzles. For example, you might know that the Doctor is in a cafe, and that cafe has a power cut. You might then discover that the place with the power cut is not going to be flooded. With this information, you can then work out that the Dcotor is not going to be flooded, and knowing this might be a vital piece of information to solving the puzzle.

As long as you keep your grid up to date by thinking about the implications of each new piece of information and how it slots into everything else you know, you'll be absolutely fine.

As the book goes on, the puzzles get tougher – for example, the detailed clues get a bit more difficult to untangle. In some places – particularly the last section – we'll even ask you to solve a small word or number puzzle first in order to fully understand a few of the clues.

Take heart! All the puzzles can be completely solved without any guesswork or prior knowledge of *Doctor Who*.

Happy puzzling!

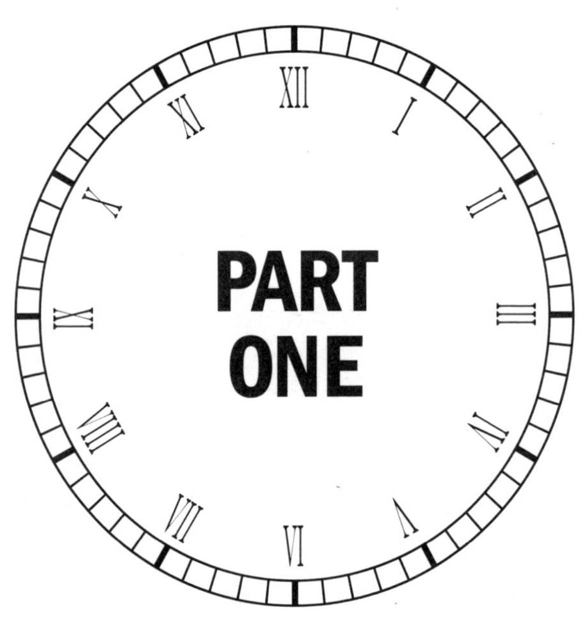
PART
ONE

THE FIRST DOCTOR
THE SECOND DOCTOR
THE THIRD DOCTOR

The Daleks

Details:

The anti-radiation drugs are in the petrified jungle or the Thal camp.

?

The poisonous metal was last seen outside, surrounded by stone.

?

Nuclear weapons are the province of science.

?

It wasn't Barbara who thought of trying anti-radiation drugs.

?

The best potential weapon was found by the most chronologically uncertain companion.

Puzzle 1: Easy

Landing for the first time on the planet Skaro, the Doctor and his companions find themselves in a peculiar stone jungle. The futuristic city visible beyond the forest is the home of the Daleks. A formerly humanoid race horribly mutated by radiation, they move around in heavily armed travel machines. They are hell-bent on the extermination of all other life on Skaro. Their particular enemies are the still-humanoid Thals, whom they have been warring with for a thousand years.

As part of their efforts to save the Thals from the Daleks, the Doctor asks his companions to think about possible weapons that they might be able to use against them. Can you figure out who correctly identified a possible weapon, and where it is located?

Using the clues opposite and overleaf, fill in the grid on page 17 to work out who identified what, and where. Then draw lines below from box to box to show your answer. Finally, circle the box with the name of the person who correctly identified the weapon.

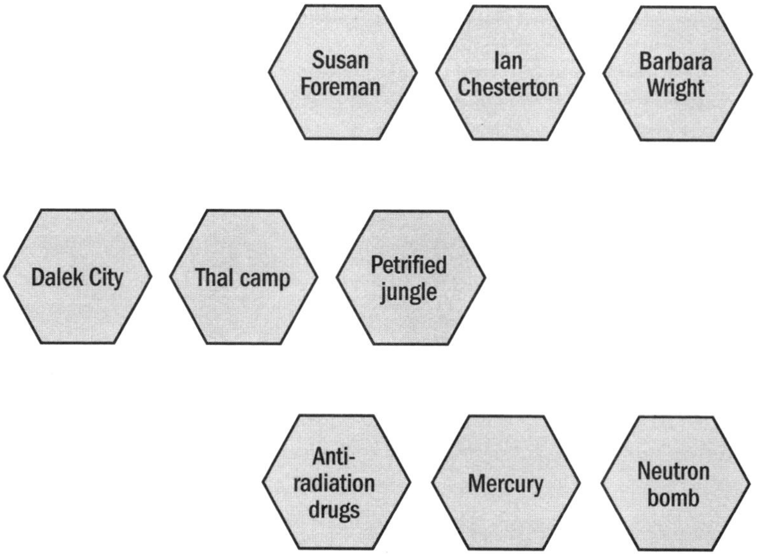

The Daleks

Who was involved · Where they were · What was used:

Susan Foreman: The Doctor's granddaughter. She has been travelling with him in the TARDIS for quite some time. She is said to have multiple, equally valid dates and places of birth across Gallifrey's history. Five foot one inch tall, black hair, green eyes.
Ian Chesterton: Science teacher at Susan's school. Trying to puzzle out the truth behind his mysterious student leads him to travel with the Doctor. Six foot tall, black hair, blue eyes.
Barbara Wright: A teacher at Susan's school who is as curious about her as Ian is, and meets the same fate. Eventually, she and Ian left the TARDIS and got married. Five foot nine inches tall, brown hair, blue eyes.

The Dalek City: Interior. A futuristic maze of metal corridors populated by murderously genocidal mutants riding around in death robots. Still, it could be worse.
The petrified jungle: Exterior. Also a futuristic maze, but of razor-sharp stone. Not much life, apart from the occasional Thal looking for food. Nicer than the Dalek City.
The Thal camp: Exterior. Not actually a maze. Populated by the Thals who, although hungry, are much better company than the Daleks. If you simply must visit Skaro at the end of the neutronic war, this is the place to pick.

Anti-radiation drugs: A serum concocted by the Thals to fight the effects of radiation poisoning. Vital for life on Skaro in the aftermath of the neutronic war.
Mercury: The only pure metal that is a liquid at room temperature and pressure. Highly poisonous to many Earth species. Famous for driving hat-makers mad.
Neutron bomb: A lethally dangerous nuclear weapon that uses radiation rather than explosive force as its primary means of destroying enemies.

Fill in the grid below as you work through the clues.

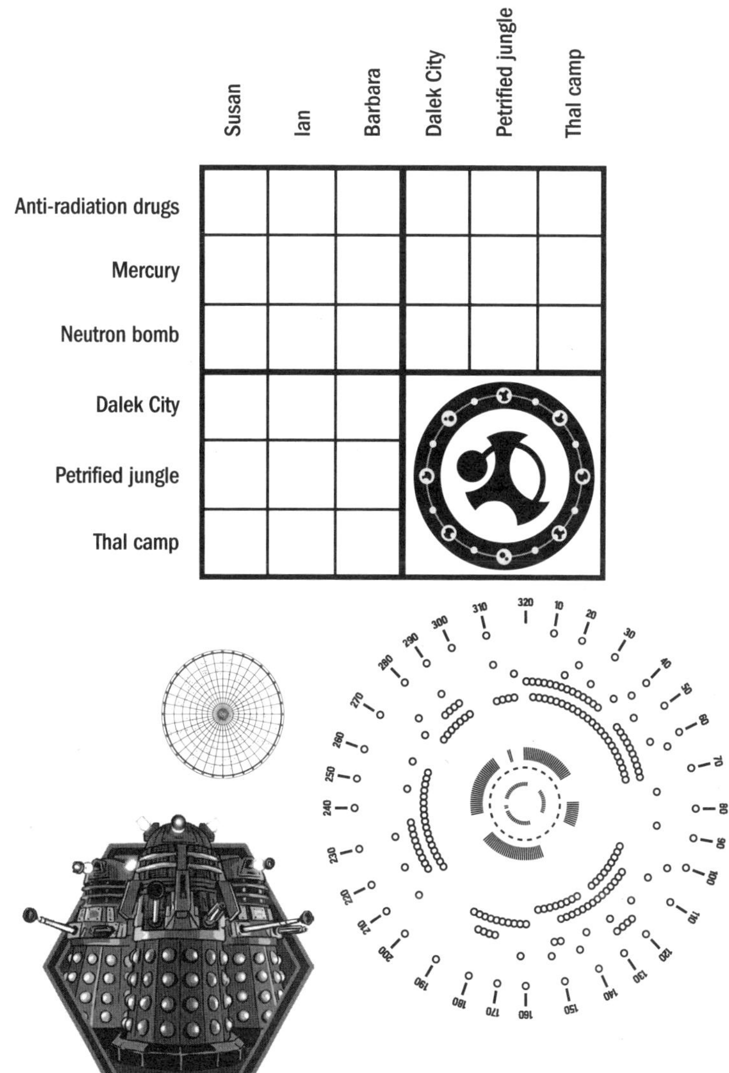

	Susan	Ian	Barbara	Dalek City	Petrified jungle	Thal camp
Anti-radiation drugs						
Mercury						
Neutron bomb						
Dalek City						
Petrified jungle						
Thal camp						

The Myth-Makers

Details:

The plan with the greatest variety of vowels is not suggested by someone with dark hair, and it is not associated with the Dardanian Gate.

?

Vicki, who the Trojans mistook for a prophetess, feels good about the Temple of Athena.

?

The Doctor does not feel pulled towards the Lower City, and Steven does not suggest slipping through the Dardanian Gate.

?

The Lower City is not a place for subterfuge.

?

It makes sense that the shortest person is drawn towards remaining unseen.

?

The most successful plan involved an important building, but it was not sneaky.

Puzzle 2: Medium

Having become mixed up in the final stages of the Trojan War, the Doctor and his companions Vicki and Steven are trapped in the city of Troy. The Trojan Horse has been brought inside the walls, so the city is filled with Greek and Trojan warriors fighting.

With the help of Katarina, one of Cassandra's handmaidens, the group plans to escape the destruction of the doomed city. Can you deduce who comes up with which plan and escape route, and which has the best chance of success?

Using the clues opposite and overleaf, fill in the grid on page 21 to work out the solution. Then draw lines below from box to box to show your answer. Finally, circle the box containing the name of the person who came up with the best plan.

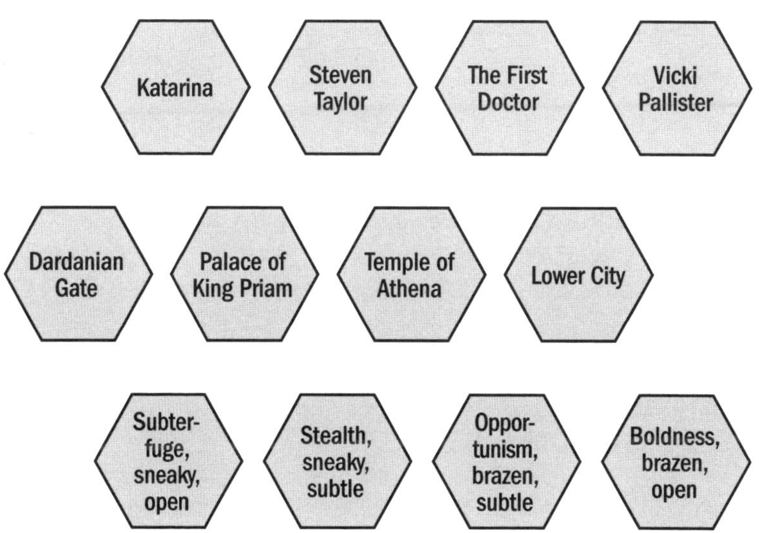

The Myth-Makers

Who was involved · Planned route · Style of escape:

Katarina: Having been lifted out of poverty by the Seventh Doctor as a child, Katarina joined the Doctor after the fall of Troy. She believed the TARDIS was a portal to the afterlife. Was she all that wrong? Five foot five inches tall, brown hair.
Steven Taylor: An ace pilot of space fighters from the twenty-fourth century. On his twenty-first birthday, he was shot in the legs by a space pirate. Not the best coming-of-age gift. Six foot one inch tall.
The First Doctor: An aging Gallifreyan Time Lord with a grumpy streak. Often mistaken for a god. Five foot eight inches tall.
Vicki Pallister: A brilliant twenty-fifth-century Earth orphan who grew up in New London and met the love of her life, Troilus, on this adventure. Five foot two inches tall.

The Dardanian Gate: Exterior. One of the six massive gates of the city. Usually well-defended, but it might be possible to slip out.
The Palace of King Priam: Interior. Kings are well-known for having handy hidey-holes that lead to safe places, particularly in troubled times.
The Temple of Athena: Interior. Where safer to escape the collapse of a city than in the arms of the gods? It is at the heart of Troy though, at the top of the hill it's built on.
The Lower City: Exterior. The poor always live in the smallest homes, and the warrens of the lower city are a good place to get lost in. Are they good to escape from, though?

Subterfuge, sneaky, open: Grab some disguises, keep your hair covered, and always, always walk as if you own the place. What could possibly go wrong?
Stealth, sneaky, subtle: Stick to the shadows, walk softly, try to move when no one is looking. Sometimes the old ways are the best.
Opportunism, brazen, subtle: Look for patches of maximum chaos, try to dash past people who are already busy fighting for their lives.
Boldness, brazen, open: You're someone else's problem, right? Don't sweat it. Just make calmly for your chosen destination.

Puzzle 2: Medium

Fill in the grid below as you work through the clues.

	Katarina	Steven	The First Doctor	Vicki	Dardanian Gate	Palace of King Priam	Temple of Athena	Lower City
Subterfuge								
Stealth								
Opportunism								
Boldness								
Dardanian Gate								
Palace of King Priam								
Temple of Athena								
Lower City								

The War Machines

Details:

The reliable, protracted investigation suggests that WOTAN will strike at first light.

?

Dodo believes that that the attack will come at sunset, while Ben thinks it will be six hours later, give or take.

?

The Doctor is investigating with the aid of the TARDIS's sensors and equipment.

?

Polly is not investigating from her place of work, but she is basing her estimate on her access to data.

?

The person in the nightclub is making an educated guess.

?

A lengthy, non-logical investigation suggests that midnight is the right time.

?

The correct time was actually discovered by the person investigating in the second-oldest location.

Puzzle 3: Hard

When the Doctor arrives in London in 1966, the TARDIS lands near the Post Office Tower. Investigating the circular, glass-fronted building, they meet Professor Brett, the creator of a powerful new computer called WOTAN (Will Operating Thought ANalogue). WOTAN was designed to centralise control of the world's computers on C-Day, but the Doctor discovered that it had decided humans needed purging. To that end, it built a series of robotic War Machines.

Can you uncover who correctly deduced when this plan was to be put into action, with information gained from which location, and using what deductive method?

Using the clues opposite and overleaf, fill in the grid on page 25 to work out the correct solution. Then draw lines below from box to box to show your answer. Finally, circle the box containing the time WOTAN is planning to act.

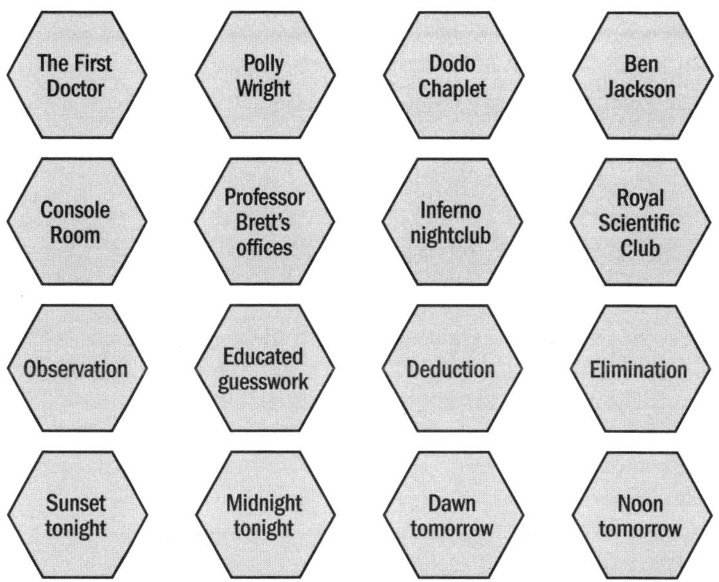

The War Machines

Who was involved · Where it takes place · How it was done · Timing:

The First Doctor: A centuries-old Time Lord prone to tripping over his tongue. A little stern, but very fond of his companions.
Polly Wright: A former model from Chelsea who works as Professor Brett's assistant. She briefly met her older self (and the Second Doctor) at the age of six.
Dodo Chaplet: A teenage runaway who was brought up by her distant great-aunt. Real name Dorothea, rather good at tennis.
Ben Jackson: Ben joined the Royal Navy at the age of fifteen, rising to Able Seaman before deciding to travel with the Doctor in 1966.

The Console Room: Inside the TARDIS. Where the Doctor has spent most of his time for centuries, when he's not outside exploring.
Professor Brett's offices: High in the new tower. There's a panoramic view across all of London. Don't the people look small?
The Inferno nightclub: A plush nightclub in Covent Garden, run by a woman named Kitty. She introduced Dodo and Polly to Ben.
The Royal Scientific Club: A well-respected institution based in a tasteful Victorian building, the Club is run by Sir Charles Summer.

Observation: You can't beat having unusual levels of access to the right data. Well informed is well prepared! Logical. Fast.
Educated guesswork: Many of the finest breakthroughs in human endeavour have been educated guesses. It's not luck, it's vast amounts of study, experience and talent. Intuitive. Fast.
Deduction: Given enough data, patterns can become visible. Following these patterns can reveal all sorts of information, and it's usually extremely reliable. Logical. Slow.
Elimination: When you have eliminated the impossible, as Sherlock Holmes was fond of saying, whatever remains, however improbable, must be the truth. Intuitive. Slow.

Sunset tonight.
Midnight tonight.
Dawn tomorrow.
Noon tomorrow.

Puzzle 3: Hard

Fill in the grid below as you work through the clues.

	The First Doctor	Polly	Dodo	Ben	Observation	Educated guesswork	Deduction	Elimination	Console Room	Brett's offices	Inferno nightclub	Royal Scientific Club
Sunset tonight												
Midnight tonight												
Dawn tomorrow												
Noon tomorrow												
Console Room												
Brett's offices												
Inferno nightclub												
Royal Scientific Club												
Observation												
Educated guesswork												
Deduction												
Elimination												

The Abominable Snowmen

Details:

The person interested in the Abbot's chambers is of middling height.

?

The Holy Ghanta does not belong in the Yeti cave.

?

Victoria is not considering the coldest location.

?

The lightest object is associated with the most prestigious location inside the monastery.

?

The correct solution was found by the blue-eyed human.

Puzzle 4: Easy

The Yeti of the Himalayan mountains are peaceful creatures, shy of contact with humans. Arriving near the Det-Sen Monastery in 1935, the Doctor is astonished to find it besieged by the creatures. People have been killed, and the monks fear that they might have to evacuate.

The Doctor discovers that the Yeti are actually robots that look like the real creatures. They're being controlled by the Great Intelligence, an eldritch being from beyond the borders of reality. To foil its plans, the Doctor and his companions have to find a way to stop the robot Yeti. Can you deduce who has identified the right tool and where to use it?

Using the clues opposite and overleaf, fill in the grid on page 29 to work out the solution. Then draw lines below from box to box to show your answers. Finally, circle the box containing the right tool.

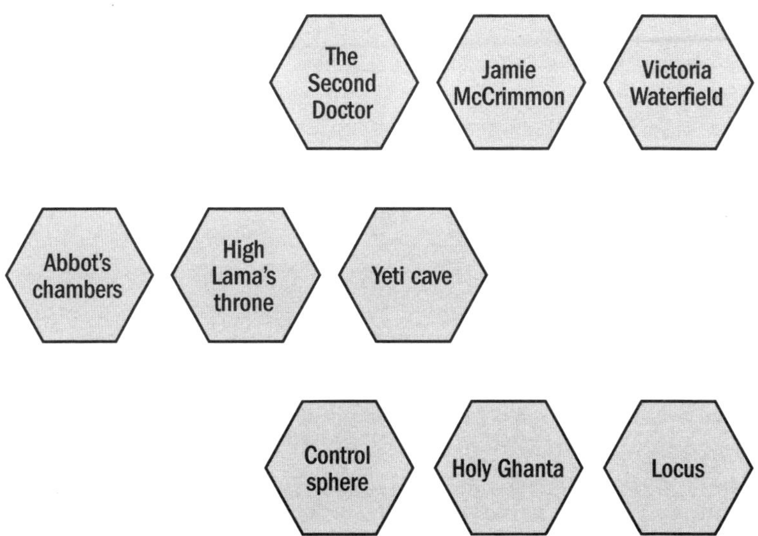

The Abominable Snowmen

Who was involved · Where they were · Which tool:

The Second Doctor: Younger-looking, scruffier, and more whimsical than his previous incarnation. But then, nobody said Time Lords have to always be elegant. Five foot seven inches tall, black hair, blue eyes.
Jamie McCrimmon: A Highlander of Clan MacLeod from the eighteenth century, Jamie was a piper who joined the Doctor after the Battle of Culloden. Five foot eight inches tall, brown hair, brown eyes.
Victoria Waterfield: The daughter of a well-to-do Victorian scientist who was orphaned in 1866 when Daleks killed her father. Four foot eleven inches tall, brown hair, blue eyes.

The Abbot's chambers: Interior. The Abbot of Det-Sen Monastery, Songsten, is in charge of the daily affairs. Does he hold the key?
The High Lama's throne: Interior. The guru of Det-Sen, Padmasambhava, is an immortal master who has guided the monks for centuries. Surely he is above reproach?
The Yeti cave: Interior. An enigmatic frozen cave in the snowy mountainside. It appears to be of some importance to the robot Yeti, but how?

A control sphere: Five pounds, sphere. A mysterious silver orb that can be found inside the chest cavity of each Yeti robot. The robot shuts down if the sphere is removed. Not great if you're faced with a small army of them.
The Holy Ghanta: Two pounds, bell. The Holy Ghanta of Yeshe Tsogyal is a holy relic of the Det-Sen Monastery that the Doctor has had in his possession for a while. He's excited to return it.
A Locus: Six ounces, model. A chess piece – or something close to it – carved to look like a Yeti. There's a fair few of them. The plural term is 'Loci'.

Puzzle 4: Easy

Fill in the grid below as you work through the clues.

	The Second Doctor	Jamie	Victoria	Abbot's chambers	High Lama's throne	Yeti cave
Control sphere						
Holy Ghanta						
Locus						
Abbot's chambers						
High Lama's throne						
Yeti cave						

The Invasion

Details:

Neither of the two people closest in height thought it likely that the Cybermen would attempt to hypnotise Earthlings.

?

Big Ben was too familiar to be hypnotic.

?

The Brigadier feared that the attack signal would come from somewhere within the TARDIS, and that they would never stand a chance of finding it in time.

?

It was clear that because of the way the underground layers of London were built, if Cerebration Mentors were going to cause paralysis, it wouldn't be possible to send the signal from the sewers.

?

As a Scot, Jamie discounted Big Ben as not being significant enough.

?

The Brigadier, worried about spies,
sent the Doctor a note, which read:

THE YWI LLM
AKE EVE RYO
NEB LIN DACK

?

It has been said that even the smallest person can change history.
That was certainly so in this case.

Puzzle 5: Medium

While in lunar orbit, the TARDIS is damaged in a missile attack. The Doctor lands it in England, 1973, to seek the assistance of Professor Travers, who he befriended in Tibet. Travers is away, but a colleague, Watkins, has gone missing. The trail leads to an enigmatic company called International Electronics.

The military task-force UNIT is also investigating IE. The Doctor learns that International Electronics is planning to help the Cybermen take over the world via Cerebration Mentors, which have been put in place everywhere. But what will the Cybermen use the machines to do to humanity's minds, and from where? Even Professor Watkins isn't sure. With the information given, can you work out who is correct?

Using the clues opposite and overleaf, fill in the grid on page 33 to work out who did what, and where. Then draw lines below from box to box to show your answer. Finally, circle the box containing name of the person who is correct.

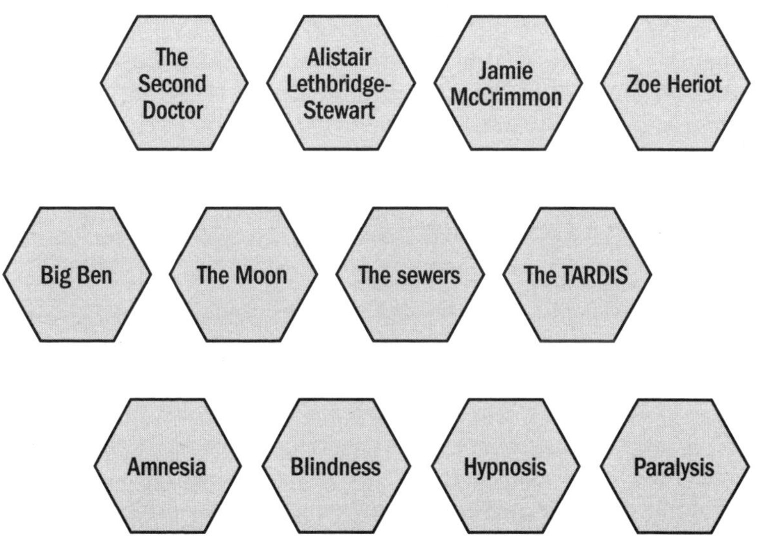

The Invasion

Who was involved · Where it takes place · How they will do it:

The Second Doctor: Beneath his light-hearted exterior and his fondness for whimsy, this Doctor hid a darkly pragmatic streak. Five foot seven inches tall, black hair, blue eyes.
Alistair Lethbridge-Stewart: Head of UNIT, a Brigadier. He eventually works with at least seven of the Doctor's incarnations. Six foot one inch tall, brown hair, blue eyes.
Jamie McCrimmon: A Highlander of the Clan MacLeod. His battle-cry is '*creag an tuire*', which means 'the boar's rock'. Five foot eight inches tall, brown hair, brown eyes.
Zoe Heriot: A twenty-first-century librarian. She stows away on the TARDIS aged fifteen. Five foot tall, black hair, blue eyes.

Big Ben: Exterior. The Clock Tower of the Palace of Westminster – Big Ben is the bell – is at the heart of British society and consciousness. Where better to attack the world from?
The Moon: Exterior. Sure, it's a long way off, but electronic signals travel at the speed of light, and you get superb coverage across the globe. You also don't typically have to worry about UNIT soldiers on the Moon. Not in the 1970s, anyway.
The sewers: Interior. London's sewers are endlessly labyrinthine, and they're linked to every home in the capital. They might be just the right place to broadcast an enemy signal from.
The TARDIS: Interior. Damaged in a "missile" attack, huh? That must have been a sophisticated missile. What was its payload? An attack signal from the depths of the TARDIS could be devastating.

Amnesia: Once no one remembers anything, they'll all latch on gratefully to anything they're told. They'll come willingly if you tell them you're returning their memories.
Blindness: In the kingdom of the blind, a legion of Cybermen is going to have a very easy time rounding everyone up.
Hypnosis: Why go to the effort of gathering humans for processing when it's simpler to make them walk into the factories themselves?
Paralysis: If people can't move, they can't run, they can't hide, and they certainly can't scream.

Puzzle 5: Medium

Fill in the grid below as you work through the clues.

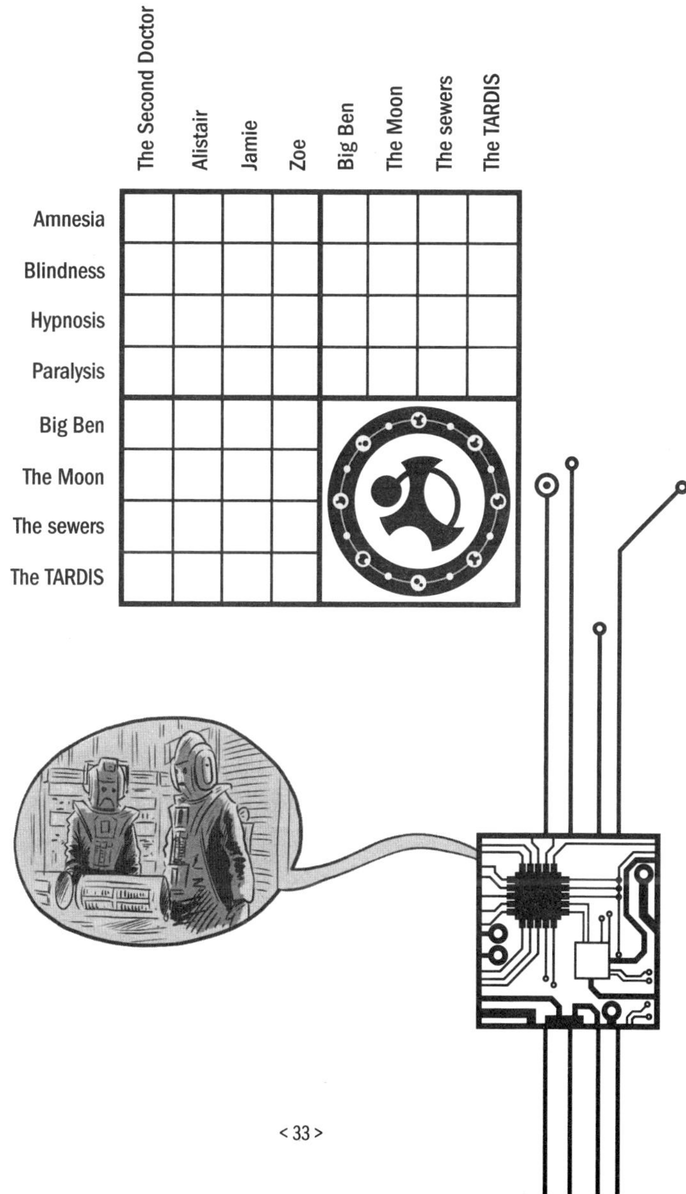

	The Second Doctor	Alistair	Jamie	Zoe	Big Ben	The Moon	The sewers	The TARDIS
Amnesia								
Blindness								
Hypnosis								
Paralysis								
Big Ben								
The Moon								
The sewers								
The TARDIS								

The War Games

Details:

A former soldier could have upset the men while they were eating.

?

The person who proposed the longest escape distraction made up for it by suggesting the second-shortest tool.

?

It takes a direct mind to recommend both chopping a door down and feigning an attack on the base.

?

Jamie thought that picking the lock would be a nicely low-profile way of springing the Doctor.

?

Any ambulance driver knows precisely how to take a vehicle out of commission – and temporarily, too, to avoid lasting damage.

?

The person who favoured the crowbar thought a disturbance at the gate would attract more eyeballs than a food fight in the mess – or any other potential scene.

?

Zoe was sure she could draw the attention of everyone in the medical ward with some lipstick, water and impassioned shrieking.

?

Lieutenant Carstairs knew the precise terminology and code words to convince the base that a major attack was incoming.

?

The best plan began with a scene in the most private location.

Puzzle 6: Hard

An alien race, named the War Lords, have been kidnapping Earth soldiers from across history and making them fight in an endless series of war games. A renegade Time Lord, the War Chief, has been helping. His plan is to forge his captives into a deadly army.

The Doctor and his companions are viewed with hostility. Before long, the Doctor has been imprisoned as a spy, and he's due to be executed. Jamie and Zoe have some help from a couple of kidnapped humans who've managed to throw off their programming. They need to make a scene, find a tool to spring the Doctor with, and devise a distraction to help them escape. Can you work out who made the best plan to free the Doctor?

Using the clues, fill in the grid on page 37 to establish who did what. Then draw lines from box to box below to demonstrate your answers. Finally, circle the box with the name of the person who came up with the successful plan.

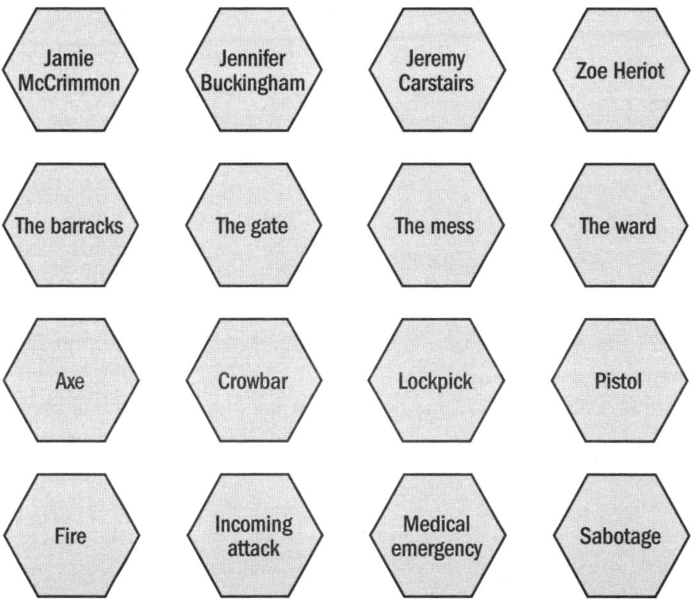

The War Games

Who was involved · Where it took place · What weapon · What distraction:

Jamie McCrimmon: A Clan MacLeod Highlander from the eighteenth century, Jamie is a master of the bagpipes.
Jennifer Buckingham: A nurse and ambulance driver during the First World War, who worked with the Doctor again afterwards.
Jeremy Carstairs: A British army officer during the First World War who later married Lady Jennifer.
Zoe Heriot: Ex-librarian from a twenty-first-century space station, a genius with an IQ to match the Doctor, and a photographic memory.

The barracks: Not just where soldiers go to sleep; it's a place where they have some space of their own.
The gate: A military base is designed to be defensive. If you make the occupants think they're vulnerable, you will get their attention.
The mess: Soldiers love to eat, just as they love to moan about food, officers and the weather. Any disruption here would be powerful.
The ward: War hospitals are chaotic, full of screaming, moaning, and pleas for help. It wouldn't take much to feign an emergency.

Axe: No need to worry about the sturdiness of the lock when you can hack your way through a door in a few hearty swings.
Crowbar: The tool of ne'er-do-wells all over. Said Archimedes: "With a long enough lever and somewhere to set it, I will move the world."
Lockpick: A flat-edged screwdriver and a bobby pin can be used to defeat any lock from 1917. If you know what you're doing.
Pistol: It's loud, but it's fast, and if you can damage the door frame, it'll be easy to open. And a gunshot won't draw attention in a war.

Fire: It's not tough to fake a fire near a sensitive place – an ammo dump or commander's quarters. Just get a convincing source of smoke.
Incoming attack: Get everyone looking for enemies outside the walls, and they won't notice what you're doing behind their backs.
Medical emergency: Spike the water with something that will wear off with no ill effects, and nobody will pay you any attention.
Sabotage: Disable something important, like the electricity or the vehicles, and you'll cause problems that will keep everyone busy.

Puzzle 6: Hard

Fill in the grid below as you work through the clues.

Spearhead from Space

Details:

You won't find any suits, button-down shirts or ties on the dummies in the central display.

?

The display located by the doors only ever features the most fashionable additions to the shelves.

?

The bestsellers display this month featured a luxurious tropical diorama, and the fruit on display naturally attracted the deep suspicion of one person in particular.

?

The Doctor was not wary of the dummies near the tills.

?

The Auton had disguised itself using the most elevated of the clothing options.

Puzzle 7: Easy

Meteorites do not normally come with plastic polyhedrons, so Brigadier Lethbridge-Stewart is particularly concerned when this odd arrival coincides with a visit from the Doctor in a new body. Brilliant Cambridge scholar Liz Shaw reluctantly agrees to study this meteoric find, and with the Doctor's help, uncovers the truth – Earth has been invaded by the Nestene Consciousness, a hostile alien intelligence that can create murderous automatons from plastic.

When the Consciousness activates these Autons, they go on a rampage. Trying to find the Nestene Consciousness's own vessel to shut the Autons down, the Doctor finds himself in a clothes shop with Liz and the Brigadier. They're being stalked by an Auton, which looks exactly like a clothes dummy.

Can you tell who correctly identified the Auton, which area of the store it was in, and its most distinctive item of clothing?

Using the clues opposite and overleaf, fill in the grid on page 41 to work out the solution. Then draw lines below from box to box to show your answer. Finally, circle the box containing the name of the person who spotted the Auton.

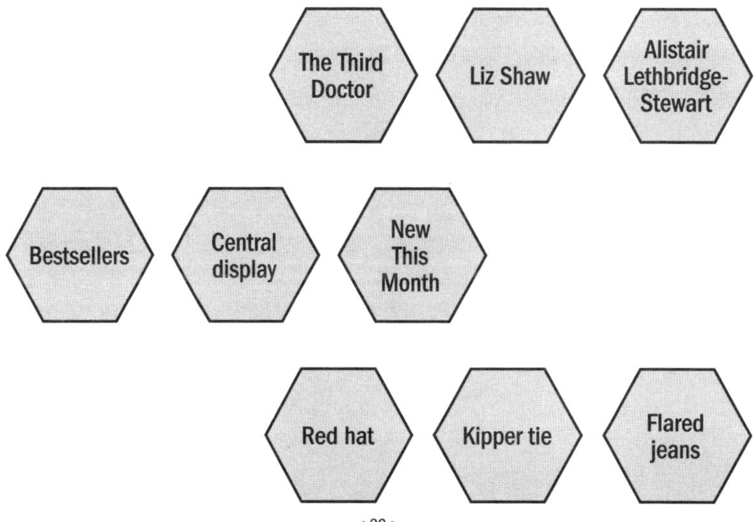

Spearhead From Space

Who was involved · Where in the store · What article of clothing:

The Third Doctor: Fashionably dapper and possessed of a mean Venusian aikido chop, the Third Doctor is a lot more hands-on than in previous incarnations. Six foot two inches tall, white hair, blue eyes.
Liz Shaw: Liz is a scientific genius with more than a dozen degrees, and one of the world's leading authorities on meteorites. She happens to be allergic to pineapple. Five foot five inches tall, brown hair, blue eyes.
Alistair Lethbridge-Stewart: The Brigadier runs UNIT, and works particularly closely with the Doctor while he's stuck on Earth. Six foot one inch tall, brown hair, blue eyes.

Bestsellers: Interior. About half-way into the shop, this island of dummies pretending to have fun features the most popular clothing lines.
Central display: Interior. Several dummies of both sexes are arranged in front of the checkout island, dressed to showcase a range of products from across the store.
New This Month: Interior. Two male, two female and two child dummies lounge around innocently by the entrance, clad in the newest arrivals.

Red hat: Whimsical, £3. With an unusually wide brim and stylish black band, this scarlet fedora is a must-have for any would-be jet-setting megalomaniac villainess.
Kipper tie: Sober, £1.50. Navy blue with a thin gold pinstripe, and a modest one and a half hand's width at its widest, this tie could hardly be more sedate if it tried.
Flared jeans: Trendy, £5.99. They cost a pretty penny, but these jeans are It, and if you want to be It too, you have to have them. Two-foot bell bottoms are the only way.

Puzzle 7: Easy

Fill in the grid below as you work through the clues.

The Dæmons

Details:

Causing harm to another, or even leaving them to come to harm, was out of the question for both people who are the same height.

?

Captain Yates was sure something could be done at the barrow which was, after all, where Azal had stashed his spaceship.

?

Fond as Sergeant Benton was of the pub, he didn't consider it a good place to try to defeat the Master's plans.

?

Jo was not a fan of graveyards.

?

There is definitely some common ground between very loud noises, massive releases of energy, and kicking an oval ball into touch.

?

As a rule of thumb, do not attempt to exchange energy fields in a graveyard, particularly not when you're operating on a reversed polarity. Who knows what you might disturb?

?

You wouldn't sacrifice someone in a pub, not even a pub named The Cloven Hoof. It's just not cricket.

?

The trick, it turned out, was using the most obscure location.

Puzzle 8: Medium

Archaeologists are about to open the Devil's Hump, an ominously named long-barrow in the village of Devil's End, but peculiar events are occurring, including a man dying of fright. The Doctor investigates and finds old enemy – the Master – posing as a vicar, corrupting the villagers into what seems to be a black magic cult.

The Master summons Azal, last member of the Dæmons, an alien race. They have lived on Earth for a hundred thousand years. The Master wants Azal to give him power over the Earth, and the Dæmon is inclined to grant his wish. The Doctor must persuade Azal otherwise. Can you uncover who came up with the best idea for stopping the Master, where it could be done, and how?

Using the clues opposite and overleaf, fill in the grid on page 45 to work out who did what. Then draw lines below from box to box to show your answer. Finally, circle the box containing the name of the person who had the best idea.

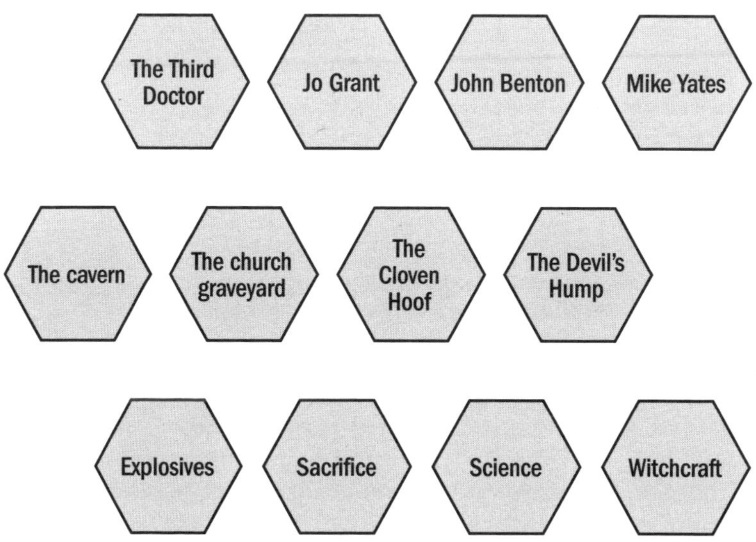

The Dæmons

Who was involved · Where it took place · How they did it:

The Third Doctor: A renegade alien from Gallifrey and former star pupil of the Time Lord Academy, just like his old friend the Master. Don't tell anyone, but the Master did better in exams. Six foot two inches tall tall.
Jo Grant: A child of the 1950s, Jo got her job in UNIT by having her civil servant uncle pull some strings. She is fiercely anti-bullying, and a skilled martial artist, dancer and abseiler. Five foot one inch tall.
John Benton: Turned down a promotion to captain in favour of Mike Yates, as he didn't want to be an officer. His grandfather met the Ninth Doctor and Rose during WWI. Six foot two inches tall.
Mike Yates: A no-nonsense army captain who works for UNIT. He grew up in Scotland and is a keen rugby player. Six foot tall.

The cavern: A secret ritual chamber deep beneath the church apparently used for black magic by the Master – and by the eighteenth-century rake Lord Aldbourne before him.
The church graveyard: Devil's End Church has an extensive graveyard containing a rich assortment of people, some of them actually blameless. Shocking, I know.
The Cloven Hoof: A somewhat unsettling pub run by a demented and moderately murderous cultist.
The Devil's Hump: An ancient barrow in a field outside the village of Devil's End. Other local villages included Witchwood and Satanhill. Not the happiest of areas.

Explosives: If you can't beat them, blow them to smithereens. A popular solution to problems throughout the twentieth century.
Sacrifice: Let's face it, dark forces always loved a sacrifice, the more human the better. The Old Ones are the best.
Science: Specifically, a brilliant gadget: the Dyothermic Energy Exchanger, which can hurt Azal when its polarity is reversed.
Witchcraft: Cold iron – in the form of a trowel on this occasion – has long been used by witches to drive off faeries and malign spirits. Surely it'll do the trick.

Puzzle 8: Medium

Fill in the grid below as you work through the clues.

	The Third Doctor	Jo	John	Mike	The cavern	The church graveyard	The Cloven Hoof	The Devil's Hump
Explosives								
Sacrifice								
Science								
Witchcraft								
The cavern								
The church graveyard								
The Cloven Hoof								
The Devil's Hump								

The Time Warrior

Details:

The Brigadier didn't have any interest in foreign spies.

?

One person suggested that perhaps tiny scientists could be used to drive off insects, and the Doctor, in a flippant moment, retorted that perhaps a madman was to blame.

?

Sarah Jane felt that maybe the scientists were being hidden in the darkness of space, while Professor Rubeish thought it more likely that the kidnap victims were being hidden locally.

?

The highest-ranking person felt that the kidnappers were driven, but not by a fear of creepy-crawlies.

?

If profit was the motive, it only made sense that it would be criminals who were to blame.

?

It was suggested that making a secret base near – or even in – a secret research institute would be an act of idle whimsy.

?

The person thinking about aliens was closest to being on the right track.

Puzzle 9: Hard

A number of well-respected scientists have vanished from a research institute. While investigating, Brigadier Lethbridge-Stewart and the Doctor meet a scientist, Rubeish, and a journalist, Sarah Jane Smith. All are puzzled by the kidnappings. It turns out that they are being snatched by a Sontaran warrior named Linx, and hypnotised into repairing his spaceship. Sarah Jane stows away in the TARDIS, the Doctor rescues the scientists and defeats the Sontaran and Irongron, the warlord protecting him.

Everyone has an idea of what is going on. Can you work out who suggested what, and who was closest to the truth?

Using the clues opposite and overleaf, fill in the grid on page 49 to work out who thought what. Then draw lines below from box to box to show your answer. Finally, circle the box containing the name of the person who was correct.

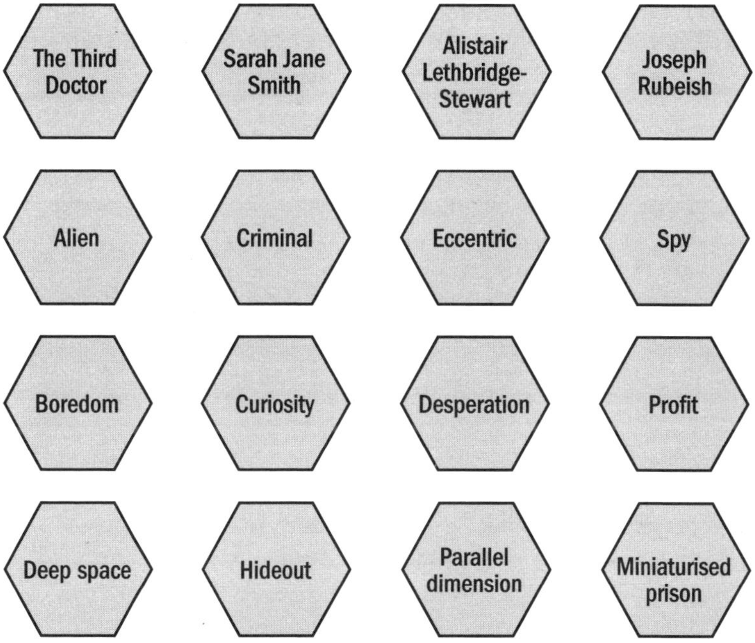

The Time Warrior

Who suggested it · What happened · Reason · Where it took place:

The Third Doctor: The first time we learn the name of the Doctor's home planet, Gallifrey.
Sarah Jane Smith: When the Doctor first meets Sarah Jane, she is pretending to be her own aunt. She's not convincing.
Alistair Lethbridge-Stewart: When leading experts go missing from a secret base, that's a problem for UNIT. Enter the Brigadier.
Joseph Rubeish: A curious fellow. Poor eyesight might not seem beneficial, but it saved him from Sontaran hypnosis.

Alien: An increasingly common hazard on Earth in the 1970s – the reason the Time Lords left the Doctor stuck there to begin with.
Criminal: The criminal mind is endlessly ingenious, and all sorts of sprees could be hatched if you controlled a clutch of scientists.
Eccentric: Sometimes, there's no clear motive that makes sense in a rational world. Perhaps someone just really wants a collection of scientists, and can't afford to pay their salaries.
Spy: As if the aliens weren't enough, the Cold War is still raging. All sorts of spies could be trying to steal research by grabbing scientists.

Boredom: If you're really bored, perhaps snatching a group of very clever people is an entertaining way to pass the time. Whimsy, idle.
Curiosity: There's no better way to familiarise yourself with the absolute cutting edge of knowledge than by interrogating the people who are revealing it. Whimsy, driven.
Desperation: Perhaps there's a really good reason for grabbing scientists. Dangerous bug infestation, maybe? Logical, driven.
Profit: Love of money is the root of all evil, so they say. Most crimes come down to money, and science can be profitable. Logical, idle.

Deep space: UNIT has a strong reputation, and if you know of him, the Doctor is terrifying to go up against. So if you're hiding victims, space is really, really big.
Hideout: If you're kidnapping several people from the same place, one at a time, you don't want to be moving them very far. So a secret base nearby would be handy.

Puzzle 9: Hard

Fill in the grid below as you work through the clues.

	The Third Doctor	Sarah Jane	Alistair	Joseph	Boredom	Curiosity	Desperation	Profit	Deep space	Hideout	Parallel dimension	Miniaturised prison
Alien												
Criminal												
Eccentric												
Spy												
Deep space												
Hideout												
Parallel dimension												
Miniaturised prison												
Boredom												
Curiosity												
Desperation												
Profit												

Parallel dimension: Banish your kidnapping victim to a nearby parallel dimension that you control, and you never need to worry about how to transport them at all. Clever, huh?
Miniaturised prison: Make your prisoners absolutely tiny, and you could easily hide them in a container such as, say, a tiny submarine you stored in a handy syringe.

Planet of the Spiders

Details:

The Doctor suspected the Daleks were behind the theft, but he did not think they planned to kill him specifically.

?

The person who was worried about the Cybermen feared that they'd take the crystal to the very depths of the Earth.

?

Spite would not motivate Lupton to place the crystal in the TARDIS.

?

If invisible spiders wanted the crystal, it was thought that they'd take it back to Metebelis III.

?

The mind-control plan did not feature either the Cybermen or the Great Intelligence.

?

The plan involving Buckingham Palace had an end result that was the total obliteration of the planet.

?

If the Daleks were to blame, they used either bribery or mind control.

?

Sarah Jane didn't think the Cybermen or the Ice Warriors were responsible, but she suspected the villains wanted to rule the Universe.

?

If Lupton was blackmailed, it was part of a plot to destroy UNIT.

?

The plan to eliminate the Doctor did not hinge on mind control.

Puzzle 10: Extreme

The blue crystals growing deep within the planet of Metebelis III possess numerous strange powers related to the mind, consciousness and psychic abilities. In the wrong hands, they are extremely dangerous. The Doctor retrieved a particularly magnificent specimen and brought it back to Eartzh. He gave it to Jo Grant as a wedding present. Later, Jo posted the crystal back, as she'd been told it was bad luck. Hours later, it was stolen by Rex Lupton, on behalf of an alien species. Everyone had a theory on why Lupton did it, for whom, where the crystal would be used, and to which end. Can you work out who suggested which complete theory, and which of them was correct?

Using the clues opposite, below and on pages 54–55, fill in the grid on pages 56–57 to work out the solution. Then draw lines from box to box overleaf to show your answer. Finally, circle the box containing the name of the person who was right.

The plan involving the Ice Warriors suspected that the real Lupton had been killed and switched with an evil duplicate.

?

The Ice Warriors did not occur to Benton as a source of trouble.

?

The proposed plan that involved bribing Lupton included taking the crystal back into the past.

?

Of the five proposed plans, one featured Ice Warriors, one thought the crystal was off-world, one believed Lupton had been bribed, one suspected the Doctor was the target, and one was devised by the Brigadier.

?

The actual plot to steal the crystal was conceived by forces who should be clear from the puzzle's title.

Planet of the Spiders

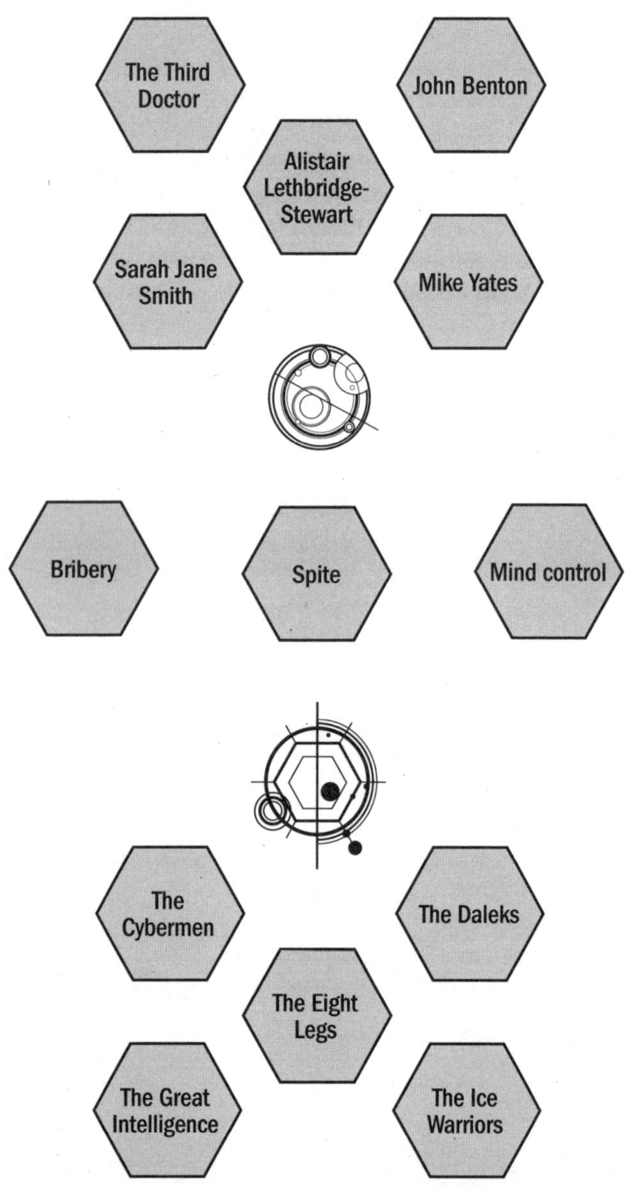

Puzzle 10: Extreme

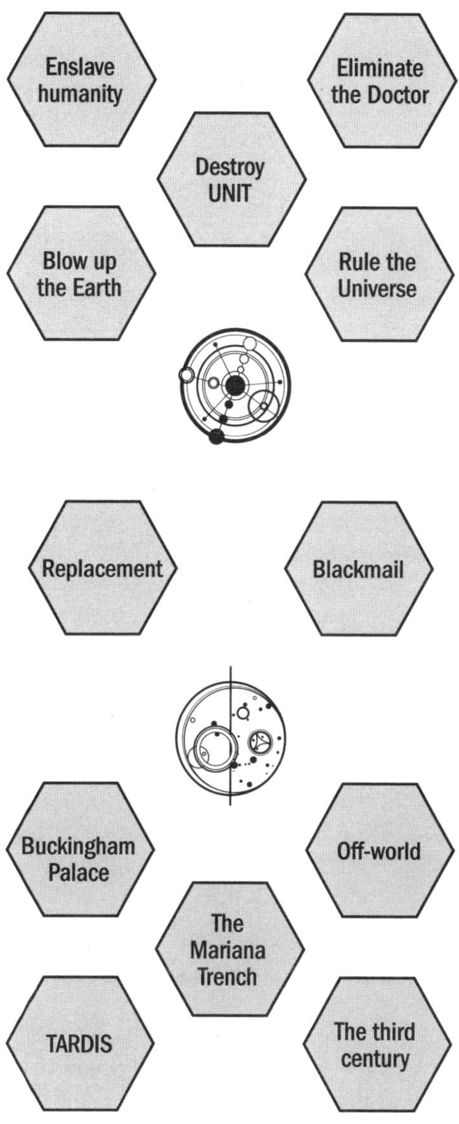

Planet of the Spiders

Whose idea · Why they did it · For whom · Where it was done · For what goal:

The Third Doctor: Frequently referred to the TARDIS as if it was a living being. These references were not accidental.
Sarah Jane Smith: Met at least nine of the Doctor's incarnations over the years, and he considered her one of his best friends.
Alistair Lethbridge-Stewart: The Brigadier was a man of action, and preferred to solve problems with weaponry, often bringing him into some conflict with the Doctor.
Mike Yates: Captain Yates spent much of his first year with UNIT hunting the UK for Silurian nests in the company of Sergeant Benton.
John Benton: Always blamed himself for his brother's accidental death, although there was nothing he could have done.

Bribery: Money and power are very strong motivators. Who knows what Lupton might have been promised?
Spite: Some men just want to watch the world burn, even if they are going to end up burning with it.
Mind control: It's entirely possible that Lupton is under the sway of malign influences. He was fond of meditation, after all.
Replacement: Sure, it looked like Lupton. But as we all know, there's any number of ways to counterfeit a specific human.
Blackmail: With a big enough lever, you could move the world. It would take far less leverage to move Rex Lupton.

Cybermen: Emotionless, cybernetically enhanced humanoids, known for turning people into new Cybermen and their desire to conquer all.
Daleks: Genetically engineered mutants from the planet Skaro, known for their lethal travel machines and desire to conquer all.
Eight Legs: A race of mutated super-intelligent spiders known for telepathy, invisibility, time travel, and their desire to conquer all.
The Great Intelligence: A bodiless interdimensional consciousness

from beyond the boundaries of time and space known for hating the Doctor and its desire to conquer Earth.
Ice Warriors: A race of reptilian humanoids known for living on Mars, their sense of aesthetics, and their warlike society.

Buckingham Palace: If you want to take control of England, the palace might well seem like a good place to start.
Off-world: There's a whole universe out there. Several of them in fact, if you consider the multiverse. Where would the crystal be the most useful?
The Mariana Trench: The deepest point in the Earth's crust. It could be a very potent spot to apply a power source.
Inside the TARDIS: The TARDIS is incredibly powerful, incredibly complex and incredibly large. With sufficient ingenuity, the crystal could be used there for all sorts of purposes.
The third century: On some occasions, the best time to start was last week. On other occasions, it was 1,800 years ago.

Enslave humanity: We're an unusually useful bunch, if the number of alien species wanting to enslave us is anything to go by.
Blow up the Earth: If enslaving humanity isn't enough, shattering the planet into tiny little pieces might be your best option.
Eliminate the Doctor: The Doctor spends most of his time foiling evil plans and saving humanity, Earth and the Universe. That wins him as many enemies as it does friends.
Destroy UNIT: There's no doubt that under Lethbridge-Stewart, UNIT became a critical part of Earth's defences. That's got to rankle.
Rule the Universe: If you're going to plan a conquest, think big. There's a whole universe out there, billions of sentient races. Might as well catch 'em all.

Planet of the Spiders

	The Third Doctor	Sarah Jane	Alistair	Mike	John	Bribery	Spite	Mind control	Replacement	Blackmail
Enslave humanity										
Blow up the Earth										
Eliminate the Doctor										
Destroy UNIT										
Rule the Universe										
Buckingham Palace										
Off-world										
Mariana Trench										
TARDIS										
Third century										
Cybermen										
Daleks										
Eight Legs										
The Great Intelligence										
Ice Warriors										
Bribery										
Spite										
Mind control										
Replacement										
Blackmail										

Puzzle 10: Extreme

Fill in the grid as you work through the clues.

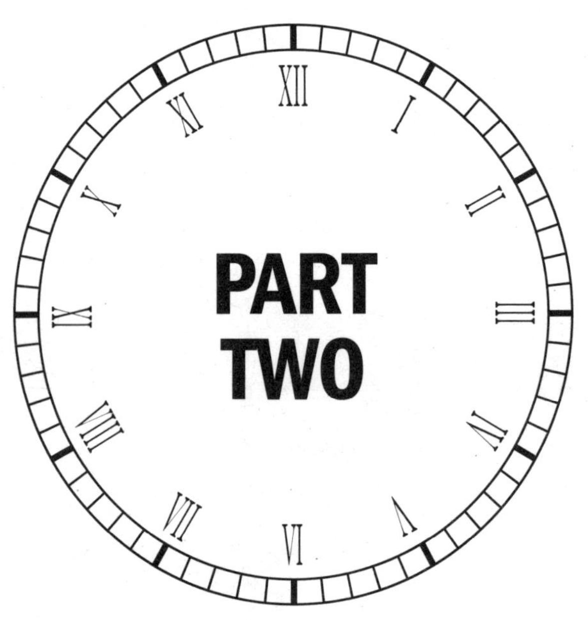
PART
TWO

THE FOURTH DOCTOR
THE FIFTH DOCTOR
THE SIXTH DOCTOR

Genesis of the Daleks

Details:

Harry investigates neither the proving ground nor the laboratory.

?

Davros's office contains the object that seems to defy photography.

?

The eyestalk is not in the laboratory.

?

The Doctor's enthusiasm goes well with a physically demanding environment.

Puzzle 11: Easy

The Time Lords snatch the Doctor and his companions out of the TARDIS and dump them on the planet Skaro back at the very creation of the Daleks. Their mission is to prevent a future where the Daleks rule, ideally by preventing them from being created.

On Skaro, the Thals and the Kaleds have been warring for generations, and the planet is almost completely devastated. The Doctor and his companions are captured by Kaleds and taken to be interviewed by a council of generals and scientists. Davros, the lead scientist, has just unveiled his 'Dalek'. One of his team, Ronson, is worried about how unethical Davros has become. The Doctor and his companions need to win Ronson over if they're going to shut down Dalek development.

Who obtains the best piece of evidence to convince Ronson, and where is it?

Using the clues opposite and overleaf, fill in the grid on page 63. Then draw lines below from box to box to show your answer. Finally, circle the box containing the name of the person who obtained the best evidence.

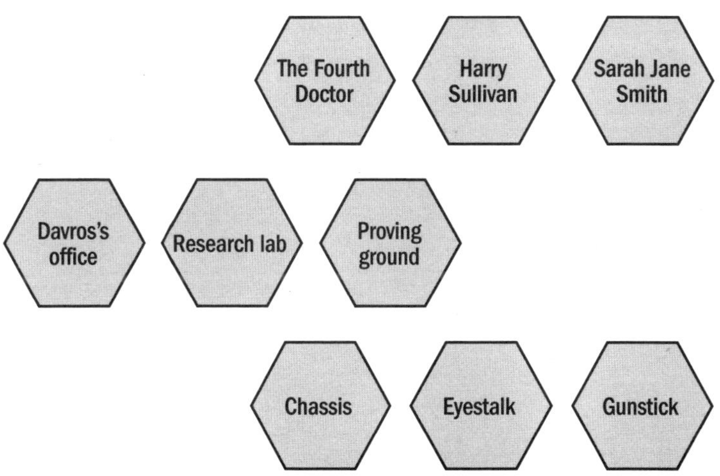

Genesis of the Daleks

Who was involved · Where the evidence was · What the evidence was:

The Fourth Doctor: Tall, curly haired and cheerfully eccentric, this incarnation of the Doctor is never without his long, multi-coloured scarf, his floppy hat, or a generously applied bag of jelly babies.
Harry Sullivan: Harry is a surgeon and navy lieutenant working with UNIT. He once managed to catch his nose in a sliding door. Unlike his friends, he arrived on Skaro bare-headed.
Sarah Jane Smith: This relentlessly dogged journalist arrives on Skaro wearing a canary-yellow jacket and a blue knit beanie. Unfortunately, there are no fishermen to interview.

Davros's office: A stark, utilitarian room for a stark, utilitarian scientist. Much like the man himself, it still manages to be unwelcoming and unnerving – even threatening.
Proving ground: The assault course and firing range where the Kaleds are testing the Mark III. Hopefully, the assault course doesn't contain much in the way of jumps, climbs, crawls or stairs.
Research lab: Lit by harsh artificial lighting, the lab is filled with ominous technology, strange instrument panels, blinking lights and computers that beep. Emphasises the 'BOR' in laboratory.

Eyestalk: A periscope-like device that allows the Dalek to see out of their travel machine. It's protected by a series of insulator discs, but it's still vulnerable. It might be monocular, but it has a wide field of vision and other useful options.
Gunstick: A deadly beam weapon powered by neutronic energy, with a variable power setting that ranges from a TASER-like stun to fully disintegrating its target. The beam is usually blue, and strikes with an effect that makes the victim look like a photo-negative.
Mark III Chassis: The prototype tank-like armoured transport that the Daleks of the future will inhabit. Made of Dalekanium and polycarbides. It's mobile, sure. Mobile enough, anyway.

Puzzle 11: Easy

Fill in the grid below as you work through the clues.

	The Fourth Doctor	Sarah Jane	Harry	Davros's office	Proving ground	Research lab
Chassis						
Eyestalk						
Gunstick						
Davros's office						
Proving ground						
Research lab						

The Robots of Death

Details:

Neither D84 nor Leela are interested in what passes for food aboard *Storm Mine 4*.

?

The human from Kaldor suspects the engineer or the crewman.

?

D84 is certain that the commander is innocent.

?

The Doctor is not investigating the aristocrat.

?

Zilda never needed to visit the workshop.

?

Borg spent a lot of time in the mess.

?

The commander always ate in his own quarters.

?

Poul believes the killer is on the control deck.

?

The murderer strongly identifies with robots.

Puzzle 12: Medium

The Doctor and Leela arrive inside *Storm Mine 4*, a huge sand-crawler on the surface of a storm-wracked desert planet. Most of the crew are robots – black 'Dum' models that can't speak, green 'Voc' models that can speak, and one silver Super-Voc, which acts as controller for the others.

The human crew are being murdered one by one, and suspicion immediately falls on the Doctor and Leela. The Doctor quickly realises that a saboteur is using the robots to kill, but who could it be? Together with a pair of undercover agents, they have to identify the murderer before it is too late.

Who correctly identifies the suspect, and where are they?

Using the clues opposite and overleaf, fill in the grid on page 67 to work out who did what. Then draw lines below from box to box to show your answer. Finally, circle the box containing the name of the person who found the murderer.

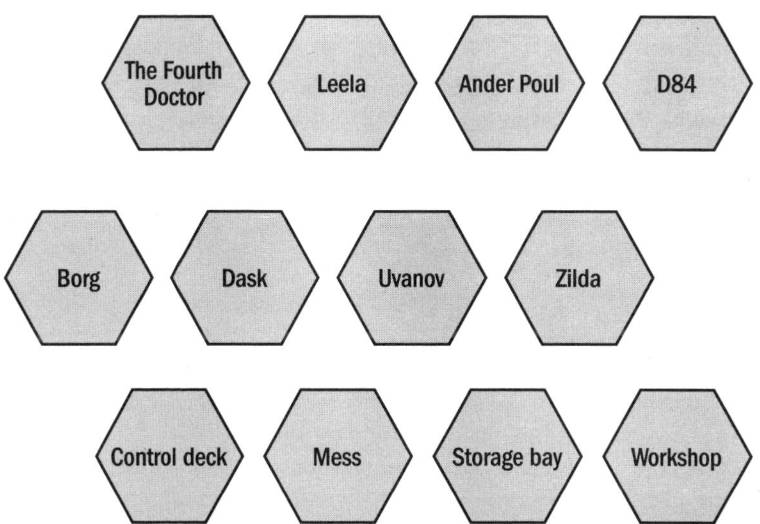

The Robots of Death

Who was involved · The suspects · Where they were:

The Fourth Doctor: The Doctor's scarf is a little oddly behaved in this episode, vanishing and reappearing a couple of times. Most curious. The Doctor didn't even get to swing on it.
Leela: Leela of the Sevateem is a warrior tribeswoman from the planet Mordee in the sixth millennium CE. She dresses in animal skins and is deadly with her knife and her poisonous Janis thorns.
Ander Poul: Watchful and cautious, Poul is a twenty-ninth-century human from Kaldor City, and a company spy put in place to keep an eye on *Storm Mine 4*.
D84: Although pretending to be a Dum unit, and decorated with the standard Dum black pattern and its name printed on its chest, D84 is Poul's highly advanced android partner.

Borg: A dark-haired crewman with a grudge against the first murder victim, the meteorologist Chub. Reacts violently to being offered a jelly baby.
Dask: The chief engineer of the sand-crawler, he bears a deep fondness for robots, and wears facial make-up in order to help look a bit more like them.
Uvanov: Commander of *Storm Mine 4*, with a reputation for keeping the mine running profitably. Has a fabulous beard.
Zilda: A trainee navigator who wormed her way on board *Storm Mine 4* under false pretences to investigate her brother's death. Secretly a Kaldor aristocrat.

Control deck: The operations centre of the sand-crawler, where all functions are controlled from. There are several computer consoles here, some quite fancy, despite the limited crew.
Mess: Where the crew eat and, occasionally, relax. As everywhere else, it's maintained by robots, so it is clean and orderly.
Storage bay: A nice, open space used for storing things. It is well-organised and kept as clean as you'd expect.
Workshop: Machinery needs maintaining, and that requires tools, spare parts, benches, and other specialised equipment.

Puzzle 12: Medium

Fill in the grid below as you work through the clues.

	The Fourth Doctor	Leela	Poul	D84	Control deck	Mess	Storage bay	Workshop
Borg								
Dask								
Uvanov								
Zilda								
Control deck								
Mess								
Storage bay								
Workshop								

Shada

Details:

The Doctor thought that the book was likely *Origins of the Universe*.

?

The book with a brown cover was at risk of burning.

?

Romana thought the book belonged on the east bookshelf, while K9 thought it was from the west bookshelf.

?

Chris was not interested in fiction.

?

The History of the Time War had a burgundy cover.

?

The book with the red cover was the object of the postgrad's interest.

?

The leatherbound book belonged on the west bookshelf.

?

The book that detailed the location of Shada was taken from the professor's desk.

Puzzle 13: Hard

The Doctor arrives in Cambridge in 1979 to visit an old friend, Professor Chronotis, formerly known as the Time Lord Salyavin.

He called the Doctor to get his help finding a significant book that he'd mislaid – one that contained the last existing record of the location of Shada, a prison the Time Lords built to keep would-be universal dictators safely locked up. The first step in finding the book is to identify it, as Professor Chronotis can't remember what it looks like.

Which book, which usually lived where, was the crucial one?

Using the clues opposite and overleaf, fill in the grid on page 71 to work out the solutions. Then draw lines below from box to box to show your answer. Finally, circle the box containing the name of the finder of the key book.

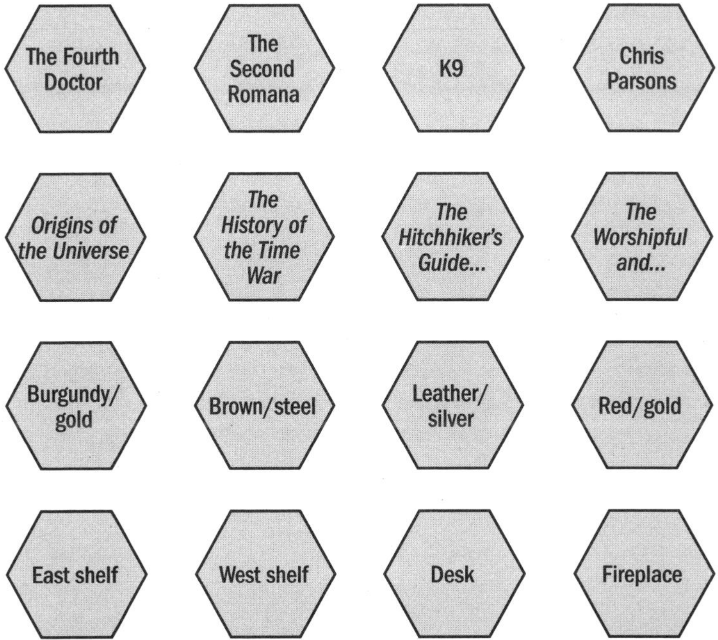

Shada

Who was involved · Book title · Colour of cover · Usual location:

The Fourth Doctor: A dab hand with a punt, the Doctor first met Chronotis in 1957, when he was still in his first incarnation.
The Second Romana: Romana, like the Doctor, the Master, and the Professor, is an aristocratic Time Lord from Gallifrey. Her parents were considered Bohemian types.
K9: A faithful cybernetic dog with a habit of taking instruction literally and logically, created by Professor Marius.
Chris Parsons: A post-graduate studying sigma particles at Cambridge University. He met the professor at a faculty party, and got talking about carbon dating.

***Origins of the Universe*:** English. Non-fiction. Laughably inaccurate.
***The History of the Time War*:** Ancient Gallifreyan. Non-fiction. No laughing matter.
***The Hitchhiker's Guide to the Galaxy*:** English. Fiction, more or less. Laugh out loud funny.
***The Worshipful and Ancient Law of Gallifrey*:** Ancient Gallifreyan. Non-fiction. Several remarkable features, none of which are funny.

A lovely **burgundy** cover with **gold** lettering on the spine.
A thick **brown** cover that features distinctive **steel** corners.
A prestige **leather**-bound cover with **silver** trim.
A faded **red** cover with five **gold** rings embossed on the spine.

East shelf: On the east wall of the professor's office. This shelf is neater and better organised than any other spot in the room.
West shelf: On the west wall of the professor's office. Cluttered, and not as well organised as the east shelf. Cosier, though.
Desk: The professor's desk is stacked with multiple messy piles of books on all manner of subjects. No plates, at least.
Fireplace: Above it, on the mantelpiece, not in the fire, and there's only a few books here. Not the safest place to keep them.

Puzzle 13: Hard

Fill in the grid below as you work through the clues.

	The Fourth Doctor	The Second Romana	K9	Chris Parsons	*Origins...*	*The History...*	*The Hitchhiker's...*	*The Worshipful...*	East shelf	West shelf	Desk	Fireplace
Burgundy/gold												
Brown/steel												
Leather/silver												
Red/gold												
East shelf												
West shelf												
Desk												
Fireplace												
Origins...												
The History...												
The Hitchhiker's...												
The Worshipful...												

Earthshock

Details:

Adric did not got to Storage Room Four.

?

A genius did not visit the tool closet.

?

The storage room did not hold a sonic screwdriver.

?

The toolkit was near the hat stand.

?

The Doctor ended up zapping the lock.

Puzzle 14: Easy

Arriving on Earth in the year 2526, the Fifth Doctor and his companions discover a cave system and are intercepted by soldiers who try to arrest them. The group comes under attack by androids, defending an odd metal hatch in the cave floor.

Later investigating the hatch, the Doctor discovers that it's hiding a worryingly powerful bomb. To defuse it, he sends his companions off to get some bits and pieces he might need.

Calculate who brings the Doctor what from where in the TARDIS and which tool turns out to be the one he needs?

Using the clues opposite and overleaf, fill in the grid on page 75 to work out who brought what, and from where. Then draw lines below from box to box to show your answer. Finally, circle the box containing the name of the person with the essential tool.

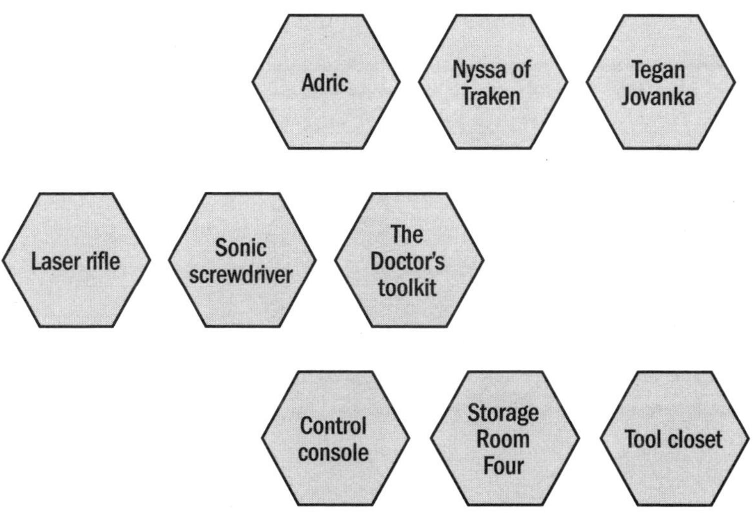

Earthshock

Who was involved · What tool was needed · Where it was:

Adric: Young, brilliant, arrogant and brash, Adric is an orphan of the thirty-second century. He always wears a star-shaped badge that he was given for mathematical genius.
Nyssa of Traken: A scientific genius, born on the planet Traken in 1961 by Earth reckoning. She is nobleborn, but recognises how lucky she has been.
Tegan Jovanka: An Australian air stewardess. She was born in 1960, and is a passionate campaigner for Aboriginal rights. She's often stubborn.

Laser rifle: A heavy black cylinder, fitted with a handy shoulder strap. It produces a harsh electronic sound when fired, but the beam is a pretty pink-purple in colour.
Sonic screwdriver: A Gallifreyan multi-tool, one of the most versatile appliances in the Universe. Produces a variety of pleasing noises.
The Doctor's toolkit: A heavy black and silver box containing tools for a variety of odd jobs, DIY, and other time-travelling shenanigans. Quiet.

Control console: Under the TARDIS control console, there are several little cubby holes one can use for storing items. There's a hat stand conveniently nearby.
Storage Room Four: The walls are wooden, the shelves are stone, it is seemingly lit by candlelight, and everything is dusty. Rather out of the way.
Tool closet: A roomy workspace containing a variety of well-used items. Smells faintly of earth, despite the absence of any soil.

Puzzle 14: Easy

Fill in the grid below as you work through the clues.

	Adric	Nyssa	Tegan	Control console	Storage Room Four	Tool closet
Laser rifle						
Sonic screwdriver						
The Doctor's toolkit						
Control console						
Storage Room Four						
Tool closet						

Terminus

Details:

If Terminus was at the bottom of a space-time crater, it was not capable of time travel.

?

Neither Tegan nor Turlough are interested in the cryptic note that read, '*Flestie mith guor ht paeli*'.

?

Nyssa thought that Terminus was rich in resources.

?

Turlough discounted the idea that the station attracted crippled and crashed craft.

?

The person who thought that the station was a trade nexus did not think that it was capable of moving quickly.

?

Nyssa was worried about the potential of sinister mind-control broadcasts.

?

The Doctor did not believe that the station was important to trade.

?

The correct solution was unmistakeably fleshier than the others.

Puzzle 15: Medium

When chunks of the TARDIS start dissolving, it makes an emergency landing at the nearest stable point in spacetime – a star liner making its way to a space station named Terminus. The station is being used to house, or imprison, victims of Lazar's disease, a debilitating, eventually fatal illness that spreads easily.

Everyone agrees that Terminus is an odd place, but no one is quite sure why its location is so critical, or what its original function was. It is vital to uncover its secrets.

Can you discover who correctly identifies the station's function and significance?

Using the clues opposite and overleaf, fill in the grid on page 79 to work out who found the function and significance. Then draw lines below from box to box to show your answer. Finally, circle the box containing the name of the person who found the answer.

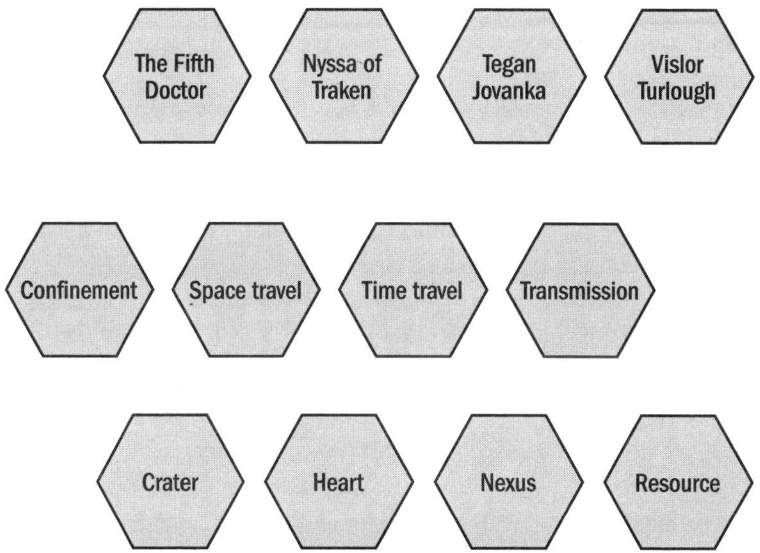

Terminus

Who was involved · What it was for · Where it was located:

The Fifth Doctor: Surprised that the emergency landing function of the TARDIS has finally worked correctly for the first time, and is curious about what caused the anomaly.
Nyssa of Traken: Quickly succumbs to Lazar's disease. Good job she's a genius in multiple scientific disciplines.
Tegan Jovanka: A career as an air stewardess is better preparation for being stuck on a space liner with a load of highly infectious disease victims than you might think.
Vislor Turlough: An erudite alien exile from the planet Trion. Turlough was placed on the TARDIS as an assassin by the Black Guardian, a god of chaos. Naughty!

Confinement: The station is surprisingly sturdy. Sure, it's being used to confine Lazar's now, but that's only a fraction of its space.
Space travel: Space, as was famously observed, is big. Very, very big. Getting across it very quickly is an immensely powerful ability that could cause all sorts of problems.
Time travel: Terminus has travelled through time. Who knows what chaos it might have sown along the way, or might be capable of moving forwards?
Transmission: The station's curious super-structure and design might make it a great way of broadcasting a signal across the galaxy.

Crater: Because of eddies in the space-time vortex, Terminus is where craft end up when they break down in this region of spacetime. What's that, Lassie? The Doctor's down the well?
Heart: Terminus somehow sits at the absolute centre of the entire Universe. You might think hitting the middle of a dartboard is tricky, but that's peanuts compared to space.
Nexus: Galactic trade is a complex beast, and safe, well-travelled routes are critical. If you think of them as ley lines, then Terminus just so happens to be Stonehenge.
Resource: Terminus is near an astonishingly dense nebula, filled to bursting with molecular hydrogen and other vital elements for fuelling spacecraft.

Puzzle 15: Medium

Fill in the grid below as you work through the clues.

Planet of Fire

Details:

The Doctor believes that the Master has come to Sarn to harness the suffering that the Time of Fire will cause.

?

Kamelion insists the Master must have used his laser screwdriver and Peri is sure that the Master used his sonic umbrella somehow.

?

One of the people who does not think that the Master arrived on Sarn through happenstance has a long-lost sibling.

?

The person suggesting the Master is hiding in the Doctor's TARDIS also thinks he used his least portable tool to get there.

?

Someone claims that the Master has gone to the Cave of Fire to meet an old subordinate.

?

Turlough believes the Master is hiding in his personal seat of power.

?

If the Master used his sonic umbrella, he must be in the Great Hall.

?

The Master is in dire need of numismaton gas.

Puzzle 16: Hard

The TARDIS goes to Sarn, a volcanic planet populated by lost colonists. The planet is about to enter its Time of Fire, a period of volcanic devastation. To make things worse, the Master is hiding nearby, planning all manner of villainy. If they are going to prevent disaster on the planet, the Doctor and his companions have to work out exactly where the Master is, what tool he used to get him there, and why he's on Sarn to begin with.

Can you help?

Using the clues opposite and overleaf, fill in the grid on page 83 to work everything out. Then draw lines below from box to box to show your answers. Finally, circle the box containing the name of the person who came up with the answer.

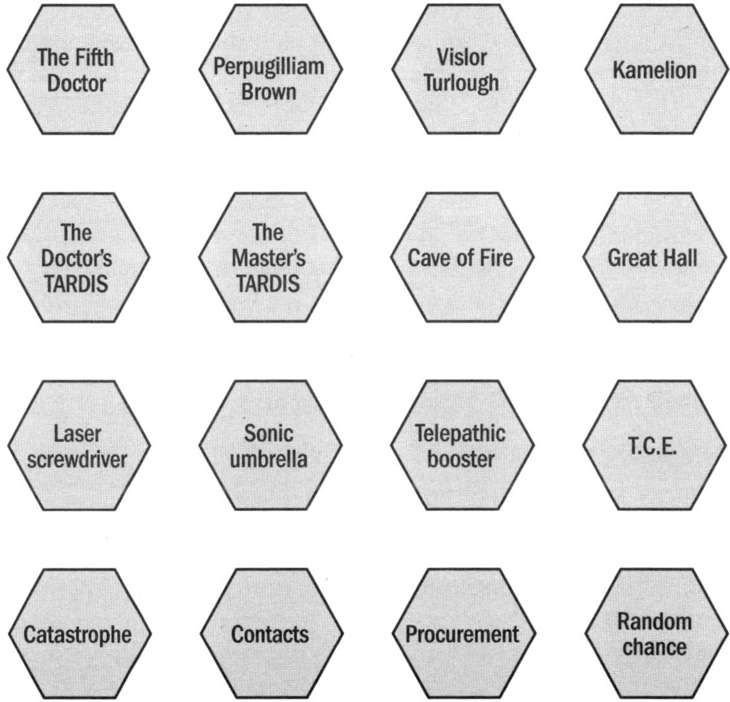

Planet of Fire

Who was involved · Where was he · What was he using · Why was he there:

The Fifth Doctor: Likes to stop for a pleasant lunchtime drinkie.
Perpugilliam Brown: Peri is a teenage botany student from 1984. A bit light-fingered, but since that saves her life, it's probably fine.
Vislor Turlough: Discovers that Sarn is populated by lost Trions, startled to discover than one of them is his baby brother.
Kamelion: A shape-shifting android from Mekalion, a planet whose name is way too close to its own for comfort. Easy to mind-control.

The Doctor's TARDIS: Spacious, brightly lit and pleasantly cool. There are an almost unmanageable number of roundels.
The Master's TARDIS: Cramped, dim and a bit too warm; lots of exposed pipes and cables, and a green tinge. Lacking in roundels.
The Cave of Fire: A great place to find hot lava, stinging clouds of black ash, or assorted volcanic gasses. A bit warm.
The Great Hall: The seat of power for the Trion population. Toasty.

Laser screwdriver: As the Master said, 'Who'd have sonic?' Fires an orange laser beam, which is cool, and still makes a great noise.
Sonic umbrella: Stylish black accessory suitable for both sun and rain, and duplicates all the functions of a sonic screwdriver. Not pocket sized, however.
Telepathic booster: Amplifies telepathic powers. Wired into the Master's TARDIS, so is not portable. Silver, looks silly when worn.
Tissue Compression Eliminator: A deadly gadget that emits a white light. But does it eliminate by compressing tissue, or does it eliminate tissue compression?

Catastrophe: The Time of Fire is about to unleash devastation on the people of Sarn. That's very useful to the Master.
Contacts: The Master has one or more allies here on the planet, and that could be very useful in facing down the Doctor.
Procurement: Sarn happens to be a great source of a substance that is vital to the Master's plans.
Random chance: The Master had to be somewhere, and he's the one that drew the TARDIS to his location. So why not Sarn?

Puzzle 16: Hard

Fill in the grid below as you work through the clues.

	The Fifth Doctor	Peri	Turlough	Kamelion	Catastrophe	Contacts	Procurement	Random chance	Doctor's TARDIS	Master's TARDIS	Cave of Fire	Great Hall
Laser screwdriver												
Sonic umbrella												
Telepathic booster												
T.C.E.												
Doctor's TARDIS												
Master's TARDIS												
Cave of Fire												
Great Hall												
Catastrophe												
Contacts												
Procurement												
Random chance												

The Five Doctors

Details:

The Fourth Doctor thought Borusa wanted to dominate the Universe.

?

The most circumspect person felt that Borusa's plan involved indestructibility. The snazziest person did not.

?

The Coronet was not thought to be part of the same plan as the Yeti.

?

The Fifth Doctor thought that Borusa's plan hinged either on the Master or the servants of the Great Intelligence.

?

Turlough was not with the Second Doctor or pondering the sash.

?

The Third Doctor was sure that cyborgs were involved somehow and The Brigadier discounted mind control as the key to Borusa's plan.

?

The Second Doctor feared that Borusa wanted to revive Rassilon and the dapper Doctor did not think that mutants were significant.

?

Sarah Jane thought Borusa planned to use the Harp to attack the Council from a secret room, and remove disloyal members.

?

The person who thought Borusa was using the Black Scrolls thought that the Daleks were a key part of the plan.

?

The Doctor who was correct identified a gemstone was involved and a staunch person was working with a dynamic one.

Puzzle 17: Extreme

The Doctor is dumped in a desolate area of Gallifrey known as the Death Zone – several different instances of him, in fact, along with several of his companions, and a host of deadly enemies. The Lord President of the Council of Gallifrey, Borusa, has gone rogue, and plans... well, nothing good at the very least, using one of the ultra-powerful Artefacts of Rassilon. As the chaos mounts, all the Doctors have their own idea as to what might be going on.

Can you unravel the theories and discover which Doctor is closest to assembling the core pieces of Borusa's plan?

Using the clues opposite, below and on pages 88–89, fill in the grid on pages 90–91 to work out the solution. Then draw lines overleaf to show your answer and circle the box with the Doctor who was right.

Neither the austere person nor his immediate successor suspected the Yeti to be of any critical importance.

The person who thought that Borusa wanted to restart the Game felt that the Raston Warrior Robot, while important for that particular event, was not a critical element in the plan.

Susan wasn't working with the third incarnation of her grandfather.

If Borusa's goal was to become immortal, then his plan definitely involved an organic opponent.

The five suggested plans each involved just one of the Third Doctor, Tegan, Borusa wanting to control the Universe, the wickedness of the Master, and the Coronet of Rassilon.

The Five Doctors

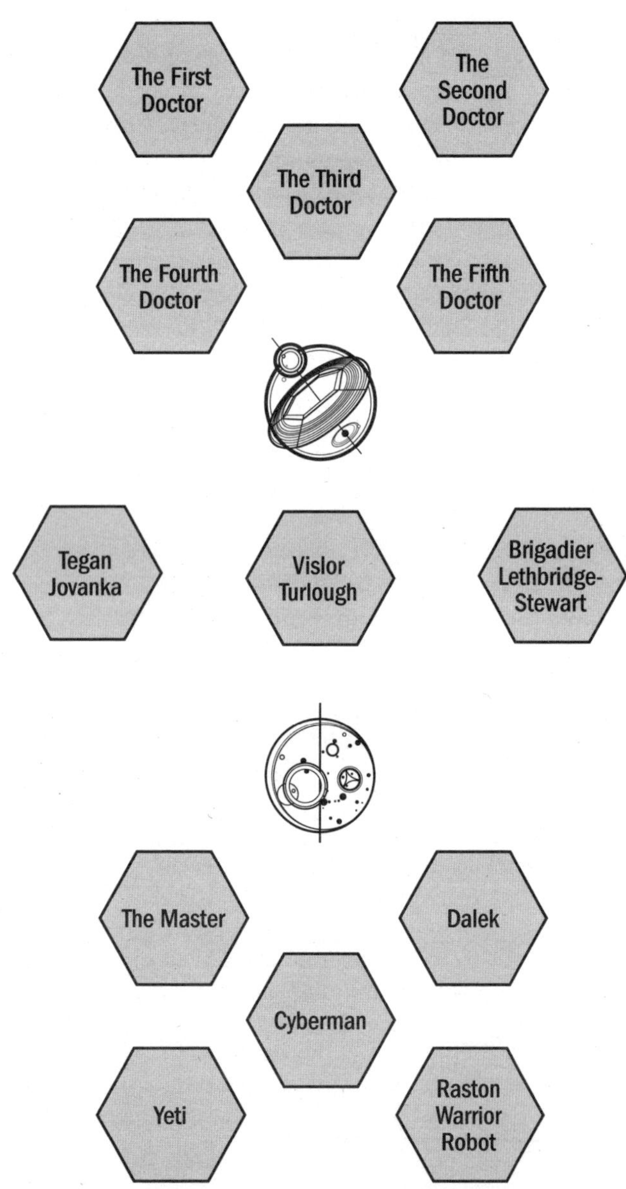

Puzzle 17: Extreme

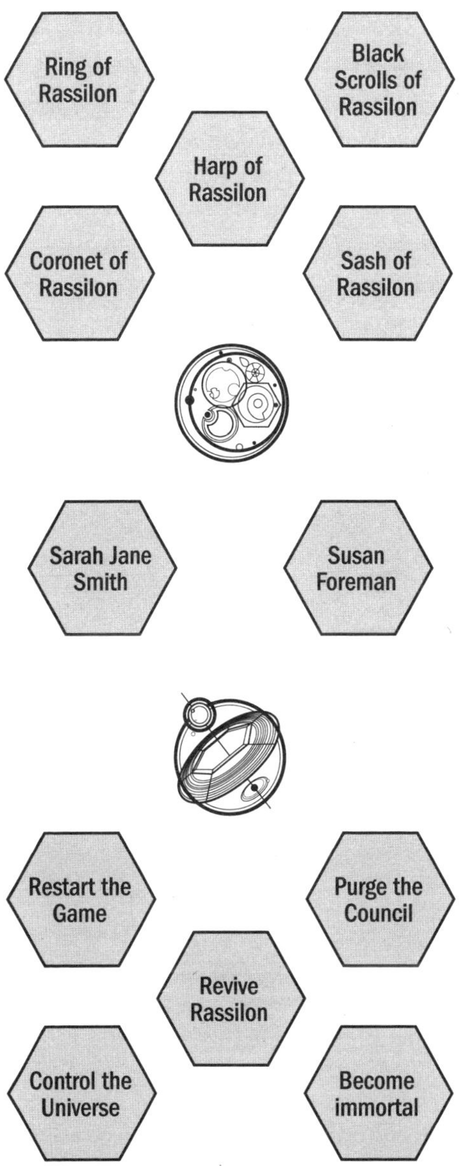

The Five Doctors

Who was involved · Who was with them · Who's planning · With what · Why:

The First Doctor: Stern. The oldest-looking, and the incarnation who has existed the longest, so far at least. That gives him seniority.
The Second Doctor: Whimsical. While his appearance may lack a certain polish, he makes up for it with his warmth and charm.
The Third Doctor: Stylish. Never less than dapper, impatient with fools, and a master of Venusian aikido.
The Fourth Doctor: Eccentric. Mostly stuck in a time vortex for this one. His sense of style is best described as 'Bohemian'.
The Fifth Doctor: Energetic, and significantly younger than his previous incarnations. A somewhat confused dress sense.

Tegan Jovanka: Headstrong. Australian former air stewardess who once unfairly described herself as 'just a mouth on legs'.
Vislor Turlough: Cagey. A clever alien from Trion, exiled when his family fell into disfavour. Prone to playing it close to his chest.
Brigadier Lethbridge-Stewart: Reliable. A talented military officer and natural leader with a fondness for heavy weaponry. Comforting to have around.
Sarah Jane Smith: Inquisitive. A stylish investigative journalist whose persistence leads her to the truth and trouble equally.
Susan Foreman: Brilliant. The Doctor's granddaughter, something of a temporal nexus in her own right. Really, really bad at lying.

The Master: Organic. The Doctor's most devout nemesis and former school friend. Participated in the Last Great Time War.
Dalek: Cyborg. A horrifying mutant inside an even more horrifying – and lethally dangerous – travel machine. Participated in the Last Great Time War.
Cyberman: Cyborg. Nothing much remains of the original human but a reprogrammed brain. Not as technologically advanced as the Daleks, but they do at least have legs.
Yeti: Robot. Beloved of the Great Intelligence for reasons that are cloudy at best. A deadly copy of the (peaceful, charming) real thing.
Raston Warrior Robot: Uh, Robot. Hunter-killer android used in the Death Zone to stalk and kill aliens for sport. Fast and deadly.

The Ring of Rassilon: A gold ring with a single red gemstone. It is said to guard the wearer from all possibility of death or destruction.
The Black Scrolls of Rassilon: Forbidden knowledge from the dark times of Gallifrey, held in a (possibly golden) casket. Many dangerous secrets are contained within.
The Harp of Rassilon: A golden musical instrument that acts as a key to a secret room in the chambers of the High Council of Gallifrey. Eventually replaced with a water feature.
The Coronet of Rassilon: A golden headband decorated with red gemstones that serves as a computer terminal of sorts, and allows mind control. Very fetching.
The Sash of Rassilon: A rather ostentatious golden sash that altered the wearer's cellular structure, making them almost indestructible. Definitely not as fetching as the Ring or the Coronet.

Restart the Game: The Game of Rassilon, of course – a lethal gladiatorial exercise where 'lesser' aliens were pitted against each other (and warrior robots). Great for controlling the masses.
Purge the Council: While all of the Doctors and many of his greatest friends and enemies were busy distracting the Time Lords, Borusa could seize the opportunity to quietly do away with various rivals and secure control of the Council.
Revive Rassilon: Death has always been a rather uncertain concept for Time Lords, and Rassilon was the greatest and darkest of them. He'd need a right-hand man.
Control the Universe: The Time Lords have often considered themselves to be the most potent and worthy species in the galaxy. Maybe Borusa is just showing a bit of ambition.
Become immortal: If Borusa was truly eternal, he could rule Gallifrey as its dictator forever and could mould the Time Lords into whatever he desired.

The Five Doctors

	The First Doctor	The Second Doctor	The Third Doctor	The Fourth Doctor	The Fifth Doctor	Tegan	Turlough	Brigadier	Sarah Jane	Susan Foreman
Restart the Game										
Purge the Council										
Revive Rassilon										
Control the Universe										
Become immortal										
Ring										
Black Scrolls										
Harp										
Coronet										
Sash										
The Master										
Dalek										
Cyberman										
Yeti										
Warrior Robot										
Tegan										
Turlough										
Brigadier										
Sarah Jane										
Susan Foreman										

Puzzle 17: Extreme

Fill in the grid below as you work through the clues.

The Twin Dilemma

Details:

You wouldn't put a drunkard in charge of a tractor beam.

?

If the villain is a duality, then the plan involves a time machine.

?

Only someone unpredictable would think a teleporter is involved.

?

Hugo does not think that the key technology is used for pulling.

?

The real villain is undoubtedly nosey.

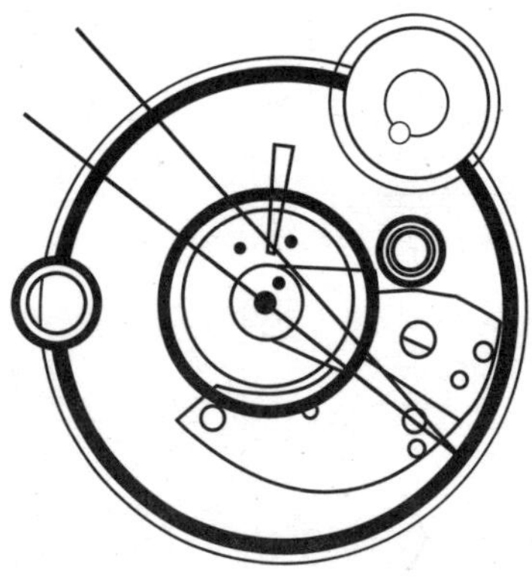

Puzzle 18: Easy

The Doctor regenerates into his sixth incarnation, who quickly shows signs of being violently unstable. Deciding to exile himself (and Peri, for no good reason) for the next few centuries, he travels to a bleak asteroid named Titan III. A space pilot named Hugo crashes on the asteroid, and then the Doctor runs into one of his old teachers from Gallifrey. He finds himself neck-deep in a mysterious plot that could doom the universe.

The Doctor and his companions have their own ideas about who is behind the scheme, and what tech is most critical. Can you decipher the clues to find out who has the right idea?

Using the clues opposite and overleaf, fill in the grid on page 95 to work out which villain did what. Then draw lines below from box to box to show your answer. Finally, circle the box containing the name of the person with the right idea.

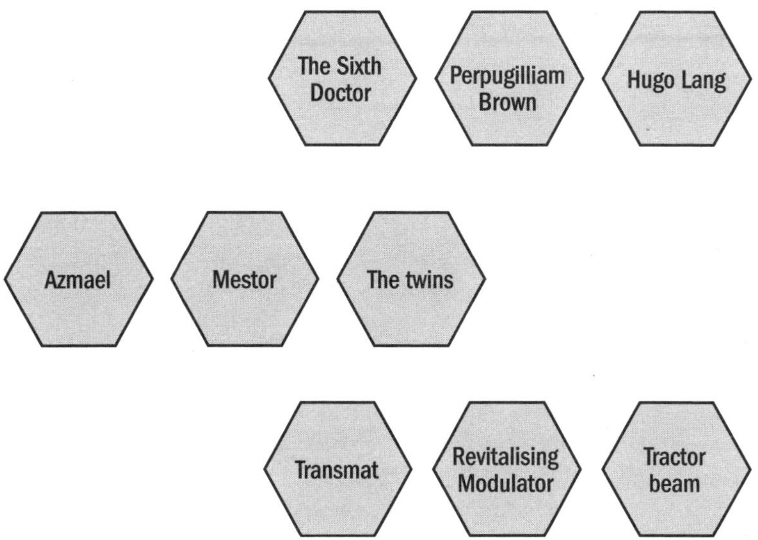

The Twin Dilemma

Who was involved · Who was behind the scheme · What did they use:

The Sixth Doctor: The new incarnation of the Doctor is out of control and knows it, but still takes exception at being judged by human standards.
Perpugilliam Brown: 'Peri' is an American botany student. Shares her name with a lovely Persian fairy.
Hugo Lang: Lieutenant Lang is a twenty-fourth-century starfighter pilot who is scared of flying. He immediately wanted to shoot the new Doctor – a relatable urge.

Azmael: An elderly renegade Time Lord on his last incarnation. He once got so drunk that the Doctor needed to throw him into a fountain to sober him up.
Mestor: A massive humanoid slug and the leader of the Gastropods, an alien race. He has a pair of deely-boppers on his head and ten – count them! – nose ridges.
The twins: Romulus and Remus Sylvest are kidnapped children who are such incredible maths geniuses that they threaten the very Universe itself. They seem fun.

Transmat: A teleport device. The name is short for 'particle matter transmission', even though 'parmatran' was right there. Some transmats send energy, others atoms.
Revitalising Modulator: A medical device invented to cure hangovers, presumably dear to Azmael's heart. The Doctor has reprogrammed this one into a time machine.
Tractor beam: A projected beam of energy used to pull one object towards another at a great distance, and with great power. The beams come in a variety of natty colours.

Puzzle 18: Easy

Fill in the grid below as you work through the clues.

	The Sixth Doctor	Peri	Hugo	Transmat	Revitalising Modulator	Tractor beam
Azmael						
Mestor						
The twins						
Transmat						
Revitalising Modulator						
Tractor beam						

The Two Doctors

Details:

Spying on your enemies to help defeat them was a long-standing tradition among the clans.

?

Neither the shorter companion nor the Second Doctor thought about trying to summon the TARDIS, not least because it was blocked from materialising right then.

?

The Second Doctor was not particularly skilled at fast talking and As a Highlander, Jamie could be quite scary when he put his mind to it.

?

The person who thought about using deceit did not waste any time worrying about the KR Module.

?

The Sixth Doctor lacked the self-control necessary to pull off a believable lie.

?

The person who considered the possibilities of the Stattenheim device was not particularly persuasive.

?

Given that the answer, as it often does, lay in misdirection of the non-physical sort, who came up with the best plan?

Puzzle 19: Medium

The Second Doctor and Jamie travel to a space station called Camera. The Head of Projects, Dastari, is experimenting with time machines on behalf of some Sontarans, and the Time Lords want him to stop. Instead, Dastari snatches the Doctor, planning to use his cell structure to complete the machine.

The Sixth Doctor and Peri dash to the rescue, but are swiftly imprisoned by the Sontarans. With everyone restrained, can you work out who found a way to get everyone free, what technique they used, and what device helped?

Using the clues opposite and overleaf, fill in the grid on page 99 to work everything out. Then draw lines below from box to box to show your answer. Finally, circle the box containing the name of the person who had the best plan.

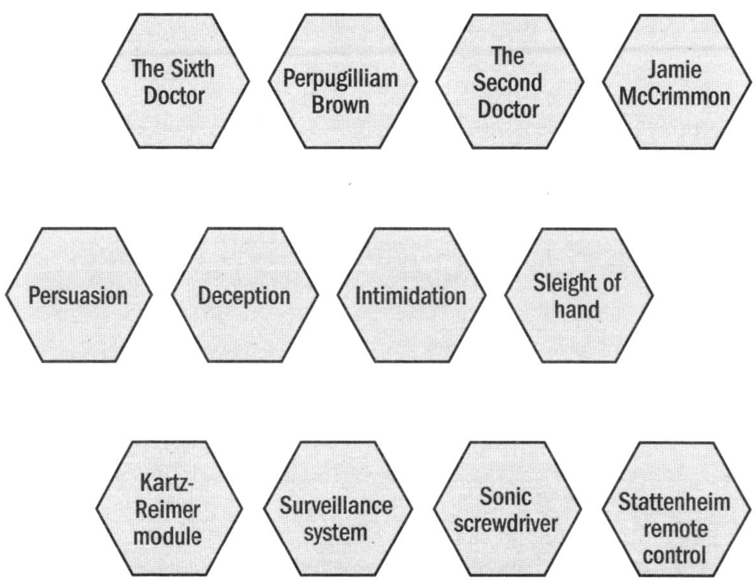

The Two Doctors

Who was involved · What technique · What device they used:

The Sixth Doctor: The Doctor is still suffering from regenerative trauma, and complains that he 'hasn't felt himself lately'. Turns vegetarian after this outing.
Perpugilliam Brown: Peri, an American student, enjoys tennis, hockey, lacrosse, and teasing the Doctor about his fashion sense.
The Second Doctor: On assignment to the Celestial Intervention Agency. Once helped a man escape from a balloon factory in Epping.
Jamie McCrimmon: A bagpipe-playing Highlander of the Clan McLeod, pronounced 'McCloud'.

Persuasion: Honeyed words can do wonders where brute force cannot. Requires a silver tongue. It helps if you're up against enemies who are a little slow, like the Androgum on the station.
Deception: Deceit is generally considered a bad thing, but needs must to prevent someone from breaking the Laws of Time. Demands a dark expression and an air of innocence.
Intimidation: Frighteningly few individuals in all of spacetime have had good results from antagonising the Doctor. What kind of fool risks going after two of them at the same time? (Apart from the Master, of course.)
Sleight of hand: The time-honoured way of parting someone from an object that they didn't intend to let you have – or, indeed, giving them something they really didn't want to take.

Kartz-Reimer module: A time-travel device in progress, stolen by Chessene, an extremely stylish evil genius. Looks like a black box with a triangular roof. You sit in it.
Surveillance system: Someone is always watching and listening to the imprisoned party. Knowing this, you can find a way to manipulate them.
Sonic screwdriver: The Second Doctor's, as the Sixth Doctor generally doesn't carry one. Looks like a pen light or laser pointer.
Stattenheim remote control: The Second Doctor can use this small rod with a gold disk and gold prongs to summon his TARDIS. A jaunty whistle is strictly optional.

Puzzle 19: Medium

Fill in the grid below as you work through the clues.

	The Sixth Doctor	Peri	The Second Doctor	Jamie	Kartz-Reimer	Surveillance	Sonic screwdriver	Remote control
Persuasion								
Deception								
Intimidation								
Sleight of hand								
Kartz-Reimer								
Surveillance								
Sonic screwdriver								
Remote control								

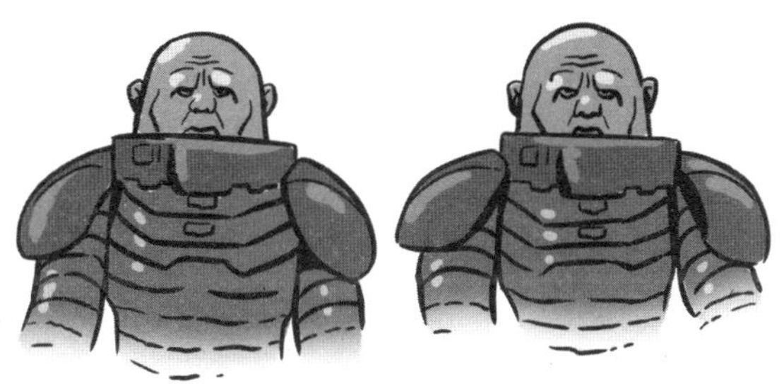

The Mysterious Planet

Details:

The best access to the hub space is kept carefully maintained.

?

Dibber prides himself on his eye for safety.

?

Peri doesn't think it's necessary to go all the way east and Glitz feels that Marble Arch is a good place to start.

?

The Doctor trusts his intuition to tell him which route is the best.

?

If you want to make sure you're not being tailed, it's best to go in past the emergency light.

?

Peri likes the idea of taking a breather along the way.

?

Instinct would suggest that you might need to pick up some handy equipment on route.

?

Given that the best entry to the catacombs is the one nearest the historical site of the Tyburn Tree, who identified the best route?

Puzzle 20: Hard

On a planet called Ravolox in the year 2,000,000, the Doctor and Peri are captured by the Tribe of the Free and the mercenaries Glitz and Dibber. It turns out Ravolox is Earth, and they're in what used to be London, ages ago. The caverns of Ravolox are watched over by Drathro the Immortal, a robot powered by black light. Both the Tribe and Glitz want to steal Drathro's secrets, but there are hazards associated with that, so the Doctor has to make sure the black light system is shut down properly.

From the information given, can you say which person's idea of how to get to Drathro is the correct one?

Using the clues opposite and overleaf, fill in the grid on page 103 to work everything out. Then draw lines below from box to box to show your answer. Finally, circle the box containing the name of the person whose idea was the best.

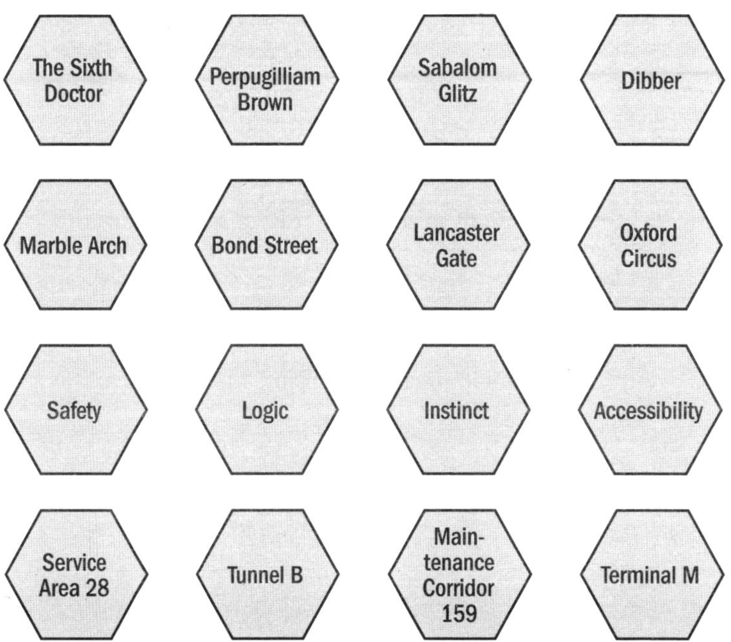

The Mysterious Planet

Who was involved · Which entrance · Why there · Through where:

The Sixth Doctor: Confused because Ravolox is two light years away from where Earth should be. Likes the universe not exploding.
Perpugilliam Brown: Peri is deeply upset over the horrendous state that her home planet is in. Aren't we all, Peri, aren't we all?
Sabalom Glitz: An avaricious rogue from the planet Salostopus in the Andromeda galaxy. Hired to retrieve some Gallifreyan files.
Dibber: Glitz's Salostopusian henchman. Short on education and sophistication, but a surprisingly wise head on his shoulders.

Marble Arch: The station's surviving sign is painted on the floor inside, partially covered by dirt. Peri and the Doctor have visited.
Bond Street: Glitz has been to this cavern entrance the most often, but that doesn't mean he thinks it's the best way in.
Lancaster Gate: The miraculously surviving half-buried sign identifying this one is lit by a flickering, dying emergency light.
Oxford Circus: Most easterly of the entrances to the caverns. It's lamentably short on actual circuses in the year two million. Shame.

Safety: The path to this entrance is covered by dense woodland, so it's the best way to approach without risking unwanted attention.
Logic: L1 maintenance robots have been sighted around this entrance recently, suggesting the caverns are in reasonable shape.
Instinct: Something about this particular entrance screams that it's the safest way. Ignore your instincts at your own peril.
Accessibility: The route to this entrance is straightforward, with no particular hazards or debris to worry about.

Service Area 28: A handy rest stop, making it a good location to use to regroup and assess possible dangers.
Tunnel B: Long, straight, and not too dingy, Tunnel B offers an excellent chance to make sure that you're not being followed.
Maintenance Corridor 159: You can find all sorts of useful stuff in here, left there by L1 robots who make use of it as a sort of store.
Terminal M: Offering an excellent range of onwards connections, a really convenient hub from which to explore routes forward.

Puzzle 20: Hard

Fill in the grid below as you work through the clues.

PART THREE

THE SEVENTH DOCTOR
THE EIGHTH DOCTOR
THE NINTH DOCTOR

Delta and the Bannermen

Details:

The Doctor thinks that the trap is either on the TARDIS or the beehive.

?

If the motorbike is trapped, then the trap is either cylindrical or disc-shaped.

?

It just wouldn't be right to leave an out-and-out deadly device strapped to a beehive.

?

The person who suspects that the trap is at the TARDIS has a great voice.

?

If the trap shares its shape with its name, who discovered it?

Puzzle 21: Easy

Doctor and Mel befriend Delta, the queen and last survivor of the Chimeron people. They're heading to Disneyland in 1959, but after an accident the tour bus lands in a Welsh holiday camp.

Delta is being hunted by the Bannermen, genocidal invaders determined to finish the job of killing her species. When Gavrok, leader of the Bannermen, learns that the Doctor and Mel are helping Delta with the aid of a local beekeeper, he sets a booby-trap. But where, and what, is it? There are multiple theories.

Can you work out which one is correct?

Using the clues opposite and overleaf, fill in the grid on page 109 to work out the various theories. Then draw lines below from box to box to show your answer. Finally, circle the box containing the name of the person with the correct theory.

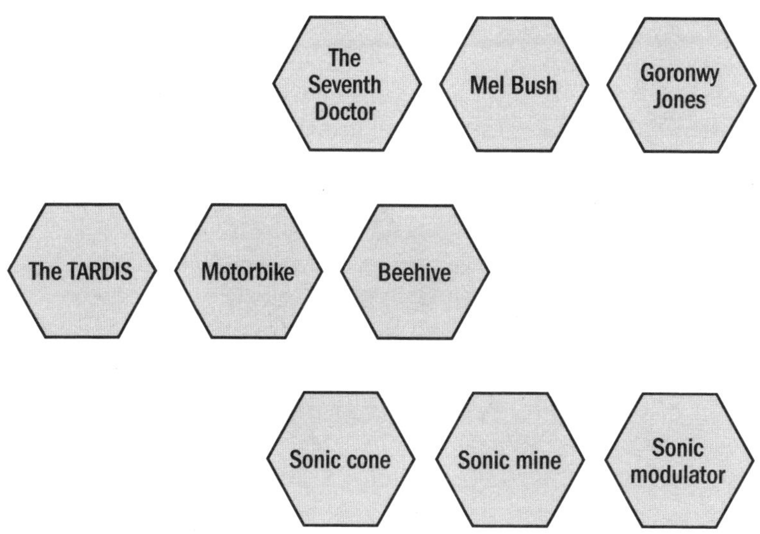

Delta and the Bannermen

Who was involved · Where was the trap · What device was it:

The Seventh Doctor: Manipulative and secretive underneath his jolly whimsy. This Doctor swapped sweaters for an umbrella with a question-mark handle. Five foot six inches tall, brown hair, blue eyes.
Mel Bush: A cheery and optimistic programming genius born on Earth in 1962, Mel has been determined to see the Earth from space since she was five. Four foot ten inches tall, red hair, brown eyes.
Goronwy Jones: A decidedly odd beekeeper who looks human, but who knows? He's very fond of singing, even by Welsh standards. Five foot seven inches tall, grey hair, blue eyes.

The TARDIS: Exterior. It could, at a pinch, possibly be described as a timey-wimey motor-home, if you were determined. Currently parked at the Shangri-La holiday camp.
Motorbike: Exterior. Having arrived in Wales, Delta fell in love with Billy, the mechanic whose bike this is. Equally besotted, he is working to become a Chimeron.
Beehive: Exterior. Tallish, boxy wooden structure owned by Goronwy. Perfectly normal and regular Earth bees live in it, nothing odd to see here. Surely, it's fine. Fine.

Sonic cone: Cone-shaped and sound-emitting, shockingly. Black. It's a powerful weapon that can potentially completely disintegrate a victim, or devastate an area.
Sonic mine: Round and disc-like, as mines tend to be. Emits sound waves. Metal-coloured, with blinking red lights. Potentially hideously destructive. Just bad all round.
Sonic modulator: A metallic cylinder that uses, yes, sound to cause horrible pain and even serious injuries. More debilitating than lethal, but that can be enough.

Puzzle 21: Easy

Fill in the grid below as you work through the clues.

	The Seventh Doctor	Mel Bush	Goronwy Jones	The TARDIS	Motorbike	Beehive
Sonic cone						
Sonic mine						
Sonic modulator						
The TARDIS						
Motorbike						
Beehive						

Remembrance of the Daleks

Details:

Unusually for a school, the cellar is not particularly smelly.

?

The turncoat instinctively fears and blames science and scientists for most things. It's all too common to hate the things we can't understand, sadly.

?

After time in the TARDIS, everything smells peculiar, particularly in London in 1963, so that's not much help.

?

The blinking lights are not coming from C4.

?

A keen student of history, the military officer does not suspect Barbara's room.

?

The Doctor doesn't much fancy the cellar.

?

Mike is hearing things, and that is never a good sign.

?

The real location of the transmat device is marked by intermittent visual clues.

Puzzle 22: Medium

Desperate to stop the Daleks from getting hold of the Hand of Omega, the Doctor and Ace travel to Shoreditch in 1963, landing near Coal Hill School. The First Doctor has just taken Susan, Ian, and Barbara travelling, so they aren't around to help. Two different factions of Daleks are fighting for the Hand.

The Imperial Dalek faction has enslaved much of the school, while the Renegade Dalek faction is working with a local fascist gang. The first step is to disable a transmat device hidden somewhere in the school. But where is it? Several people think that they've spotted a clue that reveals the location.

Can you figure out which is correct?

Using the clues opposite and overleaf, fill in the grid on page 113 to work everything out. Then draw lines below from box to box to show your answer. Finally, circle the box containing the location of the transmat.

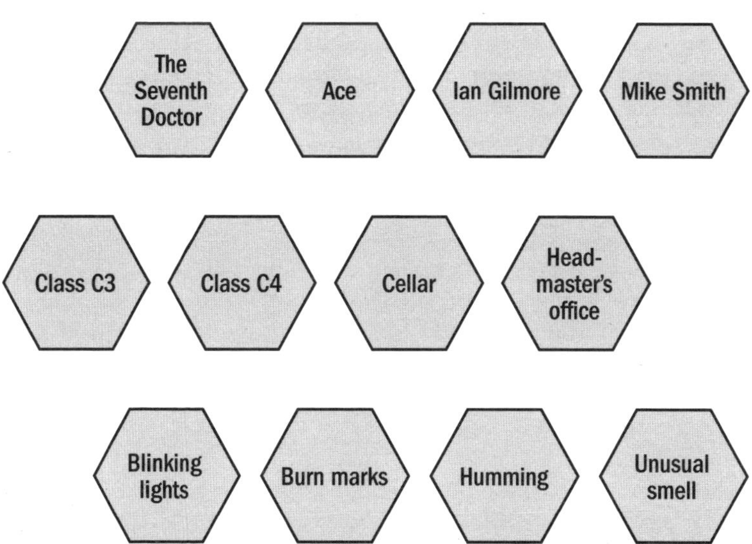

Remembrance of the Daleks

Who was involved · Where was the device · What give it away:

The Seventh Doctor: In this episode, the Doctor finally admits that he's 'far more than just another Time Lord'. Given the trail of broken foes he leaves behind, this should be no surprise.
'Ace': Dorothy Gale was a troubled child, and despite being born in London in 1970, she met the Doctor on Iceworld, a station above the planet Svartos in the year two million.
Group Captain Ian Gilmore: Reliable, resilient, and always immaculately turned out, Gilmore's men in the RAF nick-named him 'Chunky' for reasons unknown.
Sergeant Mike Smith: One of Gilmore's men. He is actually a spy for the Renegade Daleks, as well as a racist and fascist traitor. He is quite helpful until he turns, however.

Class C3: Where Ian Chesterton teaches science. 'Science Laboratory' is written on the door – feels like a needless tautology.
Class C4: Barbara Wright teaches history here. One assumes that being next door to the experiments is something of a trial at times.
Cellar: Big, maze-like, dusty, not well lit. In other words, a perfectly normal school cellar. The boiler is probably down here somewhere.
Headmaster's office: Not too ostentatious as these things go. A bit brown. The fact that the headmaster is being mind-controlled by Daleks is a downside.

Blinking lights: Visual. In 1963, machines with blinking lights were still comparatively uncommon. Still cheaper than the machine that went 'ping' though.
Burn marks: Visual. All sorts of things could leave scorch-marks on a school floor. Candles. Accidental bin fires. Pyromanic students. Flame ghosts. Daleks. Anything.
Humming: Audible. Not the tuneless attempts at quiet musical recreation so beloved of schoolchildren and teachers, but the sort of machine noise that suggests bad things.
Unusual smell: Olfactory. Schools are a horrifying source of many very unusual smells indeed, but some are just that bit more unearthly than others.

Puzzle 22: Medium

Fill in the grid below as you work through the clues.

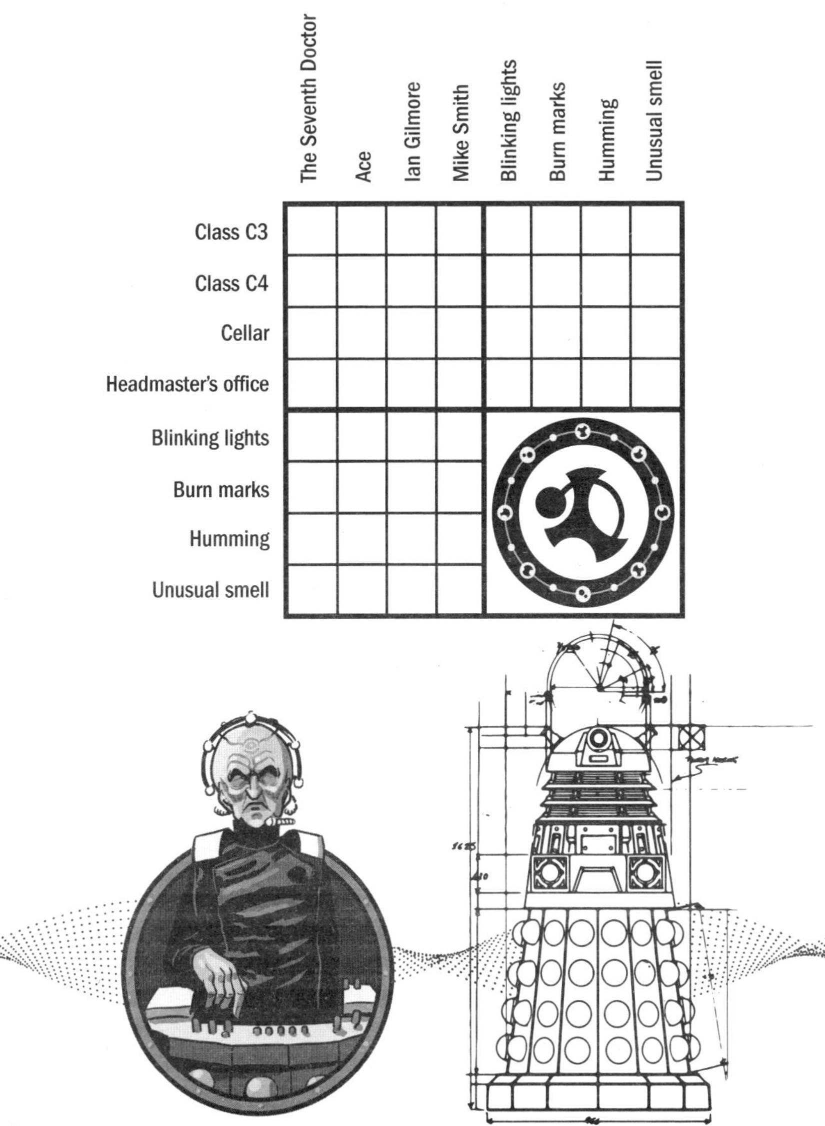

	The Seventh Doctor	Ace	Ian Gilmore	Mike Smith	Blinking lights	Burn marks	Humming	Unusual smell
Class C3								
Class C4								
Cellar								
Headmaster's office								
Blinking lights								
Burn marks								
Humming								
Unusual smell								

Battlefield

Details:

Ace expects to find Excalibur in its scabbard.

?

If the sword is where the knight landed, it is being hunted by its rightful bearer.

?

The Brigadier thinks Mordred is the one hunting for the sword.

?

The person with the darkest eyes doubts that Excalibur is in a high-tech location.

?

The Doctor believes that the seeker is loyal to Arthur.

?

The person who thinks the sword is in a sarcophagus expects to find it under the hotel.

?

Shou Yuing is sure that Excalibur is at the dig site.

?

If the sword is in or under the lake, that can only mean that Ancelyn seeks it.

?

Given that Excalibur is in a good place to go travelling, who knows where to find it?

Puzzle 23: Hard

Following an urgent distress call, the Doctor and Ace arrive in Somerset, England in 1997. An archaeologist has found the site of the Battle of Camlann. In doing so, he has drawn attention . . .

Camlann was Arthur's final battle against the evil Mordred, and the denizens of Camelot have descended from a parallel reality. Worse, a UNIT detachment with a nuclear missile is stuck too. The distress call is coming from Excalibur. The Doctor and his allies have many theories, but can you work out who is hunting Excalibur, what site it is at, and precisely where it can be found?

Using the clues, fill in the grid on page 117 to work everything out. Then draw lines below from box to box to show your answer. Finally, circle the box containing the name of the person who knows the location.

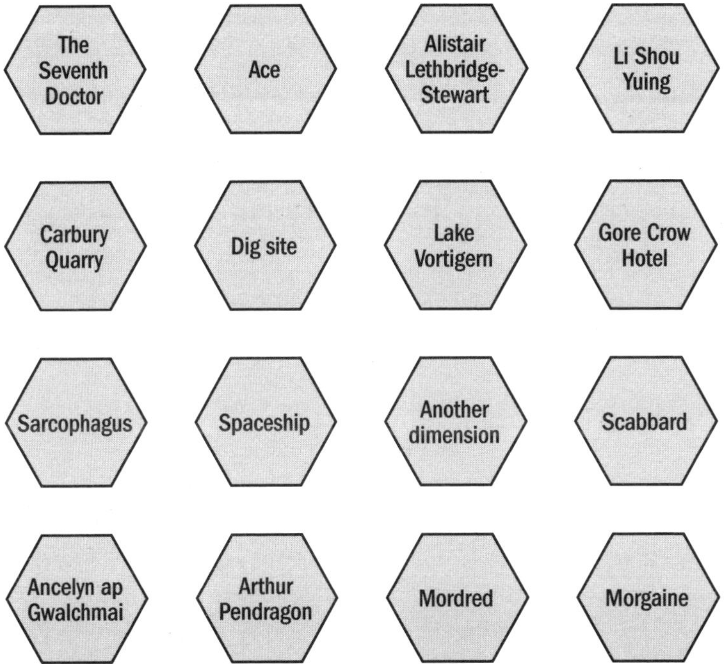

Battlefield

Who was involved · Which site · Where is it located · Who is hunting:

The Seventh Doctor: Multiple people – with little love for each other – identify the Doctor as Merlin on sight. Time travel makes for a complex social life. Blue eyes.
Ace: Having spent time in the distant future, it's no real surprise that Ace thought metal-clad figures were more likely to be robots than knights. Hazel eyes.
Alistair Lethbridge-Stewart: The Brigadier has retired. He is happy to help, of course. Blue eyes.
Li Shou Yuing: Shou Yuing works at the archaeological dig. Fond of blowing things up, so she and Ace get on like a house on fire. Name means 'Little Cloud', according to the Doctor. Brown eyes.

Carbury Quarry: Quarries have always been a key part of the Doctor's adventures. A transdimensional knight landed here.
Dig site: The Battle of Camlann is usually thought to have taken place in Cornwall or Wales, but Peter Warmsly found it here.
Lake Vortigern: A gloomy body of water outside the village which takes its name from an old warlord from Arthur's time.
The Gore Crow Hotel: Pleasant rural inn which may take its less pleasant name from folk memories of the aftermath of battle.

Sarcophagus: Many legendarily powerful artefacts end up buried in big stone boxes, at least if popular entertainment is to be believed.
Spaceship: When you are the sharpest and most deadly sword ever to have been forged, you can travel the stars with the best of them.
Another dimension: The invaders of Carbury come from a different universe. It's not hard to believe that Excalibur might be there.
Scabbard: Where else? Excalibur's scabbard was said to have the power to stop wounds bleeding – useful if you fight with swords.

Ancelyn ap Gwalchmai: The Knight Commander of King Arthur's forces, loyal to Arthur. Hates Mordred. Likes warrior women.
Arthur Pendragon: An avatar of the hyper-powerful Guardian of Might, from the times before the creation of the Universe.

Puzzle 23: Hard

Fill in the grid below as you work through the clues.

	The Doctor	Ace	Alistair	Li Shou Yuing	Sarcophagus	Spaceship	Another dimension	Scabbard	Carbury Quarry	Dig site	Lake Vortigern	Gore Crow Hotel
Ancelyn												
Arthur												
Mordred												
Morgaine												
Carbury Quarry												
Dig site												
Lake Vortigern												
Gore Crow Hotel												
Sarcophagus												
Spaceship												
Another dimension												
Scabbard												

Mordred: The illegitimate son of Morgaine, conceived thanks to the Master's interference. He is King Arthur's deadliest enemy.
Morgaine: The sorcerous Battle-Queen of the S'rax. She became intrigued by King Arthur on Earth, and was deeply offended when he married Guinevere.

Details:

The permanent building is not associated with either displacement or motion.

?

Suspect One is suspicious because of a potentially anomalous object.

?

If the Master is in the TARDIS, it is not a motion that gives him away.

?

Suspect Three is not associated with a revelatory movement.

?

If the Master is on the move, which suspect is he?

Puzzle 24: Easy

The Seventh Doctor is taking the Master's remains back to Gallifrey when he is forced to land in San Francisco at the tail end of 1999. He steps outside and is gunned down by street thugs.

The malfunction is the result of sabotage, and the Master is not yet dead. Instead, using a Deathworm Morphant, he escapes the TARDIS and possesses a human victim. Newly regenerated, the Eighth Doctor has to find the Master before his plans to stabilise his new existence destroy the Earth.

From the information given, can you work out who and where the Master is, and what gives him away?

Using the clues, fill in the grid on page 121 to work out who and where. Then draw lines below from box to box to show your answer. Finally, circle the box containing the identity of the Master.

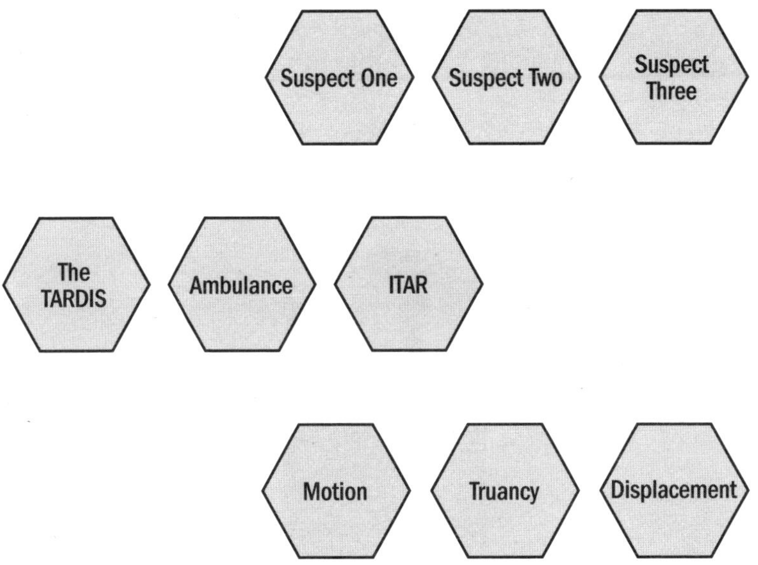

Doctor Who: The Movie

Who was the Master · Where was he · What: gave him away:

Suspect One: Wearing a dark grey business suit, black Oxford shoes, and carrying a briefcase. Very short blond hair and blue eyes.
Suspect Two: Wearing jeans, a check shirt, a black leather duster, and light boots. Not carrying anything. Slicked back hair, wearing sunglasses.
Suspect Three: A punk in a denim vest and heavy black boots, carrying a brown paper bag. Green Mohawk hair and green eyes.

The TARDIS: Currently suffering from a critical timing malfunction, thanks to the Master's interference. Offers a vast number of places to hide.
Ambulance: Capable of movement, at least, which is more than the other two. Has more hidey holes than you might think, but still limited compared to other options.
ITAR: The Institute for Technological Advancement and Research. A big, dramatic building. Only moves during earthquakes. Lots of hiding spots.

Motion: A twitch, a half-gesture, a jostle, a moment of minor clumsiness, unintended movements can reveal far more than is intended, as you would imagine.
Truancy: People abandon their posts, go places they shouldn't, don't turn up as expected. Sometimes, that rings alarm bells.
Displacement: Objects that are innocuous become deeply anomalous when out of their correct time and place, raising suspicion.

Puzzle 24: Easy

Fill in the grid below as you work through the clues.

Details:

Neither of the Doctors thought that it was just loathing behind the attacks.

?

Tegan was always suspicious of the Time Lords.

?

Having just beaten the Master, the Eighth Doctor was sure he'd be off licking his wounds.

?

Turlough couldn't imagine a being as vast as Omega bothering with attacking the Doctor.

?

Tegan figured the attack was a pre-emptive strike.

?

If it was Omega behind the attempt, he had no reason to want revenge.

?

The Master is far too calculating to act purely from malice.

?

Unscramble this – **YOUR ARCANE TIP** – to discover the reason behind the attack.

Puzzle 25: Medium

After saving the Fourth Doctor's life, the Eighth Doctor arrives in the Gallifreyan Death Zone. The Fifth Doctor, Tegan and Turlough are still there, having just stopped President Borusa from becoming the eternal dictator. They're being attacked by a Raston Warrior Robot and a passing squad of Sontaran soldiers.

The Eighth Doctor is able to save his younger self and his friends, but someone is using time technology to meddle. They're trying to kill him. Can you work out who correctly guessed the identity and motivation of the hidden enemy?

Using the clues opposite and overleaf, fill in the grid on page 125 to work out who correctly guessed the identity and motive. Then draw lines below from box to box to show your answer. Finally, circle the box containing the name of the person who was right.

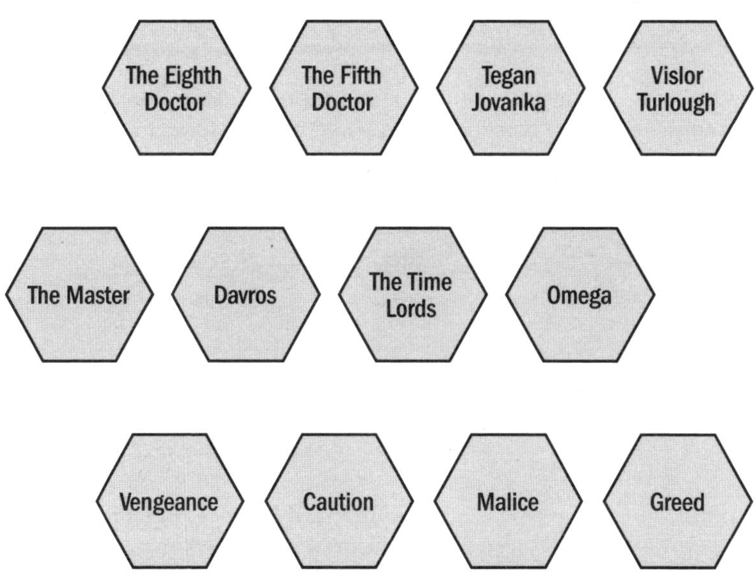

The Eight Doctors

Who was involved · Which enemy · Motivation:

The Eighth Doctor: Joyful, charming and carefree, with a fondness for red jelly babies and a flair for the dramatic.
The Fifth Doctor: Energetic, but sometimes indecisive and vulnerable. Likes iced lemonade and celery.
Tegan Jovanka: Practical, stubborn and direct, but faultlessly loyal and honest. A fan of the band Talking Heads.
Vislor Turlough: Extremely clever, but prone to selfishness and prioritising his own survival. Likes tea with milk and sugar.

The Master: The Doctor's greatest enemy, renegade Time Lord, owns his own TARDIS, near impossible to kill – he's a prime candidate.
Davros: The utterly amoral scientific genius who created the Daleks. Almost as hard to kill as the Master, and the Daleks do have time technology.
The Time Lords: Every now and again, some unpleasant Time Lord decides that the Doctor has to be killed. Never seems to work out well.
Omega: One of the founders of Time Lord society, a genius engineer twisted into hateful insanity by uncountable years in the anti-matter universe.

Vengeance: The Doctor has foiled all sorts of plans representing vast amounts of effort on the part of a great many enemies. He positively hoards grudges.
Caution: There are all sorts of reasons why it might be prudent to remove the Doctor from existence. He does, after all, meddle in a great many affairs.
Malice: Some beings just want to watch the Universe burn. There's more than enough hatred to go around, but the Doctor attracts an unusually large share.
Greed: The classic motivation for evil actions. If the Doctor is standing in the way of vast wealth or power, perhaps it's time for him to go.

Puzzle 25: Medium

Fill in the grid below as you work through the clues.

	The Eighth Doctor	The Fifth Doctor	Tegan Jovanka	Vislor Turlough	Vengeance	Caution	Malice	Greed
The Master								
Davros								
The Time Lords								
Omega								
Vengeance								
Caution								
Malice								
Greed								

Placebo Effect

Details:

A gold medal is worth nine points, a silver medal is worth three points, and a bronze medal is worth one point.

?

The person who bet on Earth isn't human.

?

The person who bet on Arcturus wants some fritters.

?

The planet Stacy bet on won the most individual medals, but did not win the most points.

?

Ssard fancies a really exquisite curry.

?

The person who wants to go to the seventy-eighth century bet on Earth.

?

Someone with dark hair bet on Arcturus.

?

Someone with blue eyes bet on Betelgeuse V.

?

Given that Arcturus got twenty-six bronze medals – and more silver medals than Earth – when did the group head there for their meal?

Puzzle 26: Hard

In the year 3999, the Galactic Olympic Games are taking place on an artificially built planetoid called Micawber's World. The Eighth Doctor's old companions Stacy Townsend and the Ice Warrior Ssard are getting married during the Olympiad.

The group decide to place a wager – the one who correctly guesses which planet's athletes do the best in the competition gets to choose when in history the group travel to for a fancy meal.

From the information provided, can you decide who won, which planet they picked, when they're going, and what their planet's medal tally was?

Using the clues, fill in the grid on page 129 to work out who bet what. Then draw lines below from box to box to show the century they will travel to.

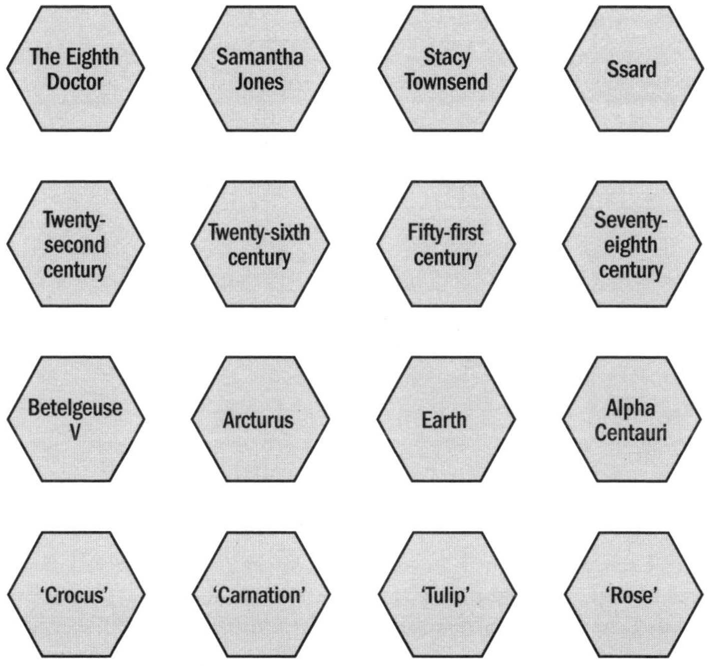

Placebo Effect

Who was involved · When they want to go · Which planet · Medal count:

The Eighth Doctor: Known to have acquired a tattoo of a man transforming into a jaguar. Brown hair, blue eyes.
Samantha Jones: Born on Earth in 1980, Sam is one of the very few beings in the universe who actually knows the Doctor's real name. Dark hair, blue eyes.
Stacy Townsend: A former deep space freighter worker, born in 2220 on Earth. Her first fiancée was turned into a Cyberman. Blonde hair, blue eyes.
Ssard: A former royal guard from Mars in the late fortieth century, a talented and cunning engineer as well as a capable warrior. No hair, red eyes.

Twenty-second century: Notable for a culinary craze involving delicate fritters made from flower petals.
Twenty-sixth century: A time of synthetic designer foods designed from the DNA up to be irresistible to the diner.
Fifty-first century: A chance encounter with an anomalous cookbook made this an unparalleled time for traditional curries.
Seventy-eighth century: Ice-cream never got finer than in the space palaces of this period.

Betelgeuse V: The Third Doctor remembered a double sunrise here, which was odd, as the Betelgeuse is not a binary star.
Arcturus: An AI terraforming probe once landed here and started work, which rather annoyed the (extensive, advanced) population.
Earth: The home-world of various intelligent space-faring species, including Humanity, the Silurians and dolphins. No dolphins competed in the 3999 Olympics.
Alpha Centauri: Captain Jack Harkness fondly remembered once having gone to a great party on Alpha Centauri, so they must know how to have a very good time.

Puzzle 26: Hard

Fill in the grid below as you work through the clues.

	The Eighth Doctor	Samantha Jones	Stacy Townsend	Ssard	Twenty-second century	Twenty-sixth century	Fifty-first century	Seventy-eighth century	Betelgeuse V	Arcturus	Earth	Alpha Centauri
'Crocus'												
'Carnation'												
'Tulip'												
'Rose'												
Betelgeuse V												
Arcturus												
Earth												
Alpha Centauri												
Twenty-second century												
Twenty-sixth century												
Fifty-first century												
Seventy-eighth century												

Codename **'Crocus'**:	37 Gold	36 Silver	26 Bronze.
Codename **'Carnation'**:	32 Gold	40 Silver	57 Bronze.
Codename **'Tulip'**:	29 Gold	54 Silver	38 Bronze.
Codename **'Rose'**:	36 Gold	33 Silver	43 Bronze.

The End of the World

Details:

The motivated individual would not be needed in the place named after a city.

?

It is safe to assume that not everyone has the bureaucratic experience required to access Control.

?

The tree is used to operating in windy conditions.

?

The Manchester Suite is not in need of a solicitor.

?

Given that motivation is probably the most important quality, who does the Doctor need help from?

Puzzle 27: Easy

The Ninth Doctor and Rose Tyler travel to the year five billion, for a party at the end of the world. The space station Platform One is in orbit around Earth to witness its final end. The great and good of the galaxy are here to enjoy the spectacle.

Unfortunately, the Adherents of the Repeated Meme have sabotaged the station under the control of the depraved last human, Lady Cassandra O'Brien.Δ17. The Doctor needs help to reboot key systems and prevent the station from being destroyed in the eruption.

From the information given, which potential ally is best placed to help, and where and why?

Using the clues opposite and overleaf, fill in the grid on page 133 to work out who is where and how they might help. Then draw lines below from box to box to show your answer. Finally, circle the box containing the name of the ally.

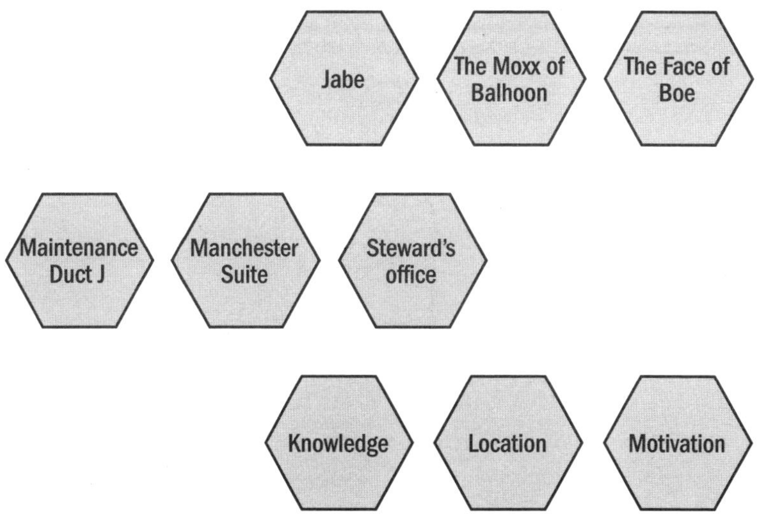

The End of the World

Which ally · Where they are · Why they may help:

Jabe of the Forest of Cheem: An Earthling descended from the rainforests of Earth, Jabe is a sapient humanoid tree. She knows the Doctor is the last of his kind.
The Moxx of Balhoon: A small, blue gentleman who floats around in a rather nice antigravity chair. The Moxx is representing a firm of solicitors.
The Face of Boe: A gigantic humanoid head in a glass case. Telepathic and immortal, the Face of Boe is the oldest creature in the Universe.

Maintenance Duct J: Platform One's power core is located here. Because it is a key route in the ventilation system, it's also very windy.
Manchester Suite: The post end-of-the-world drinks and buffet are located here. There is also a control node for the station shields.
Steward's office: Control, the computer operating Platform One and all its systems, can be accessed from here.

Knowledge: The Doctor doesn't want just any assistance, he has specific requirements that one ally meets.
Location: One of the Doctor's allies is currently in exactly the right spot to be really quite handy.
Motivation: Of the three possible assistants in this matter, one of them is particularly determined to be helpful.

Puzzle 27: Easy

Fill in the grid below as you work through the clues.

	Jabe	The Moxx	Face of Boe	Maintenance Duct J	Manchester Suite	Steward's office
Knowledge						
Location						
Motivation						
Maintenance Duct J						
Manchester Suite						
Steward's office						

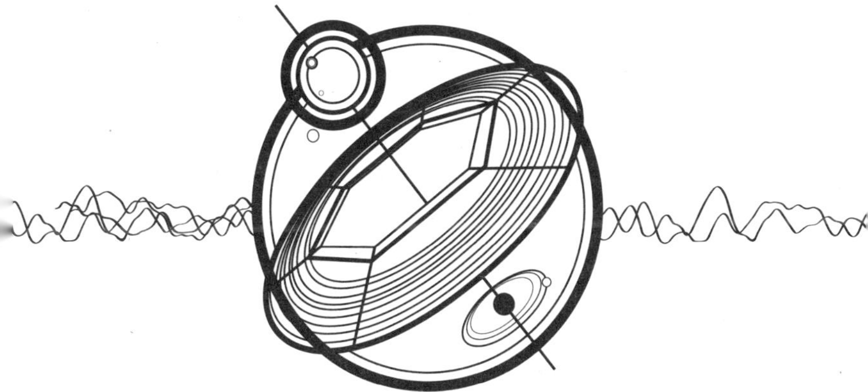

The Long Game

Details:

The person who wants to use someone's Type II port to deploy the software is excited.

?

The Dalek software can only be deployed by the sonic screwdriver.

?

Cathica wants to use the Gallifreyan software, but does not trust the superphone.

?

A person with blue eyes wants to use the superphone.

?

The Trojan could easily be deployed using a Type II port.

?

If the most subtle software is the best choice, who can access the computer?

Puzzle 28: Medium

The Doctor takes Rose and Adam to the year 200,000 CE to visit the Fourth Great and Bountiful Human Empire. Arriving in Station 5, the broadcast hub of the Empire, the Doctor quickly realises that something is decidedly wrong. There are no aliens to be seen anywhere, the Empire is nowhere near as developed as it should be, and the station's staff are disappearing.

The information needed to actually understand the current situation is stored on the station's mainframe computer. From the information given, can you figure out who is able to hack into the computer, and what hardware and software they use?

Using the clues opposite and overleaf, fill in the grid on page 137 to work out who did what, and how. Then draw lines below from box to box to show your answer. Finally, circle the box containing the name of the person who actually accessed the computer.

The Long Game

Who is involved · What hardware will they use · What software:

The Ninth Doctor: Unusually emotional and vulnerable, this incarnation has been badly scarred by recent events. Brown hair, blue eyes.
Rose Tyler: Born in the late '80s, Rose joins the Doctor in 2005. Having been depressed by the Earth's destruction, she is excited to see a good period for humanity. Blonde hair, brown eyes.
Adam Mitchell: Adam has the dubious distinction of being the only companion to be banished from the TARDIS for dire behaviour. Brown hair, brown eyes.
Cathica: Despite being a journalist, Cathica is initially reluctant to investigate the possibility that something is wrong on Satellite 5. Black hair, brown eyes.

Sonic screwdriver: The Ninth Doctor's sonic screwdriver is grey and silver with a blue emitter: nice.
Type II port: A neural implant stuck into the user's brain via a forehead port, allowing a user to connect their mind to Satellite 5's technology. Seems hygienic?
Credit stick: A metallic silver object used for transferring money within the Empire. It's like your credit card got horribly spliced with a USB stick in a teleport accident.
Superphone: Rose's twenty-first-century mobile phone, upgraded with Time Lord technology. It can make calls across time and space.

Virus: A computer virus runs hostile code on a target computer. This one is Gallifreyan, and can give total control, but it's not subtle.
Worm: Malware that repeatedly copies itself, spreading through networks, until a target is overwhelmed. This unsubtle cyber-weapon was retrieved from a Dalek ship.
Trojan: A Trojan horse disguises itself as normal software. It's comparatively slow, but really rather stealthy. This one was purchased from a Crespallion 'businessman'.
Keylogger: Spyware that records which buttons and screen spots users interact with. Extremely stealthy. This logger was designed by Judoon security experts.

Puzzle 28: Medium

Fill in the grid below as you work through the clues.

The Unquiet Dead

Details:

The shortest person fears that the presence of the zombies is motivated by a form of imperialism.

?

The person who thinks that the bodies were just handy also suspects that Sneed's is the site because of the dimensional rip.

?

Gwyneth knows all too well that the dead make for impactful envoys.

?

The Doctor does not think that anyone is out for revenge.

?

Mr Dickens suspects that someone is using zombies because they are the fastest option.

?

If the undead are here to deliver a message, then it is surely about the disrespect they've faced.

?

The Doctor suspects something hitched a ride on a meteor

?

If haste drove the selection of zombies, it was because the disturbance was centred around an individual.

?

If the zombies are merely the best option from the available resources, then who correctly identified the problem?

Puzzle 29: Hard

It's Christmas Eve in the year 1869, and the city of Cardiff is having something of a problem with the undead. In the funeral parlour of Sneed and Company, the recently deceased are exhibiting a lamentable desire to get back up and kill the living.

With the help of the novelist Charles Dickens and Sneed's kindly servant Gwyneth, the Doctor and Rose have to determine why Sneed's offices are such a hub of necromantic activity. From the information given, can you say who correctly identifies the main cause for the zombie infestation's location, nature and purpose?

Using the clues, fill in the grid on page 141 to work out the answers. Then draw lines from box to box to show them. Finally, circle the box with the name of the person who identified the problem.

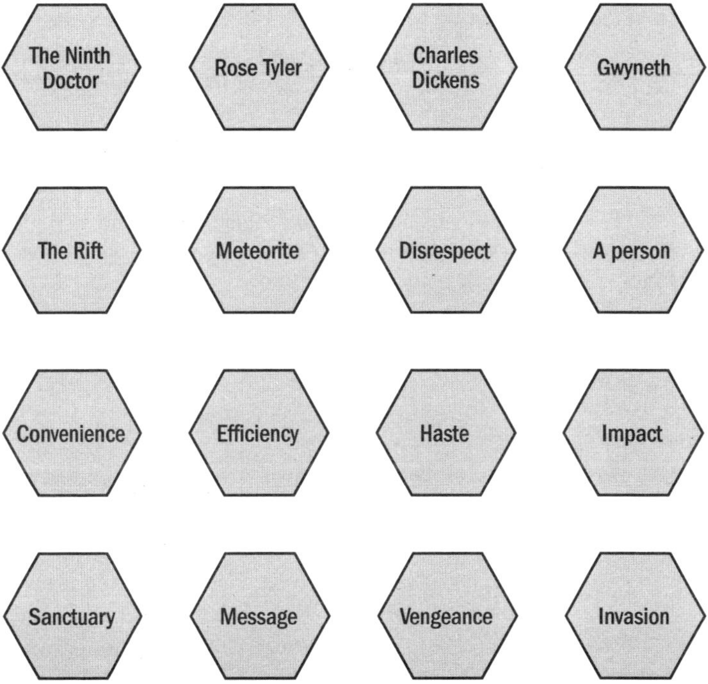

The Unquiet Dead

Who was involved · Why was there activity · Nature · Purpose:

The Ninth Doctor: This Doctor likes to live impulsively and joyfully in the moment, which makes sense given the past. Six foot tall.
Rose Tyler: Resolutely brave, curious and defiant, Rose is horrified by the working conditions that Gwyneth has to suffer. Five foot four inches tall.
Charles Dickens: One of the greatest writers of English, celebrated across centuries of Earth history. Five foot seven inches tall.
Gwyneth: A kind, friendly woman with surprisingly strong psychic powers. Works as Gabriel Sneed's servant. Five foot six inches tall.

The Cardiff Space-Time Rift: A tear in the fabric of spacetime through which all kinds of peoples and things occasionally arrive.
Meteorite: The Pied Piper of Hamelin arrived via space rock in 1283. So will a gaseous alien that possesses people. Perhaps Sneed's is built on something similar.
Disrespect: Sneed is a bad undertaker, careless with the deceased and his job. It's possible that the dead have just had enough.
A person: It might not be the funeral home that's the problem, it might be one of the people in or near it. Seen any necromancers lately?

Convenience: When times are troubled and the resources you have to hand are scarce, you work with what you've got. Even corpses.
Efficiency: Maybe using zombies is helping to achieve more than one purpose. Maybe it's a desire to avoid waste. Maybe zombies have useful skills. Who knows?
Haste: Sometimes the shortest distance between two points involves riding around inside the remains of the dearly departed. It isn't a common solution, but...
Impact: Mortal terror can help to emphasise a point, even if it is in poor taste. Whether pleading or threatening, words spoken by the dead do tend to draw attention.

Sanctuary: Whether they're kicking open the darkest gate or screaming across the void, perhaps someone is desperate to escape.

Puzzle 29: Hard

Fill in the grid below as you work through the clues.

	The Ninth Doctor	Rose Tyler	Charles Dickens	Gwyneth	Convenience	Efficiency	Haste	Impact	The Rift	Meteorite	Disrespect	A person
Sanctuary												
Message												
Vengeance												
Invasion												
The Rift												
Meteorite												
Disrespect												
A person												
Convenience												
Efficiency												
Haste												
Impact												

Message: Communication is an urgent need of almost all sentient life. Maybe someone needs to send a post-mortem telegram.
Vengeance: Rage is a great motivator. Is Sneed incompetent and callous enough to drive the netherworld mad with the urge for revenge?
Invasion: It is common for one group to arrive at another's home, claim it for their own, and annihilate the locals. Did the zombies bring a flag?

Rose

Details:

Of the five folders, one was blue, one included Article 57, one held an acclaimed article, one held a bureaucratic article, and one held an article written by six species.

?

The tangled article is not kept in the green or purple folders.

?

The terse article was compiled by five species.

?

Article 6 is not in the storage room, but it was mostly written by the Judoon.

?

The least contentious article includes a contribution by the Time Lords.

?

Somehow, the article written by the greatest number of species is not considered tangled.

?

The article that is widely dismissed is not the long one.

?

The shunned article is in a green folder.

?

The article in the red folder is either bureaucratic or tangled.

?

Article 1327 is usually held in the red folder, and it was not written with the involvement of any poets.

Puzzle 30: Extreme

Arriving in London in 2005, the Doctor finds that the Earth is – once again – threatened by alien invasion. With help from his new friend Rose Tyler, he begins working to defuse the situation.

The Doctor hopes to invoke the Shadow Proclamation in order to find a peaceful solution, but his copy of the text was scattered around the TARDIS ages ago. It doesn't help that a recent bumpy landing has jostled a number of pages loose from their various folders. With Rose's help, he sets about recompiling everything.

From the information given, can you discover which article of the Proclamation might serve him the best?

Using the clues opposite, below and on pages 146–147, fill in the grid on pages 148–149 to work out the solution. Then draw lines from box to box overleaf to show your answer. Finally, circle the box containing the correct article.

The bureaucratic article is sharply divisive on Earth.

The article in the blue folder is dull, and was not written by three species.

The article stuck in the TARDIS's wardrobe dimension is considered acclaimed.

Article 829 is not usually found inside a roundel.

?

If the article that the Doctor wants has the average number of contributors, which one is it?

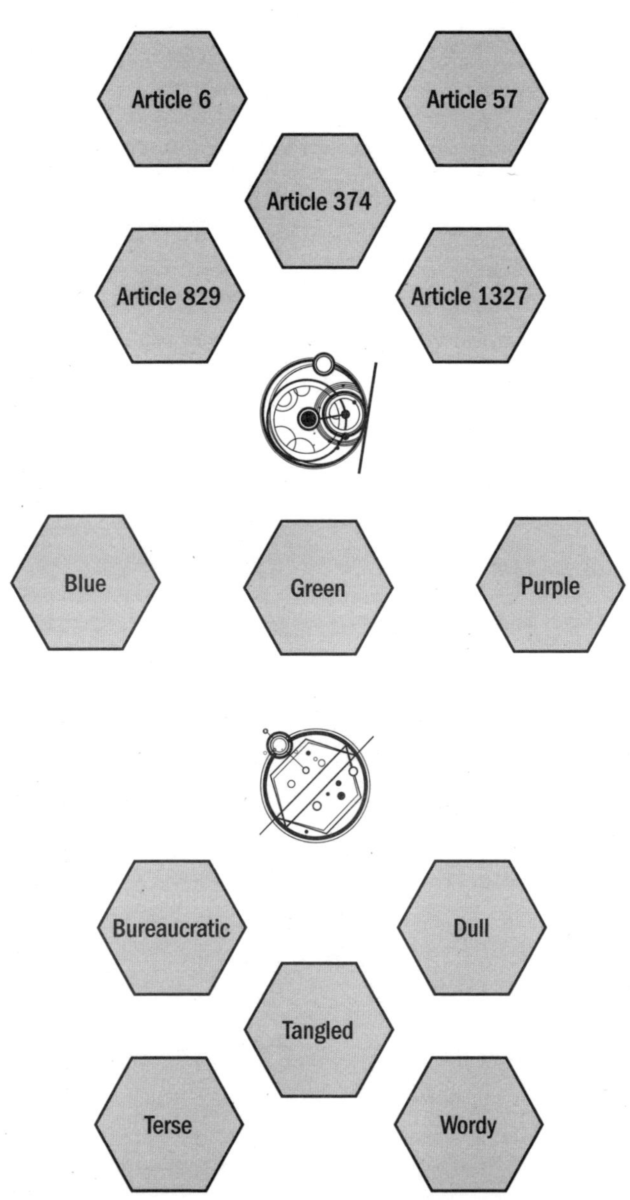
Article 6
Article 57
Article 374
Article 829
Article 1327
Blue
Green
Purple
Bureaucratic
Dull
Tangled
Terse
Wordy

Puzzle 30: Extreme

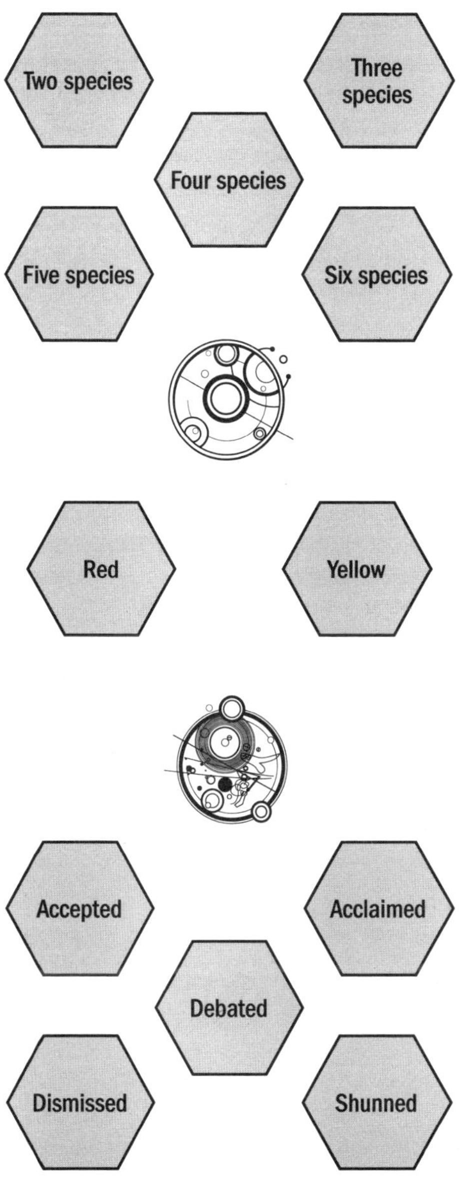

Rose

Provision · Folder stored · Contents · Number of contributors · Opinion:

Article 6.
Article 57.
Article 374.
Article 829.
Article 1327.

Blue: This folder is stored in a hollow roundel.
Green: This folder was left on a shelf in a storage room.
Purple: This folder was left on a desk in the library.
Red: This folder is stored in a cubby in the central console.
Yellow: This folder was left in a briefcase in the wardrobe dimension.

Bureaucratic: This provision references Convention P. This is the shortest provision of the five.
Dull: This provision is extremely bland and dry, but has notoriously bleak implications.
Tangled: This provision is of middling length compared to the other four.
Terse: This shortish provision banned the use and creation of certain warforms.
Wordy: A subsection of this provision covers various jurisdictions. This provision is the longest.

Two species: The Cyber-Legions submitted the first draft text of this article.
Three species: The Judoon wrote the majority of the text for this article.
Four species: The Time Lords contributed to this article accidentally.
Five species: The Krillitane submitted addenda to this article.
Six species: Several Vespiform philosopher-poets consulted on this article.

Accepted: This is the least contentious article among the major signatories.
Acclaimed: The Daleks actively hate this article, but the Atraxi respect it.
Debated: Humans and the Silurians have wildly differing views of this article.
Dismissed: The Sycorax and the Isolus both dispute this article of the Shadow Proclamation.
Shunned: The Ba-El Cratt have frequently quibbled over the wording of this article.

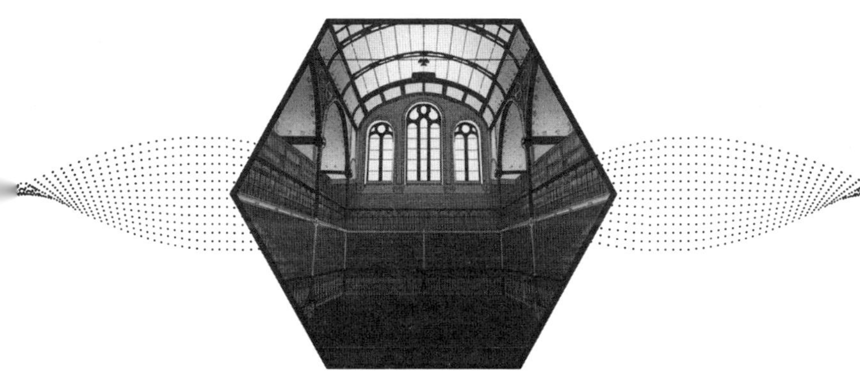

Rose

	Article 6	Article 57	Article 374	Article 829	Article 1327	Blue	Green	Purple	Red	Yellow
Accepted										
Acclaimed										
Debated										
Dismissed										
Shunned										
Two species										
Three species										
Four species										
Five species										
Six species										
Bureaucratic										
Dull										
Tangled										
Terse										
Wordy										
Blue										
Green										
Purple										
Red										
Yellow										

Puzzle 30: Extreme

Fill in the grid below as you work through the clues.

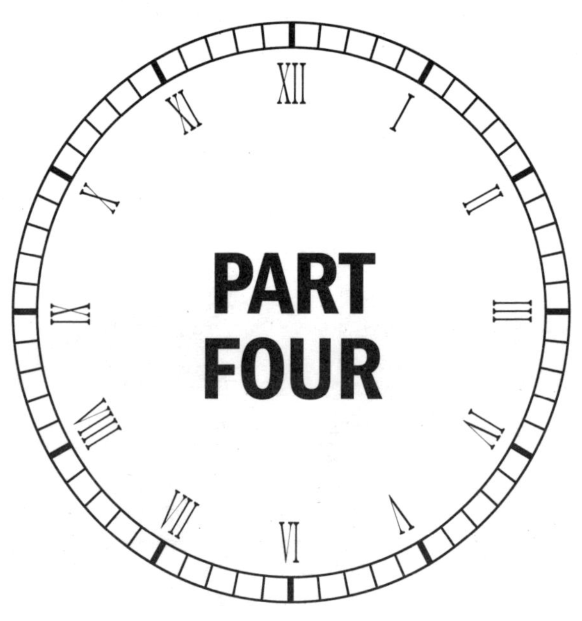

PART FOUR

THE TENTH DOCTOR THE ELEVENTH DOCTOR

Details:

If the cup is to be kept at room temperature, a teapot is not needed.

?

If you're boiling your tea, you'll need to cool it swiftly.

?

If you're brewing your tea in your cup, you need a nice, flat pouch.

?

Pyramid bags do not belong in a teapot.

?

On the assumption that you do not like to curdle your milk, where should you brew your perfect cup of tea?

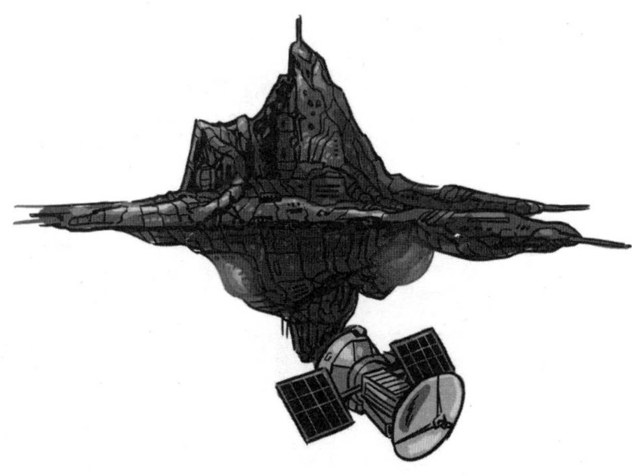

Puzzle 31: Easy

After absorbing the cataclysmic energies of the time vortex, the Doctor's ninth regeneration is unusually difficult. He manages to get the TARDIS to land outside Rose's home on Christmas Day 2006, and then collapses.

All he really needs is time for his system to recover, but there's an alien invasion going on. In lieu of some rest, it turns out a good cup of tea will do the trick.

What's the secret to a good cup of tea?

Using the clues opposite and overleaf, fill in the grid on page 155. Then draw lines below from box to box to show your answer. Finally, circle the box containing the best vessel for brewing tea.

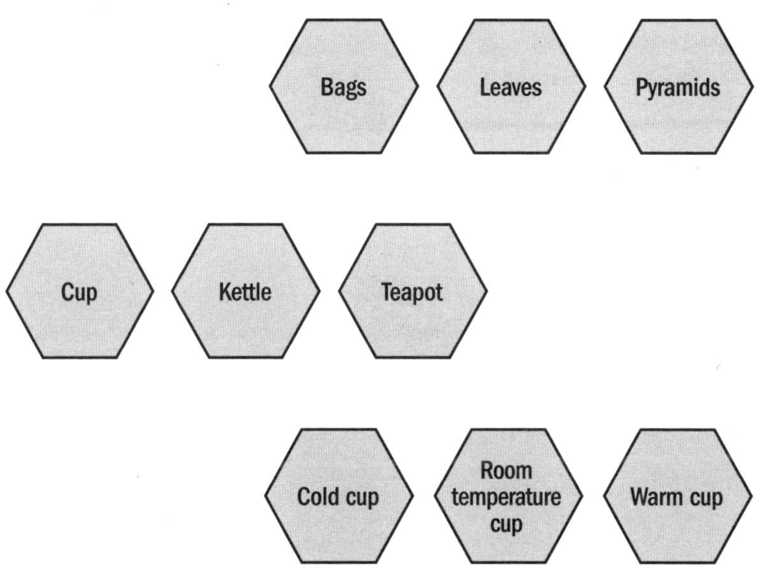

Which tea · What to brew it in · Teacup type:

Bags: Teabags have survived the test of time for one very good reason – they really are the perfect mix of concentration and permeability to prepare tea for brewing.
Leaves: Loose tea is able to swirl around freely in the boiling water, getting maximum exposure and providing ideal flavour.
Pyramids: Teabags are clever, but they are a bit restrictive. Pyramid bags have that bit of extra space that makes all the difference.

Cup: Put the dry tea into the cup and pour the boiling water over it. As it cools, it'll hit the perfect taste.
Kettle: Put your tea directly into the kettle before you start boiling the water. It's not only quicker, you get the most flavour.
Teapot: Use a decent-sized teapot to maximise water flow without over-diluting the tea, and always remember to warm it first.

Cold teacup: Chill your teacup down in the freezer for a minute to bring out the tea's crispness. Milk goes in afterwards.
Room temperature teacup: Keep the teacup at room temperature to avoid interfering with the milk or the tea. Put either in first; it's fine.
Warm teacup: You need to make sure the teacup is toasty warm. To keep the milk from curdling, put it in before the hot tea.

Puzzle 31: Easy

Fill in the grid below as you work through the clues.

	Bags	Leaves	Pyramids	Cup	Kettle	Teapot
Cold cup						
Room temperature cup						
Warm cup						
Cup						
Kettle						
Teapot						

Rise of the Cybermen

Details:

Email is not what supposedly gave Jackie away, nor is it mentioned by the Doctor or Mrs Moore.

?

Mickey knows he's not responsible, even if he's not himself.

?

Mrs Moore doesn't fancy Jackie for the spy.

?

Rose has always felt her dad was a bit of a hero.

?

Some bodily decorations are secret from everyone and everything except the wearer and the artist.

?

The person who was clued in by an odd décor choice wasn't thinking about Ricky.

?

Gemini is – obviously – living a double life, but in one of them, they are a bit of a huckster.

Puzzle 32: Medium

The TARDIS accidentally lands in another version of London in 2007. The Doctor discovers that a new variant of an old enemy has designs on this Earth. The Cybermen are making a resurgence.

The metal warriors are being developed in this time and place by a megalomaniac named John Lumic, the president of Cybus Industries. Thanks to the heroic efforts of a secret source known only as 'Gemini', a resistance group, the Preachers, have been able to start working against the Cybermen. But who is Gemini?

The Doctor and his companions all have their own theories on who Gemini is, and are happy to explain their thinking. From the information given, can you say who is right?

Using the clues opposite and overleaf, fill in the grid on page 159 to work everything out. Then draw lines below from box to box to show your answer. Finally, circle the box containing the name of the person who identified Gemini correctly.

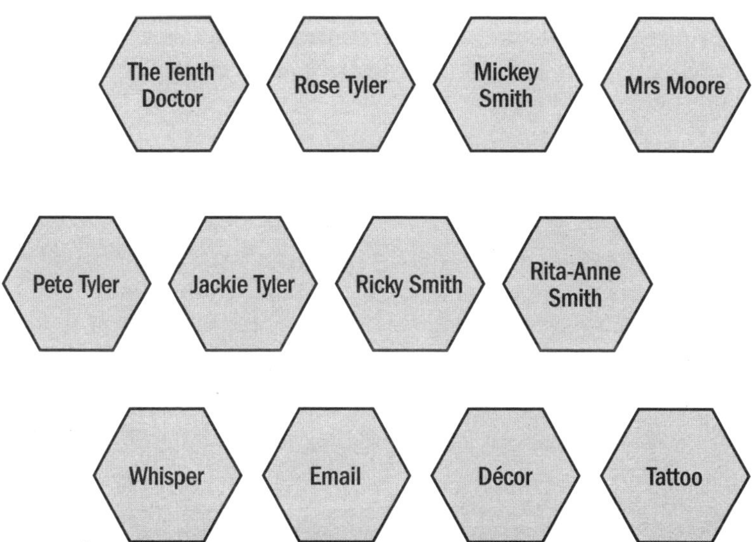

Rise of the Cybermen

Who was involved · Gemini's identity · Hint:

The Tenth Doctor: Skinnier than his usual incarnations, he has a sociable, silly manner he uses to hide a relentlessly ferocious side.
Rose Tyler: Recently spent time as a de facto god of time and space, but managed to come out of it with her humour and bravery intact.
Mickey Smith: Rose was his childhood sweetheart, but she never entirely reciprocated his feelings. He's had to grow up a lot recently.
Mrs Moore: A Cybus Industries employee, she goes on the run after learning their plans. Even her family don't know she's alive. Her real name is Angela Price.

Pete Tyler: Parallel version of Rose's dad. He's the rich and reasonably responsible founder of Vitex, a company that sells a 'healthy' soft drink.
Jackie Tyler: Parallel version of Rose's mum. Still married to Pete for now. No daughter, but she has a dog: Rose.
Ricky Smith: Parallel version of Mickey Smith. He's a brave, resolute freedom fighter, leading his group, the Preachers, against the Cyberman menace.
Rita-Anne Smith: Parallel version of Mickey's grandma. She's a fearless firebrand and has never let her blindness slow her down or erode her sense of justice.

Whisper: If you're responsible for leaking vitally sensitive criminal information to an underground resistance group, you really ought to keep your voice down.
Email: As a rule of thumb, the trash folder of your private email only empties itself once a month. Best not to leave sensitive correspondence lying around.
Décor: Something as simple as an unusual lawn ornament can raise unwelcome suspicions. Discretion is absolutely the better part of discretion. Yeah, sure, valour too.
Tattoo: It is sometimes necessary to prove your commitment, and to offer something tangible to a secret group that they can hold over your head. But why there?

Puzzle 32: Medium

Fill in the grid below as you work through the clues.

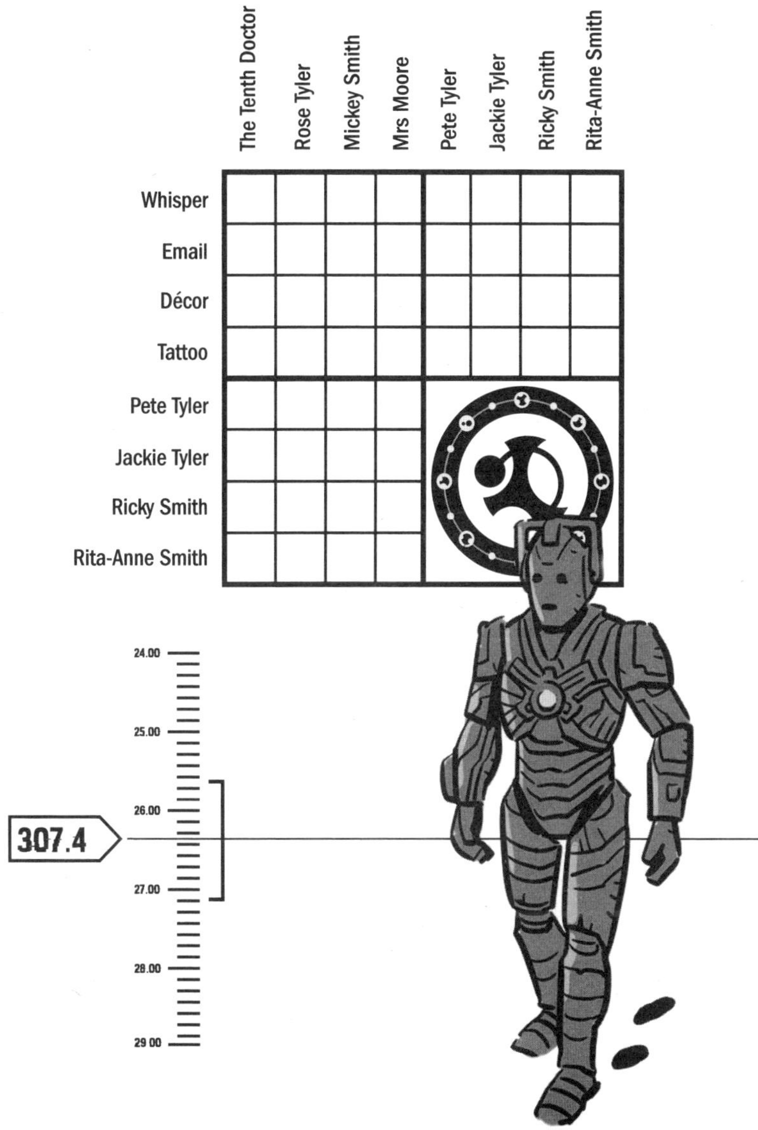

	The Tenth Doctor	Rose Tyler	Mickey Smith	Mrs Moore	Pete Tyler	Jackie Tyler	Ricky Smith	Rita-Anne Smith
Whisper								
Email								
Décor								
Tattoo								
Pete Tyler								
Jackie Tyler								
Ricky Smith								
Rita-Anne Smith								

The Shakespeare Code

Details:

The Doctor rather fancies that the oldest site is the right spot, but the actor thinks the spell needs to be of Babylonian origin.

?

The hendecasyllabic spell would need to be read at Bedlam.

?

The Sumerian spell is an epic, but the Akkadian one has a witchy meter.

?

Martha was rather taken with iambic pentameter, but did not like fourteen-sidedness.

?

Shakespeare believed the right spell was written to rescue warriors.

?

If the correct site requires planetary alignment, who has the right spell?

Puzzle 33: Hard

The Doctor takes Martha to London in 1599 to thank her for her help, so that she can see Shakespeare. He is working on a play, *Love's Labour's Won*, which the Doctor knows is lost to history.

Behind the scenes, Shakespeare is being manipulated by three witches from the Dark Times. Their magic uses patterns of sound, and if they can get the right lines into the play, they can bring their whole evil species into reality and take over the Earth. The Doctor and allies must devise a counter-spell to drive them back. Can you uncover who finds the right language and poetic meter for the spell, and where it is to be performed?

Using the clues opposite and overleaf, fill in the grid on page 163. Then draw lines below from box to box to show the answers. Finally, circle the box with the person who identified the right spell.

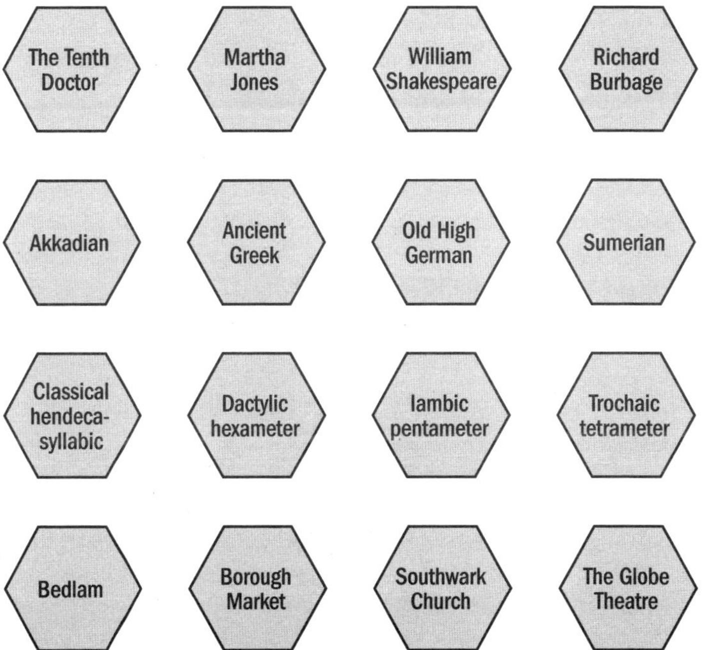

The Shakespeare Code

Who was involved · Language used · Meter employed · Performance location:

The Tenth Doctor: Unusually fond of his own appearance in this incarnation, even finding a way to recreate it during regeneration.
Martha Jones: A medical student who started travelling with the Doctor after her hospital was shifted to the Moon.
William Shakespeare: Shakespeare remains the greatest English poet and writer in history, and one of the greatest of all humankind.
Richard Burbage: The lead actor of the Lord Chamberlain's Men, Burbage is a friend of Shakespeare's, and has met various Doctors.

Akkadian: The Maqlû is a lengthy Babylonian ritual to drive off witches and other forms of evil, written in cuneiform on clay tablet.
Ancient Greek: The Voces Mysticae, enigmatic magical formulas from the fourth century BCE.
Old High German: The First Merseburg charm, to rescue warriors from evil witches, was written in Old High German and recorded on parchment in the tenth century.
Sumerian: The Udug Hul incantation, an extensive set of spell-prayers to banish evil from the third millennium BCE.

Classical hendecasyllabic: Line of eleven syllables with complex stress, popular in Ancient Greece. 'Flame as fierce as the fervid eyes of lions.'
Dactylic hexameter: The meter of epic, mixing six metrical 'feet' of two kinds. Difficult to read in English. 'Stand like Druids of eld, with voices sad and prophetic.'
Iambic pentameter: Shakespeare's favourite, five pairs of syllables, alternately stressed, starting with the second: 'So foul and fair a day I have not seen.'
Trochaic tetrameter: Used in *Macbeth* by the witches. Four pairs of syllables, again alternately stressed, but starting with the first: 'Double, double, toil and trouble.'

Bedlam: The Hospital of St Mary Bethlehem was founded in 1247. It has become a byword for mania, chaos and mental illness.
Borough Market: Although the stalls and sellers come and go over the centuries, Borough Market has been in existence since 1014.

Puzzle 33: Hard

Fill in the grid below as you work through the clues.

	The Tenth Doctor	Martha Jones	Shakespeare	Richard Burbage	Akkadian	Ancient Greek	Old High German	Sumerian	Bedlam	Borough Market	Southwark Church	The Globe Theatre
Classical hendecasyllabic												
Dactylic hexameter												
Iambic pentameter												
Trochaic tetrameter												
Bedlam												
Borough Market												
Southwark Church												
The Globe Theatre												
Akkadian												
Ancient Greek												
Old High German												
Sumerian												

Southwark Church: Started in 1106 but not completed until 1538, the church we now know as Southwark Cathedral is a beautiful and historic construction.

The Globe Theatre: Famous for performing Shakespeare's plays. Not so much a globe as a fourteen-sided shape designed to echo the Rexel planetary configuration.

Blink

Details:

Of the five messages, one was left in 1908, one was great to receive, one was written in spray paint, one was in the living room, and one was found fourth.

?

The scariest message was written in drippy black paint, while the scratched message was in the living room.

?

The fourth message was not in the stairwell, but the message about the key was either in the stairwell or the living room.

?

Sally and Larry found the message from the year the wall fell first, and it didn't mention going into the kitchen.

?

The great message was located on the porch, but it wasn't the first message found.

?

The message written in chalk was, frankly, worrying, but the second message was written in pen.

?

The message in the hall was found third, while the message in the stairwell was neither worrying nor obvious.

Puzzle 34: Extreme

After being attacked by Weeping Angels, the Doctor and Martha are trapped in the year 1969. They need to summon the TARDIS to escape, which means a set of very carefully coordinated messages to Sally Sparrow and Larry Nightingale in 2007. However, the Angels have attacked other people, sending them to different time periods, and they too are sending information.

To help the Doctor, Sally and Larry need a firm idea of the timeline of the various pieces of information. Can you help figure out which message comes from which year, in what format, where it's been left, and what order Sally and Larry find them in?

Using the clues opposite, below and on pages 168–169, fill in the grid on pages 170–171 to work out the solution. Then draw lines from box to box overleaf to show your answers. Finally, circle the box showing where the fifth message was found.

The message from the year beginning midweek was definitely useful, but it was not found fourth, and the message from 1920 was not great.

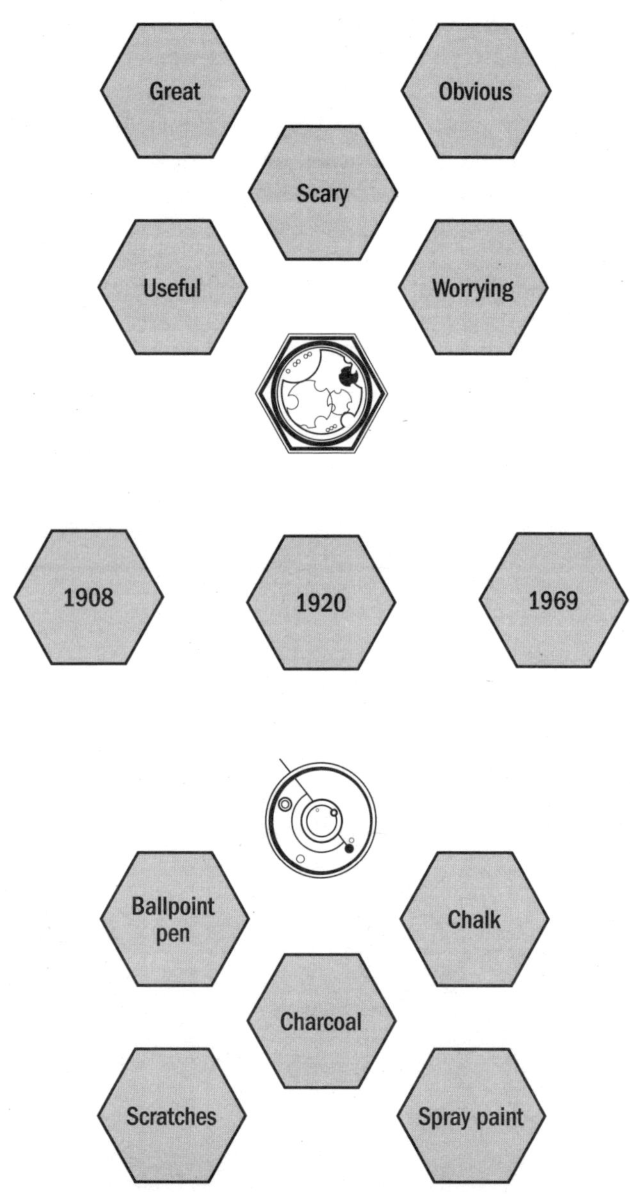
Great
Obvious
Scary
Useful
Worrying
1908
1920
1969
Ballpoint pen
Chalk
Charcoal
Scratches
Spray paint

Puzzle 34: Extreme

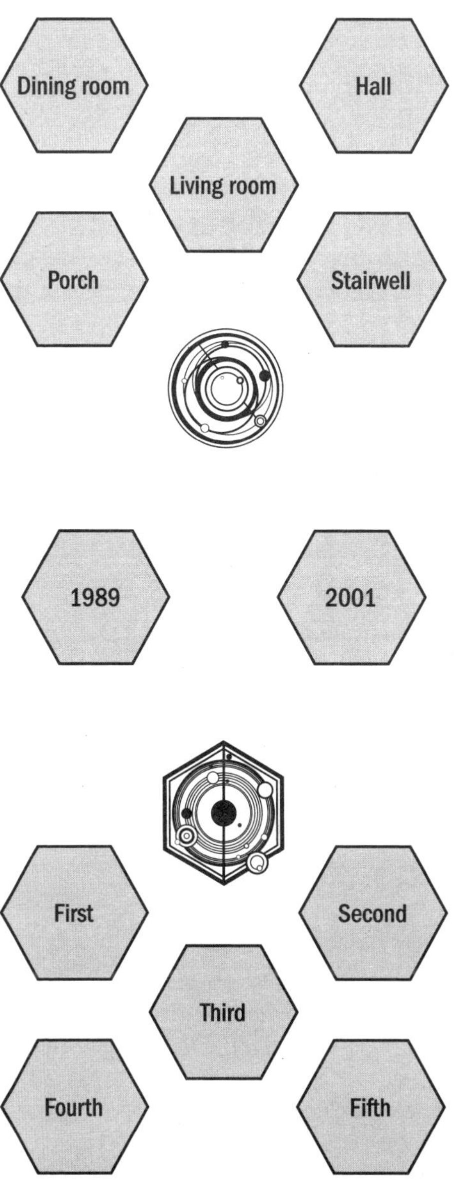

Blink

Message text · When sent · Message format · Where left · Finding order:

Great: 'You'll be here for a while the next time. Bring sandwiches.'
Obvious: 'If you're lost, call Larry.'
Scary: 'Watch out for the statue in the attic.'
Useful: 'Don't forget the key.'
Worrying: 'The next time you enter the kitchen, walk in backwards.'

1908: This leap year started on a Wednesday.
1920: A leap year, starting on Thursday. Denmark gets a little bigger when Germany gives them northern Schleswig.
1969: This year began with a Wednesday. It was an important year for the Moon, at least in human culture. The Moon itself wasn't overly delighted.
1989: This year started on a Sunday. The Berlin Wall came down, to a wild explosion of joy. Berlin was whole again.
2001: This year began on a Monday. *The Lord of the Rings: The Fellowship of the Ring* was in the cinema this year.

Ballpoint pen: A sensible medium; everyone should carry a pen. This one is holding blue ink.
Chalk: The sender was obviously not in a hurry, as this message is very artistic and well-drawn in white. They end their message with a little heart.
Charcoal: A highly stylised message reminiscent of nothing so much as a black metal band logo.
Scratches: Some pointy implement was used to chisel a message into bare stonework. The letters are all composed of straight lines.
Spray paint: The sender of this message was not ad ept with a spray paint can; the whole thing has a very drippy quality to it. Black paint.

Puzzle 34: Extreme

Dining room: A larger room. Quite well lit until mid-afternoon.
Hall: Possibly the least dusty space in the house, given the through-draft.
Living room: Also larger. Gets more natural light in the latter half of the day.
Porch: This is an open porch, so anyone standing within it is outside.
Stairwell: Creaky, and not as well-lit as one might like.

First
Second
Third
Fourth
Fifth

Blink

	Great	Obvious	Scary	Useful	Worrying	1908	1920	1969	1989	2001
Dining room										
Hall										
Living room										
Porch										
Stairwell										
First										
Second										
Third										
Fourth										
Fifth										
Ballpoint										
Chalk										
Charcoal										
Scratches										
Spray paint										
1908										
1920										
1969										
1989										
2001										

Puzzle 34: Extreme

Fill in the grid below as you work through the clues.

Planet of the Ood

Details:

Ood Sigma was not in the same location as the gas canisters.

?

The crackly Ood was at the warehouse.

?

It would take a keen eye to spot the importance of the pylons.

?

Ryder wanted to tackle the pylons or the warehouse.

?

If Sigma is at the right location, who found the best plan?

Puzzle 35: Easy

The Ood Sphere is the homeworld of the Ood, a race of kindly, tentacled telepaths enslaved by the Second Great and Bountiful Human Empire. The corporation Ood Operations lobotomised the Ood for two centuries, selling their victims across the empire.

The Doctor and Donna arrive on Ood Sphere accidentally, and set about trying to free the Ood. They have an ally on the Moon – Dr Ryder, an undercover member of Friends of the Ood. There's a number of things that need to be done, but can you say who thought of the most important action and where assistance could be most reliably found?

Using the clues opposite and overleaf, fill in the grid on page 175 to work out who did what, and who helped. Then draw lines below from box to box to show your answer. Finally, circle the box containing the name of the person who had the best plan.

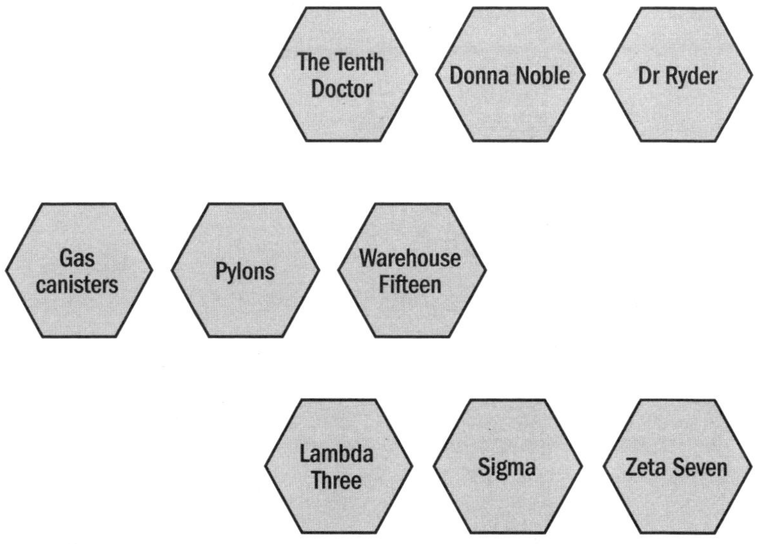

Planet of the Ood

Who was involved · What needs to be done · Who helped:

The Tenth Doctor: The Doctor once accidentally hijacked Donna from her own wedding, and didn't return her until the reception was well under way. Six foot one inch tall, brown hair, brown eyes.
Donna Noble: Donna is defiantly feisty, and although she insists that she's stupid, she is in fact quick-witted, observant and deeply compassionate. Five foot seven inches tall, red hair, blue eyes.
Dr Ryder: Joined Ood Operations and spent ten years working for them, all the time waiting for his chance to take down the corporation. In the end, he gets it. Five foot nine inches tall, brown hair, blue eyes.

Gas canisters: Deadly weaponised gas that could be used to kill all the Ood in the facility. It must be vented harmlessly outside.
Pylons: This hexad of pylons generates a crackling ring of electrical energy, encircling the Ood Brain. It should be shut down.
Warehouse Fifteen: The Ood Brain is in here. Probably some other stuff too. It must be seized from the corporation.

Lambda Three: Lambda Three's translation sphere glows an unusual shade of forest green.
Sigma: The patient, gentle personal Ood of Klineman Halpen, Sigma has a large Greek letter on the right-hand side of his uniform.
Zeta Seven: The speaker in Zeta Seven's translation sphere is faulty, lending his voice an electronic buzz.

Puzzle 35: Easy

Fill in the grid below as you work through the clues.

	The Tenth Doctor	Donna Noble	Dr Ryder	Gas canisters	Pylons	Wareshouse Fifteen
Lambda Three						
Sigma						
Zeta Seven						
Gas canisters						
Pylons						
Wareshouse Fifteen						

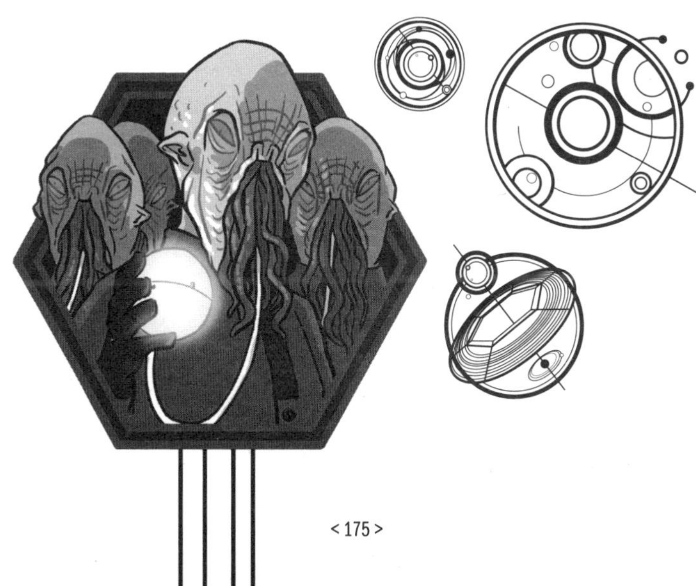

Cold Blood

Details:

Either Amy or Nasreen thinks that they'll need to resort to shenanigans to stop the drill safely.

?

Nasreen wants to target the drill's software, because that's nice and easy to patch later. Rory doesn't want to target the machinery, for the same reason.

?

Amy isn't convinced that changing where the drill is aiming is good enough.

?

The mine entry is favoured by the industry insider.

?

You wouldn't want to adjust the drill's aim from the Silurian city.

?

The TARDIS is not the place to monkey-wrench the drill machinery from.

?

If there's only time for the fast and flashy approach, whose plan must it be?

Puzzle 36: Medium

In the year 2020, the Discovery Drilling Project is starting in the small Welsh village of Cwmtaff. Unfortunately the massive exploratory drilling machine is pointed at a subterranean city filled with hibernating Silurians. Negotiations led by the Doctor manage to get the drilling paused.

Radicals cause a breakdown in the negotiations, both sides becoming steadily more hostile. Disaster looms. The humans are considering using the drill to eradicate the Silurians, and the Doctor decides to disable it. From the information given, can you work out who has the best idea of how to target the drill and from where?

Using the clues opposite and overleaf, fill in the grid on page 179 to work out who, what each person wants to target and where from. Then draw lines below from box to box to show your answer. Finally, circle the box containing the name of the person who had the best plan.

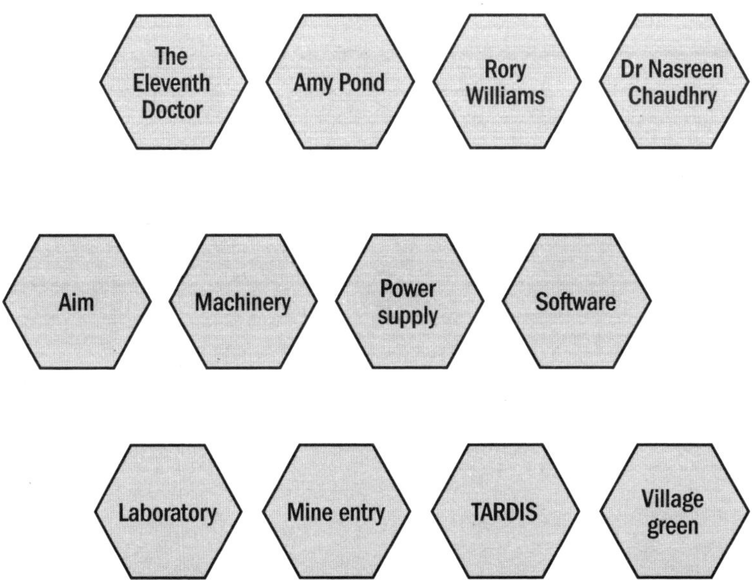

Cold Blood

Who was involved · How to target · From where:

The Eleventh Doctor: This incarnation of the Doctor is always looking for excitement, and he gesticulates expressively when talking.
Amy Pond: Amy is intelligent, insightful and stubborn.
Rory Williams: Humble, sarcastic and hard to freak out, Rory is a trained nurse and carries a handful of medical supplies in his pockets.
Dr Nasreen Chaudhry: A brilliant geologist, and the head of the Discovery team. They plan to dig deeper than any human has before.

Aim: Fairly obvious to anyone watching, and requires a bit of time and skill, but it might be possible to redirect the drill. Different stone deposits mean the drill will sustain some damage.
Machinery: The most visible solution. This requires the least expertise, and is potentially the quickest option, but will certainly cause major damage to the drill.
Power supply: This could be fast or slow depending on finesse, patience and technical aptitude. Will possibly inflict minor damage to the drill.
Software: Hack the program running the drill. The subtlest option, but it requires the most technical knowledge. Will not cause any damage to the drill.

Laboratory: This lab in the Silurian city has some impressive technology.
Mine entry: The location where the drill is accessed from.
TARDIS: The central console allows for all manner of shenanigans.
Village green: The point on the surface exactly above the drill head.

Puzzle 36: Medium

Fill in the grid below as you work through the clues.

	The Eleventh Doctor	Amy Pond	Rory Williams	Dr Nasreen Chaudhry	Aim	Machinery	Power supply	Software
Laboratory								
Mine entry								
TARDIS								
Village green								
Aim								
Machinery								
Power supply								
Software								

A Good Man Goes to War

Details:

Madame Vastra produced the fastest estimate.

?

The person who would have worked with Ood Sigma owed the Doctor a favour because of personal growth.

?

The Doctor once helped Henry Avery against the Lux.

?

Strax did not agree with the Doctor's own estimate, while Dorium Maldovar was returning the same favour he'd received.

?

The person who guessed the slowest time would have had Liz Ten on their team if it had been safe, and had not been rescued by the Doctor.

?

Captain Jack would have been working with the nurse.

?

The person who would have had Cyber-soldiers on their squad went with the Doctor's estimate.

?

If the real time was two seconds different to the Doctor's, and provided by someone who was almost teamed with a human, who guessed correctly?

Puzzle 37: Hard

All the greatest villains of the Universe are absolutely terrified by the Doctor. Turns out there's an excellent reason for that.

Amy Pond and her daughter Melody are imprisoned on the asteroid Demon's Run. Calling in favours, the Doctor gathers an army of allies to rescue them. When he declares it will take three minutes and forty seconds to seize Demon's Run, his allies speculate about how accurate that guess might be. Can you work out which team leader correctly estimates the time, why they owe the Doctor a favour, and who else was almost on their team?

Using the clues opposite and overleaf, fill in the grid on page 183. Then draw lines below from box to box to show your answers. Finally, circle the box containing the name of the person who was correct.

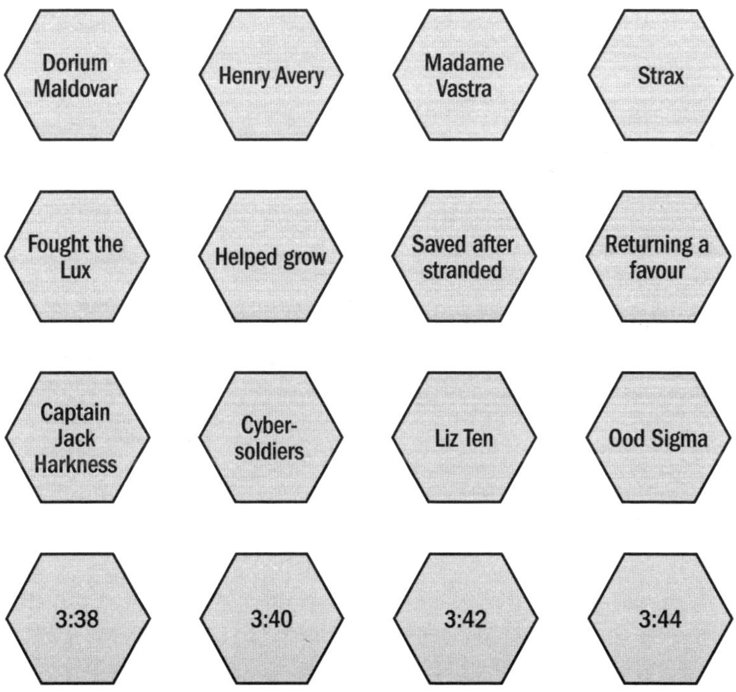

A Good Man Goes to War

Team leader's name · Why they helped · Almost on the team · Time estimate:

Dorium Maldovar: A Crespallion businessman from the fifty-second century who owns and operates the Maldovarium – a black market technology trading post.
Henry Avery: A naval officer turned pirate from seventeenth-century Earth. Henry and the crew of the *Fancy* abandoned traditional piracy for a Skerth spaceship.
Madame Vastra: A Silurian who works as a detective in Victorian London. She and her maid Jenny Flint are deliciously in love.
Strax: A Sontaran soldier who became a nurse in order to restore the honour of his clone batch after they disgraced themselves in combat. He's an excellent marksman.

The Doctor helped this person **fight the Lux.**
The Doctor helped this person **grow.**
The Doctor saved this person after they became **stranded.**
They're **returning the same favour** the Doctor did for them.

Captain Jack Harkness: Would have been excellent, but would have been beheaded. It wasn't the right time for that, so the Doctor retrospectively uninvited him.
Cyber-soldiers: Rory, as the Last Centurion, was initially going to conscript some Cybermen to help. The Doctor abandoned this plan, since they were not trustworthy.
Liz Ten: Liz Ten was supposed to join the assault, but would accidentally reveal future knowledge to the Doctor. River Song made sure she was elsewhere. No spoilers.
Ood Sigma: Due to assist with a telepathic song that forced the Headless Monks into prayer, but he might have been shot by a plasma pistol. Not worth the risk.

3:38
3:40
3:42
3:44

Puzzle 37: Hard

Fill in the grid below as you work through the clues.

	Dorium Maldovar	Henry Avery	Madame Vastra	Strax	Fought the Lux	Helped grow	Saved after stranded	Returning a favour	3:38	3:40	3:42	3:44
Captain Jack												
Cyber-soldiers												
Liz Ten												
Ood Sigma												
3:38												
3:40												
3:42												
3:44												
Fought the Lux												
Helped grow												
Saved after stranded												
Returning a favour												

The Snowmen

Details:

If 'Who' is the word to use, then it is to be spoken in the coach or the house. The same is true if Clara is the one to speak to the Doctor.

?

If 'Run' is the word, it should be spoken while the Doctor is in motion.

?

If the word is to be spoken at Darkover, it should not be delivered by a woman.

?

If the word is a noun, who speaks it to the Doctor?

Puzzle 38: Easy

It's 1892, and the Doctor's TARDIS is stationary in the skies above Victorian London. He's deep in mourning, taking some time away from saving the Universe, and using the Paternoster Gang – Madame Vastra, her wife Jenny Flint and Strax, who is now working as their butler – to keep people away.

However, something sinister is afoot. Snow that shouldn't be possible is falling. Dark forces are stirring. Clara Oswald and the Paternoster Gang know that he is needed again. What is the key word that can bring the Doctor out of his retirement slump, who speaks it to him, and where is he at the time?

Using the clues opposite and overleaf, fill in the grid on page 187 to work out who did what, and how. Then draw lines below from box to box to show your answer. Finally, circle the box containing the person who speaks the key word.

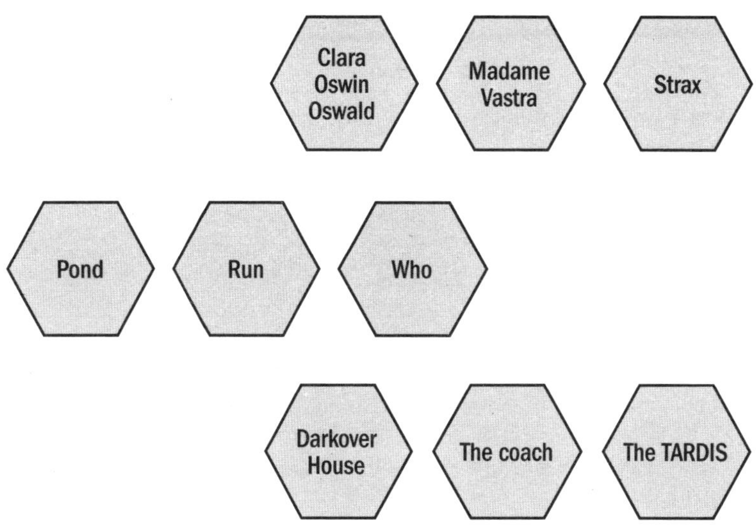

The Snowmen

Who was involved · What was the word · Where was he:

Clara Oswin Oswald: Feisty and warm-hearted, Clara is a perceptive and slightly odd Victorian barmaid and governess who enjoys baking soufflés. Five foot two inches tall, long brown hair, brown eyes.
Madame Vastra: Vastra inspired the character of Sherlock Holmes, and wears a black veil in public to hide her Silurian features. Five foot ten inches tall, no hair, blue-grey eyes.
Strax: A Sontaran. Well-meaning, but has trouble with Earthling nuances. The Doctor once unfairly described him as a 'psychotic potato dwarf'. Five foot two inches tall, no hair, brown eyes.

Pond: A poignant word for the Doctor, as well as a handy term describing a small, deliberately created body of still water smaller than a lake.
Run: One of the Doctor's most commonly used words, and the first thing that both the Ninth and Tenth Doctors ever said to Rose Tyler.
Who: The oldest question, and of particular relevance to the Doctor. Definitely not a question to be answered on the Fields of Trenzalore.

Darkover House: A posh Victorian house containing a lot of wood panelling, many expensive-looking portraits, and gardens featuring at least one ill-fated pond.
The coach: Black, four wheels, driven by a coachman and pulled by a black horse. Might have a secret, camouflaged hatch in the roof.
The TARDIS: Has lots of roundels, now ringed by blue light and with an orange central glow. The Tenth Doctor admitted having no idea what they were for.

Puzzle 38: Easy

Fill in the grid below as you work through the clues.

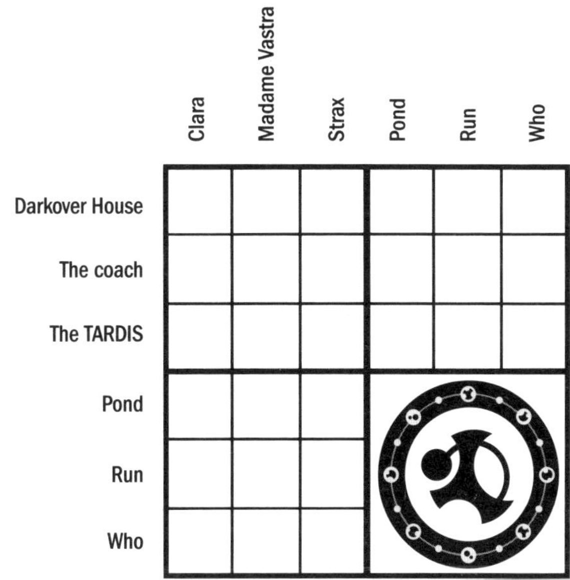

Hide

Details:

If Vortex-hopping is required, the key person has a professional title, but the required tool is not a crystal.

?

If the Doctor is the key, then the tool is Rassilon's Star.

?

The Metebelis crystal would not be needed if Clara was the key, while the vortex manipulator would not be needed if it was Alec.

?

There's only one person in the group who regularly gets broken down to atomic components and rebuilt.

?

You wouldn't use the vortex manipulator to open a portal.

?

If the appropriate tool for the job is highly sought after, who is the key person?

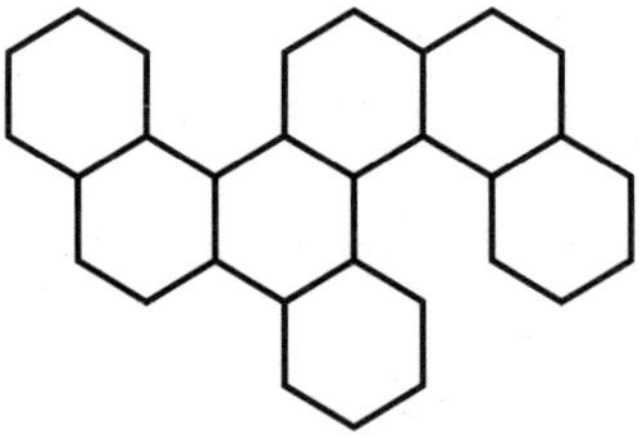

Puzzle 39: Medium

It is November 1974, and the Doctor and Clara are at Caliburn House, a famously haunted mansion that stands alone on the moors. The ghost, the Witch of the Well, is currently being investigated by Professor Alec Palmer, with the help of his psychic assistant, Emma Grayling.

Having discovered that the famous ghost is actually a time-traveller trapped in a pocket dimension, the group have to find a way to safely rescue her. From the information given, can you discover who is the key to rescuing the traveller, and what tool and technique are required?

Using the clues opposite and overleaf, fill in the grid on page 191 to work everything out. Then draw lines below from box to box to show your answer. Finally, circle the box containing the name of the person who found the correct tool.

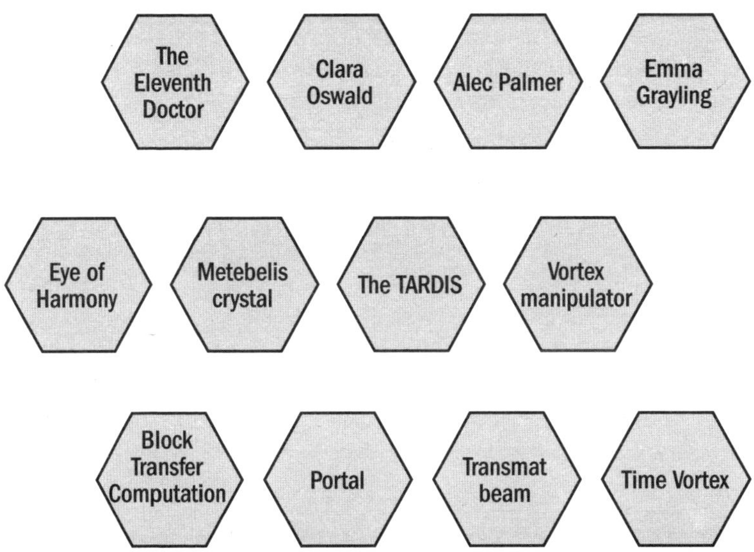

Hide

Who was involved · What tool was used · What technique:

The Eleventh Doctor: Has difficulty keeping still. Tells Professor Palmer that he's from 'the Ministry', but doesn't specify which one.
Clara Oswald: Warm-hearted Clara has a brilliant mind, and is able to quickly master alien technologies. She claims that she and the Doctor are 'Ghostbusters'.
Professor Alec Palmer: A member of the Baker Street Irregulars in World War II, Alec has multiple degrees, the military rank of major, and a talent for watercolours.
Emma Grayling: An empathic psychic working as Alec's assistant. Her powers are intermittent. Alec and Emma are quietly in love with each other.

Eye of Harmony: Sometimes known as Rassilon's Star, or the Eye of Time, it allows space-time travel. It, or a piece of it, sits inside the TARDIS.
Metebelis crystal: A blue-hued sapphire from Metebelis III. Can increase the potency of psychic powers. Numerous races covet them.
The TARDIS: Much more than just a time machine, the TARDIS is alive in some fashion, and possesses some manner of consciousness.
Vortex manipulator: A wrist-mounted device, fuelled by Chronoplasm, that opens a hole in the Time Vortex allowing travel through time and space.

Block Transfer Computation: A mathematical process used to affect space-time. Calculations have to be carried out in an organic mind.
Portal: Poke a hole through space-time, creating a bridge between two points. There are many kinds of portal with various qualities and quirks.
Transmat beam: Also known as matter transmission, or teleportation. Would reduce the time traveller down to atoms, and reconstitute them in Caliburn House.
Time Vortex: A dimensional plane where time and space intersect at non-Euclidean angles. Can be hopped across and can reach almost any point in existence.

Puzzle 39: Medium

Fill in the grid below as you work through the clues.

	The Eleventh Doctor	Clara Oswald	Alec Palmer	Emma Grayling	Eye of Harmony	Metebelis crystal	The TARDIS	Vortex Manipulator
Block Transfer Computation								
Portal								
Transmat beam								
Time Vortex								
Eye of Harmony								
Metebelis crystal								
The TARDIS								
Vortex manipulator								

The Impossible Astronaut

Details:

The person with time of 07:00 is given coordinates for the cafe, while Amy and Rory are sent to the meet-up spot, and Canton is sent to the lake.

?

The Doctor's envelope is marked with the number one, while number four is not River's.

?

River's card is green, but the envelope delivered second holds a blue card, and the person with the white card was told to go to a still point.

?

To get the year that the Doctor is shot at Lake Silencio, add the two Doctors' ages together and subtract the number on the Doctor's envelope.

?

The number of the month is the same as the number of Canton's envelope.

?

To find the day, first add up the differences in inches of height between Rory and all three of Amy, River and Canton, then multiply that total by three, and finally add one.

?

To find the time, add the number on River's envelope as minutes to the time of Canton's invitation.

Puzzle 40: Hard

At the ripe old age of 1103, the Eleventh Doctor sends a series of envelopes to various people, including his past self, and asks them to meet in Utah. Each of the envelopes is numbered, and contains a time, the same date, and coordinates that specify a location. The invitees don't know it, but the Doctor is going to his death. He is scheduled to be assassinated by a mysterious figure in a spacesuit.

Can you use the information provided to work out the precise date and time of the Doctor's assassination?

Using the clues opposite and overleaf, fill in the grid on page 195 to work out the details. Then draw lines below from box to box to show your answer. Finally, circle the box with the time of the deed.

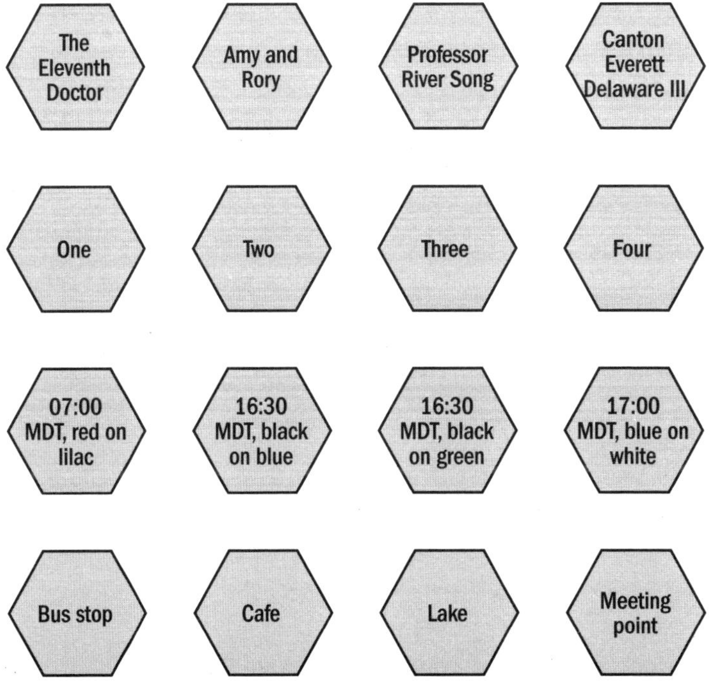

The Impossible Astronaut

Who was involved · Envelope number · Time · Place of assassination:

The Eleventh Doctor: At this point in his timeline, the Doctor is 909 years old, and as enthusiastic as ever about his bow tie. Five foot eleven inches tall, brown hair, green eyes.
Amy Pond and Rory Williams: They are shocked and overjoyed to see the younger version of the Doctor after his older self's death. Amy is five foot ten inches tall, red hair, green eyes. Rory is five foot eleven inches tall, brown hair, blue eyes.
Professor River Song: The Doctor's wife. River is very hard to keep imprisoned. Her timeline and the Doctor's generally run in opposite directions. Five foot seven inches tall, exceptional hair, green eyes.
Canton Everett Delaware III: Terribly, Canton was kicked out of the FBI in the late 1960s because he was in a relationship with an African-American man. Five foot nine inches tall, no hair, hazel eyes.

One: This is the last envelope to be delivered.
Two: This is the third envelope to be delivered.
Three: This is the second envelope to be delivered.
Four: This is the first envelope to be delivered.

07:00 MDT: Written in red on a lilac card.
16:30 MDT: Written in black on a TARDIS-blue card.
16:30 MDT: Written in black on a soft green card.
17:00 MDT: Written in blue on a white card.

Bus stop: A dusty bus stop along U.S. Route 163.
Cafe: An all-American diner complete with checkered floor and Elvis statue.
Lake: Lake Silencio is a still point in time, on the Plain of Sighs in Utah.
Meeting point: A designated spot to meet up along U.S. Route 163.

Puzzle 40: Hard

Fill in the grid below as you work through the clues.

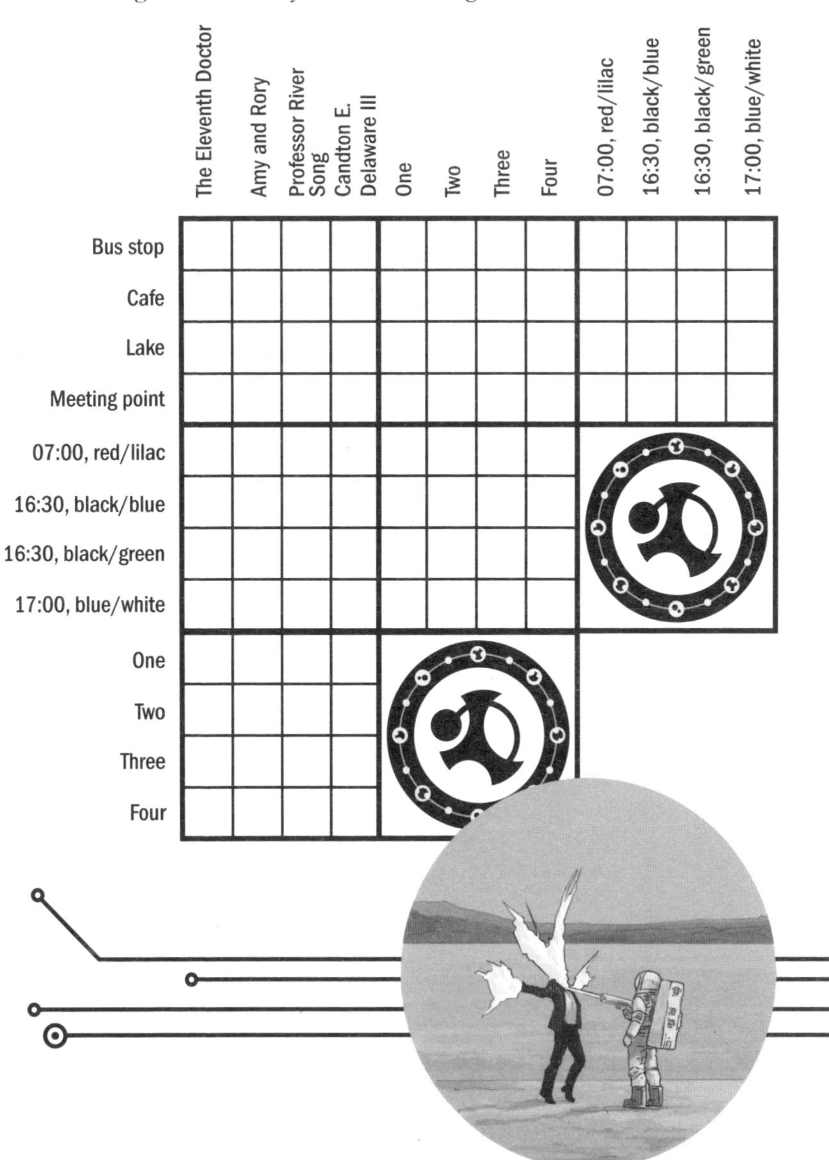

PART FIVE

THE TWELFTH DOCTOR
THE THIRTEENTH DOCTOR

Robot of Sherwood

Details:

The stone object was not in the highest location.

?

Parchment should not be stored in damp conditions,
and yet here we are.

?

Clara was feeling peckish, while Robin disliked draughty spots.

?

If the Sheriff's plans could be said to be the most forward-thinking,
who found them?

Puzzle 41: Easy

The Doctor reluctantly takes Clara to Robin Hood's Sherwood Forest to discover to his complete astonishment that not only is the legendary hero real, he's demanding a duel. Sensing that something isn't right, the Doctor pokes around to discover that the Sheriff of Nottingham is hoarding gold with the help of robotic knights from a crashed spaceship.

With the planet itself in possible danger, it's vital to find out what the Sheriff's plans are. From the information provided, can you say who finds the plans, where they're located in the Sheriff's castle, and what form they take?

Using the clues opposite and overleaf, fill in the grid on page 201 to work out who found what and where. Then draw lines below from box to box to show your answer. Finally, circle the box containing the name of the person who found the plans.

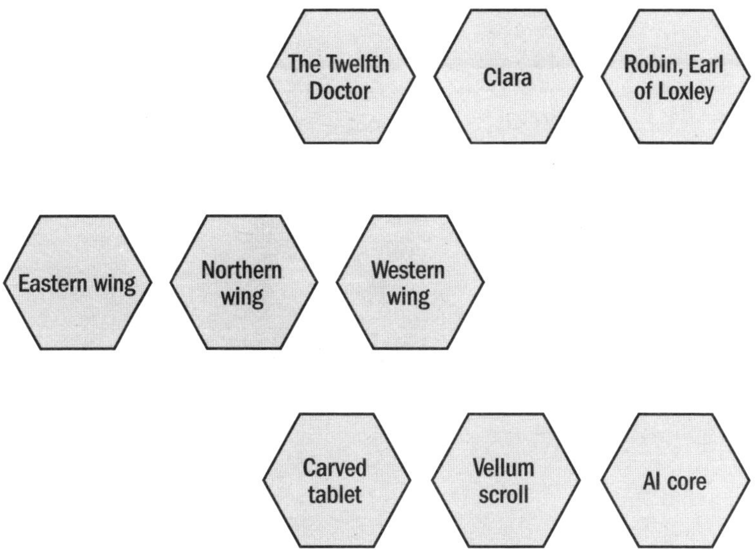

Robot of Sherwood

Who was involved · Where were the plans · What form they take:

The Twelfth Doctor: Having saved Gallifrey and beaten his guilt, this incarnation of the Doctor felt free to be blunt, insensitive and even ruthless if needed. Six foot tall, silver hair, blue eyes.
Clara Oswald: Frequently impossible in a number of literal senses, Clara took on the Doctor's identity on several occasions, and spent a while splintered into millions of echoes. Five foot two inches tall, brown hair, brown eyes.
Robin, Earl of Loxley: Despite the Doctor's stubborn disbelief, Robin Hood proved to be a real person who turned his back on a privileged life to help the oppressed. Much like the Doctor himself. Five foot ten inches tall, blond hair, brown eyes.

The eastern wing: Interior, underground. It is damp down here, and it smells of wet earth. Noises made down here have a tendency to echo.
The northern wing: Interior, ground floor. The dining room is here. The smell of food wafts through at meal times, and you can always hear the roaring fire.
The western wing: Interior, first floor. A branching corridor leads to a number of doors. It's breezy up here, making the torch flames flicker in their sconces.

Carved tablet: A stone tablet carved by a master mason of the eighth century who believed the gods of Asgard were showing her the formulas to get blessings.
Vellum scroll: A delicate scroll penned by tenth-century monks at the behest of a talented seer, containing explicit instructions on how to avoid sin.
AI core: A computer from a spaceship originally built in the twenty-ninth century, holding information about the afterlife and some (unusual) ways to get there.

Puzzle 41: Easy

Fill in the grid below as you work through the clues.

	The Twelfth Doctor	Clara	Robin, Earl of Loxley	Eastern wing	Northern wing	Western wing
Carved tablet						
Vellum scroll						
AI core						
Eastern wing						
Northern wing						
Western wing						

Time Heist

Details:

If the blood control matrix is the most useful object, the person to open the vault is either Clara or Psi.

?

If Clara is first, then the vault is one which has three digits in its name that add together to produce an even number.

?

If Saibra opens the vault, it is not in the HEX wing, but if Psi opens the valut, it is not in the CHEM wing.

?

If the mutation switch is the most useful object, the person to open the vault is the shortest.

?

If the neophyte circuit is critical, the vault is not the one with lowest number, but if it's the blood control matrix that's vital, then the vault is not the one which has three digits that add up to the lowest total.

?

If the vault has an energy source beneath, who is the one to open it?

Puzzle 42: Medium

Picking up the phone in the TARDIS, the Doctor discovers that he and Clara are now inside the Bank of Karabraxos, the most secure bank in the Universe. With them are a hacker named Psi and a shapeshifter called Saibra, and none of them know how they got there or why.

Recorded footage shows the four of them agreeing to have their memories erased, and documents on a table show they're robbing the bank on behalf of 'the Architect'. From the information below, can you work out which vault is their goal, who opens it first, and what piece of equipment will be the most useful?

Using the clues opposite and overleaf, fill in the grid on page 205 to work out who, what and where. Then draw lines below from box to box to show your answer. Finally, circle the box containing the name of the person who opened the vault first.

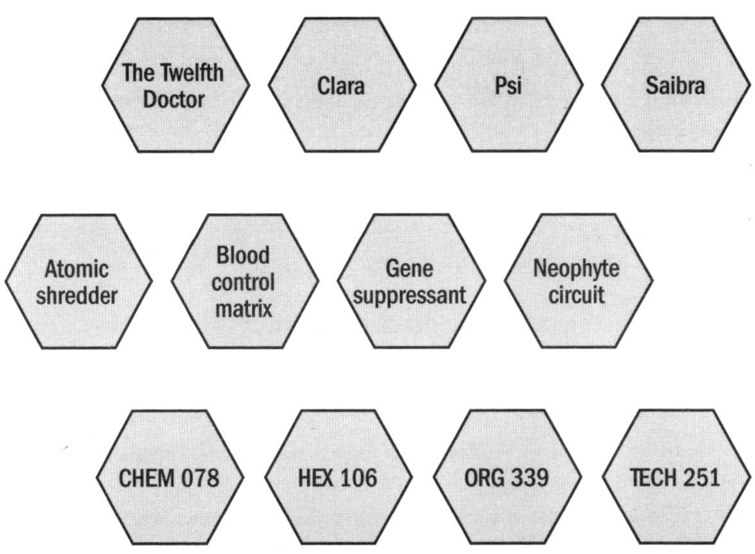

Time Heist

Who was involved · What was used · Which vault:

The Twelfth Doctor: The Doctor spent a lot of time staying in single locations in this incarnation, unfortunately including four and a half billion years stuck inside a torture device. Six foot tall, silver hair, blue eyes.
Clara Oswald: Eventually Clara steps outside of the passage of time, becomes immortal, claims a TARDIS, and goes off adventuring with companions. Yes, really. Five foot two inches tall, brown hair, brown eyes.
Psi: Cybernetically augmented, Psi can store data in his brain cryptographically, project images onto flat surfaces, and recharge from plug sockets. Five foot eleven inches tall, brown hair, brown eyes.
Saibra: A mutated human who automatically takes on the form of anyone she touches. She uses holographic clothing to make sure she stays modest. Five foot five tall, black hair, brown eyes.

Atomic shredder: A small, circular device that, when activated, dismantles the holder into their component atoms for an instant, painless death.
Blood control matrix: A rare piece of Sycorax technology that allows the user to control a group of people who share the same blood type.
Gene suppressant: A medicinal substance that can be used to stabilise or even deactivate specific genetic mutations.
Neophyte circuit: A highly advanced technological gadget that can restore any data wiped from a computer system. Very rare.

CHEM 078: This vault is towards the heart of the bank, and features red trim.
HEX 106: This vault has a soothing blue-green tint to its ambient lighting.
ORG 339: This vault is directly above a section of dangerous plasma ducting.
TECH 251: This vault's door is facing thirty degrees left of the main entrance.

Puzzle 42: Medium

Fill in the grid below as you work through the clues.

	The Twelfth Doctor	Clara	Psi	Saibra	CHEM 078	HEX 106	ORG 339	TECH 251
Atomic shredder								
Blood control matrix								
Gene suppressant								
Neophyte circuit								
CHEM 078								
HEX 106								
ORG 339								
TECH 251								

Heaven Sent

Details:

If the critical item is the sand, then the critical factor is gravity.

?

If the castle is a sort of symbolic Petri dish, then the decisive element of the Veil's nature is its reluctance to actually catch the Doctor.

?

The duplicated clothing being the most important item would suggest that the Veil is most interested in discomfort.

?

If the consistency of the size of the castle and its environs is critical, then the night sky is not.

?

Should the teleporter be the most significant item, then the enemy's blatant activity is its defining nature.

?

If the castle is truly a conundrum, then the painting reveals the most critical factor.

?

If the night sky is the critical physical evidence, then the castle is designed to extract answers.

?

The castle being a very sophisticated prison cell would fit well with the Veil's visibility.

?

If the Doctor's innate senses are the definitive factor – which they are – then what is the castle's purpose?

Puzzle 43: Hard

Teleported into an ancient circular castle in the middle of seemingly endless ocean, the Doctor finds himself trapped. A monstrous entity, the Veil, is stalking him through the corridors. Worse, the TARDIS is sealed behind a twenty-foot-thick wall that is made of a mineral three hundred times harder than diamond.

It's clear that he's not in the castle by accident. But what is unclear is what his captors actually want. Can you piece the critical bits of evidence together to discover why the Doctor has been imprisoned?

Using the clues opposite and overleaf, fill in the grid on page 209 to work out the correct explanation. Then draw lines below from box to box to show your answer. Finally, circle the box containing the purpose of the Doctor's imprisonment.

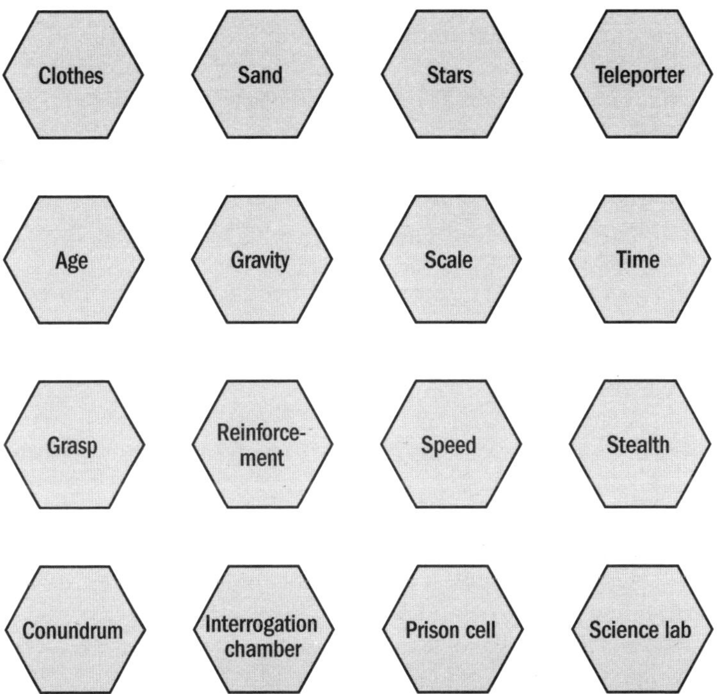

Heaven Sent

Critical items · Factor · Enemy nature · Reason for capture:

Clothes: After getting wet, the Doctor finds a spare set of dry clothes by a fireplace. They are identical to the ones he's wearing.
Sand: Near the teleporter that he arrived in there's a pile of sand, and a word is written in it, in the Doctor's own handwriting: 'BIRD'.
Stars: Not right. From his sense of time and the plausible locations he could be in, the sky should be thousands of years in the future.
Teleporter: From the technology used, it is clear that the Doctor has only been moved an absolute maximum of one light-year.

Age: There is a painting of Clara in the castle. Close examination reveals that it is in fact thousands of years old.
Gravity: Easy to test – just ask any cat near a table. The gravity in the castle is very close to that of Earth, but it is not quite identical.
Scale: Distances can be deceptive, but to throw a stool through a window and see it hit water below confirms the drop is survivable.
Time: As a Time Lord, the Doctor has an exquisite sense of his personal timeline. This tells him beyond doubt that he has not jumped across time to get here and now.

Grasp: The Veil's touch burns, and although it is lethal, it takes time and agony to kill. This suggests that inflicting pain is more important than killing.
Reinforcement: The Veil pauses for a while every time the Doctor reveals a secret. This implies it wants the Doctor to tell the truth.
Speed: The Veil never stops stalking the Doctor, but it moves slowly and deliberately. Maybe the chase is more important than the catch?
Stealth: A lack of it, to be specific. The Veil makes certain to stay visible to the Doctor. Perhaps it wants to be seen, wants the Doctor to know he is being chased.

Conundrum: If the castle is effectively a puzzle box, then perhaps those who put the Doctor in it hope he can solve what they couldn't.
Interrogation chamber: It might be that the castle is an eccentric, indirect way of getting some knowledge that the Doctor is reluctant to divulge.

Fill in the grid below as you work through the clues.

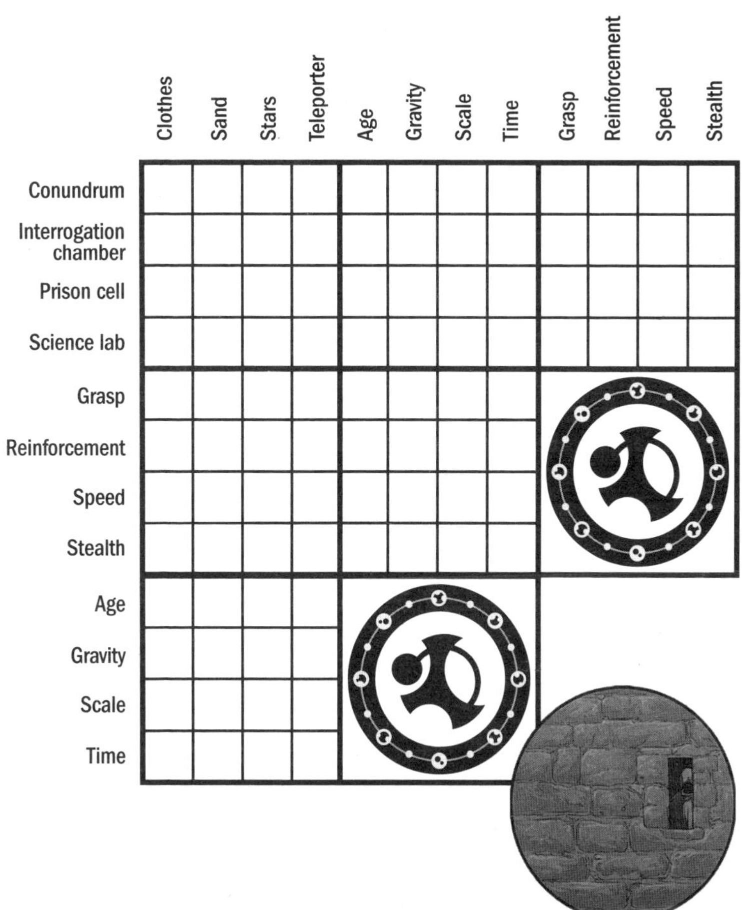

Prison cell: The castle could be a jail, a specially customised oubliette designed to keep the Doctor indefinitely locked up, too distracted to escape.

Science lab: Possibly, the Doctor is being tested in some fashion. The castle and its contents could form some kind of psychological examination.

The Pilot

Details:

If the puddle's reflection is a bit fidgety, it's silent, and its origin is not in doubt.

?

If the image's line of symmetry is in question, then the puddle has stayed put and not apparently sprung up out of nowhere.

?

If the puddle isn't where it was, then it's not a path to anywhere useful.

?

If the weather has been suspiciously nice for the puddle's existence, then it isn't in an occasional parking spot.

?

Assuming that the puddle has actually been muttering to itself, where is it?

Puzzle 44: Easy

The Doctor is a professor, specifically at St Luke's University in Bristol, where he has been lecturing for the last seventy years. His assistant and valet at the university is Nardole, a partly cybernetic human-like alien. Together, the pair have been secretly guarding the university's vault for all this time.

The Doctor's new private student, Bill Potts, is a canteen worker at St Luke's. Things start to go wrong when Bill's prospective girlfriend Heather takes her to witness a very strange puddle. From the information below, can you discover where the puddle is and what is wrong about it?

Using the clues opposite and overleaf, fill in the grid on page 213 to work out what is going on, and where. Then draw lines below from box to box to show your answer. Finally, circle the box containing the location of the puddle.

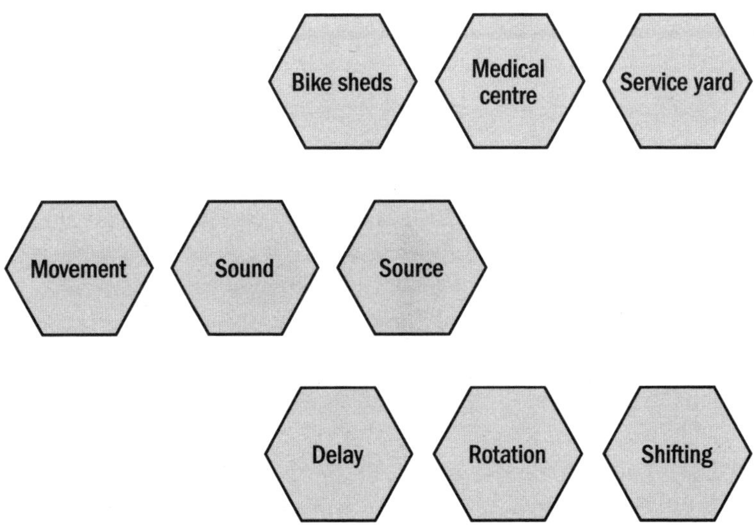

The Pilot

Puddle location · Unusual feature · Reflection status:

Bike sheds: Although hanging out behind the bike sheds is popular at secondary school, by the time students get to university, they've got better places to hide.
Medical centre: There's a patch of paved-over space down the east side of the medical centre. It's not on the way to anywhere useful, and no one much uses it.
Service yard: A quiet chunk of the grounds that is used as a delivery spot and tradesman's parking for the surrounding buildings.

Movement: The puddle is not in the precise position it was in the last time Heather saw it. It's on perfectly flat ground. It really shouldn't be moving.
Sound: A voice has been heard coming from the puddle. It's too shallow to be hiding speakers, in either sense of the word. Surely there isn't a rogue ventriloquist at large?
Source: It looks like normal rainwater, but the puddle is the only one in sight, and in fact it hasn't rained in a week. There's nowhere the water could have leaked from. So why is it here?

Delay: This puddle reflects images correctly, but it's a little... slow. Make a quick, unexpected movement, and the puddle needs an instant to catch up. It's nothing to do with light reflecting slowly either, as it's fine unless you fool it by being fast.
Rotation: If you were cloned and facing yourself, your left side would line up with your clone's right side. Mirrors don't rotate you in the same way, so things seem back to front. In this puddle however, you are rotated exactly as if facing your clone. Odd.
Shifting: Buildings don't wiggle around a bit to get comfy. Neither do people's reflections, unless it's something that the person being reflected is also doing. Except, it seems, in this particular puddle, which is unusually squirmy.

Puzzle 44: Easy

Fill in the grid below as you work through the clues.

	Bike sheds	Medical centre	Service yard	Movement	Sound	Source
Delay						
Rotation						
Shifting						
Movement						
Sound						
Source						

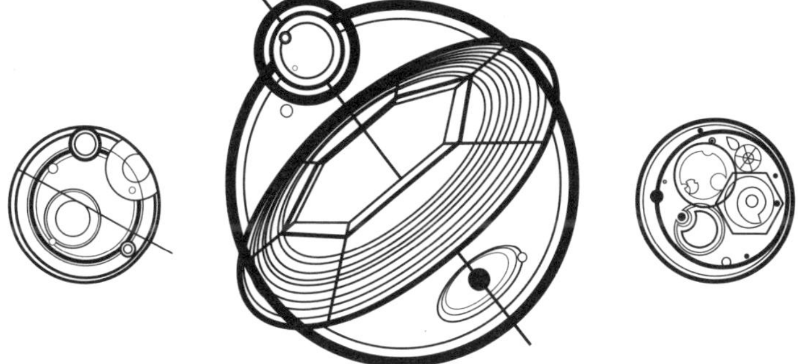

Extremis

Details:

Neither the Doctor nor Bill found the collection where entering wrongly puts you in danger of drowning.

?

Nardole was very interested in the usually chatty talisman.

?

The Doctor knew Pope Benedict IX, but did not find her library.

?

Angelo doesn't know how to get into the Goetic Vault.

?

Having cybernetic lungs, Nardole is unusually precise with his whistles.

?

The Goetic Vault is not accessed by candle, while the Haereticum is not accessed by plaque.

?

If the switch to the correct collection is on the fiery side, who found it?

Puzzle 45: Medium

The Veritas is a parchment translated into ancient Latin by a very early Christian sect. Anyone reading it commits suicide afterwards, making the work only slightly less dangerous than *The Necronomicon* and *The King in Yellow*. Unfortunately, it has been translated again, and leaked onto the Internet.

The Pope himself reaches out to the Doctor to investigate the original and try to find out how it got out. The manuscript is locked away in one of the Vatican's many secret collections of forbidden knowledge, but no one is exactly sure where. From the information given, can you say who finds it, where it is hidden, and how the collection is accessed?

Using the clues opposite and overleaf, fill in the grid on page 217 to work out who, where and how. Then draw lines below from box to box to show your answer. Finally, circle the box containing the name of the person who found the manuscript.

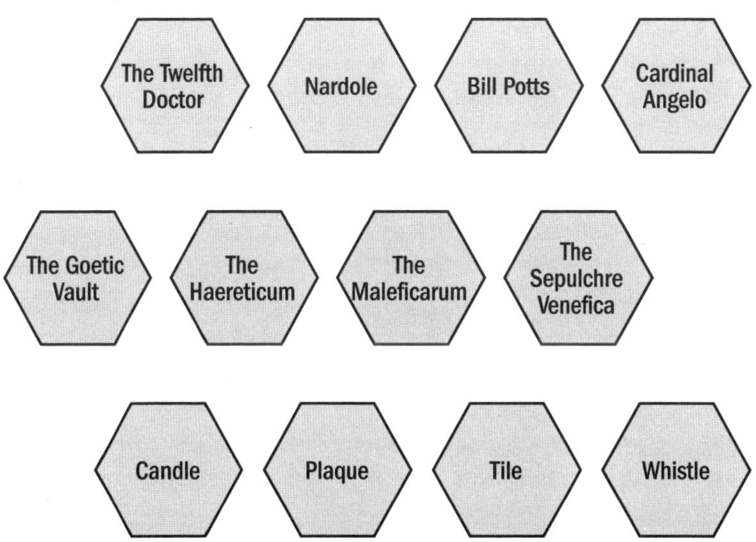

Extremis

Who was involved · Where was the collection · How was it accessed:

The Twelfth Doctor: This Doctor has a 'tell' – as he grows increasingly angry, his accent becomes increasingly thick. If he sounds like a Glaswegian, it's time to run.
Nardole: Former con-man and Tarovian martial artist, this cyborg is unimpressed with humans, but is very protective of the Doctor.
Bill Potts: Inquisitive, clever and sweary, Bill is optimistic and relentlessly brave.
Cardinal Angelo: A pious and humble translator assigned to help the Doctor, since the Pope doesn't know about translation circuits.

The Goetic Vault: This archive is hidden behind a case displaying *The Voynichese Concordance*. It could translate the Voynich manuscript but the Third Doctor forbade it.
The Haereticum: The secret entrance to this archive is concealed behind a portrait of Pope Benedict IX, who set up the collection.
The Maleficarum: A statue called *L'Ange du Mal*, or the 'Angel of Evil', hides this library. The statue was removed from Liège to the Vatican for making Satan too saucy.
The Sepulchre Venefica: Hidden beneath movable floor tiles, this collection includes the Moon Talisman of Scire, which told the Doctor that it refused to add to his burdens.

Candle: There's a candle sconce a little to the right of the secret door. Extinguish the candle, grab the sconce and twist. Anticlockwise, unless you're feeling radically cold.
Plaque: There's an innocuous-looking bronze information plaque towards the base of the secret door. Push it gently. Push too hard, and you'll need to hold your breath.
Tile: Using your heel, put your weight on one specific corner of one specific tile on the floor in front of the secret door. Definitely not to be attempted by children.
Whistle: Facing the secret door, emit a loud whistle of precise length and pitch, then another half as long. If you get the tone wrong, duck.

Puzzle 45: Medium

Fill in the grid below as you work through the clues.

	The Twelfth Doctor	Nardole	Bill	Cardinal Angelo	Candle	Plaque	Tile	Whistle
The Goetic Vault								
The Haereticum								
The Maleficarum								
The Sepulchre Venefica								
Candle								
Plaque								
Tile								
Whistle								

The Ghost Monument

Details:

The Doctor took her action in the ruins.

?

In the threatening-each-other game,
a laser rifle beats a blaster pistol.

?

Graham dealt with the angry cloth pieces
while Ryan talked down Angstrom.

?

It took some calm investigative skills to get
through the underground tunnels.

?

The gas pocket proved to be the perfect place for a spark of fire.

?

Yaz was given charge of the sonic screwdriver.

?

The threat of the EMP was enough to bring the Albarian in line.

?

If the decisive action was the most explosive, who took it?

Puzzle 46: Hard

The Thirteenth Doctor and her companions are rescued from deep space by contestants in an intergalactic rally. The last leg of the race is across a hostile planet, Desolation. The winner will be retrieved, the loser will be stranded. The TARDIS is being used as the finish line, but it is seriously malfunctioning.

As well as environmental hazards, Desolation is seething with SniperBots and other hazards, and the rally contestants are unfriendly. Can you establish who made the key move that helped the Doctor and her friends reach the finish?

Using the clues opposite and overleaf, fill in the grid on page 221 to work out who did what. Then draw lines below from box to box to show your answer. Finally, circle the box containing the name of the person who took the decisive action.

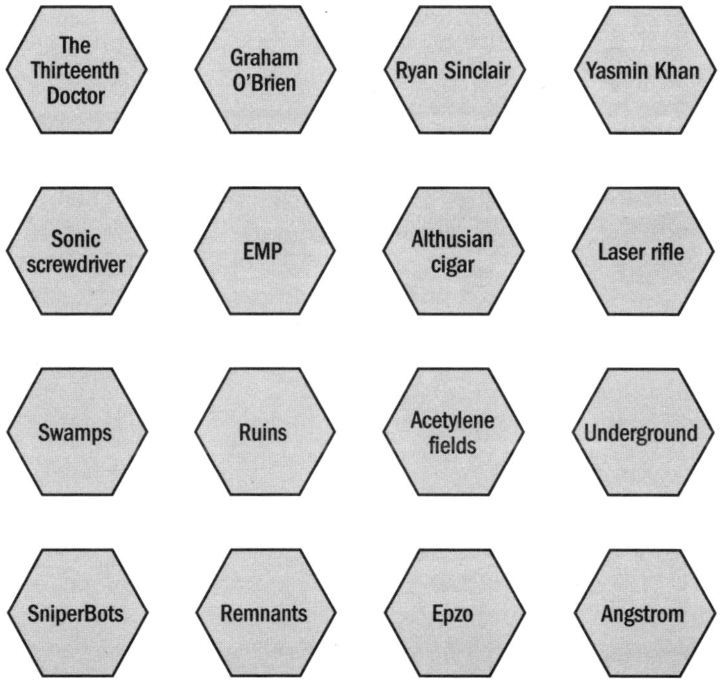

The Ghost Monument

Who took the move · What was used · Where were they · Which route:

The Thirteenth Doctor: This incarnation of the Doctor loves biscuits so much that her TARDIS has a custard cream dispenser built into the console.
Graham O'Brien: A retired bus driver, Graham is the voice of common sense on the TARDIS. He's fiercely anti-bigotry, and rather keen on houseplants.
Ryan Sinclair: Trainee engineer Ryan is impulsive, but trying to improve. He works hard to learn all sorts from the Doctor.
Yasmin Khan: Very loyal, Yaz was a police officer before joining the Doctor. She's a skilled investigator, interviewer, and voice of calm.

Sonic screwdriver: Assembled by the Thirteenth Doctor in a workshop in Sheffield. It has a steel case and a clear crystal tip.
EMP: Stands for 'Electro-Magnetic Pulse'. Excellent for disabling technological devices. Salvaged from a broken SniperBot.
Althusian cigar: Incredibly rare and equally expensive, these premium cigars have a thin metal band that ignites to light the cigar for you when you click your fingers.
Laser rifle: An imposingly designed long, sleek, black weapon. Shoots lasers, and looks like a futuristic version of an Earth rifle.

Swamps: The swamps of Desolation are misty, which limits vision, allowing enemies the element of surprise. Also, flesh-eating microbes.
Ruins: Belonging to a lost civilisation. Heaps of SniperBots, more Remnants than anywhere else, and sensor traps. Be careful.
Acetylene fields: Flat terrain hosting a vast pocket of acetylene gas. Remnants stalk the area at night, and it is profoundly flammable.
Underground: Tunnels criss-cross half of the planet. Fairly safe, but the air supply can be shut off by those with the know-how, and SniperBots have been sighted in the area.

SniperBots: These metallic automata are armed with laser rifles and possess a single eye which glows in a threatening shade of red.
Remnants: A bioengineered race of living weapons that look like sentient strips of cloth. They're active at night.

Puzzle 46: Hard

Fill in the grid below as you work through the clues.

	The Thirteenth Doctor	Graham	Ryan	Yaz	Swamps	Ruins	Acetylene fields	Underground	SniperBots	Remnants	Epzo	Angstrom
Sonic screwdriver												
EMP												
Althusian cigar												
Laser rifle												
SniperBots												
Remnants												
Epzo												
Angstrom												
Swamps												
Ruins												
Acetylene fields												
Underground												

Epzo: A Muxteran pilot competing in the rally. He sacrificed his ship to ensure everyone on board survived the crash on Desolation. Has a blaster pistol.
Angstrom: An Albarian pilot competing in the rally. She wants to use the prize money to get her family to safety. Has a neck tattoo.

Kerblam!

Details:

The Doctor gave the sonic screwdriver to someone leaving the console room.

?

Some incredible heavy clothes racks had to be painstakingly shifted around in the wardrobe dimension.

?

The translation matrix databanks picked up the impression of blue eyes.

?

Yaz wasn't working directly with the Doctor.

?

If the chameleon circuits needed authorisation to reboot, who fixed them?

Puzzle 47: Easy

Arriving in the endless, oppressive warehouses of Kerblam!, the Doctor discovers that there's a problem with the chameleon circuits, and the TARDIS keeps changing appearance.

While the Doctor pulled up large chunks of wiring in the console room, she equipped her companions and sent a couple of them off to other parts of the TARDIS to try things, keeping one with her to help with some fiddly stuff.

Using the clues opposite and overleaf, fill in the grid on page 225 to work out who did what and where. Then draw lines below from box to box to show your answer. Finally, circle the box containing the name of the person who fixed the circuits.

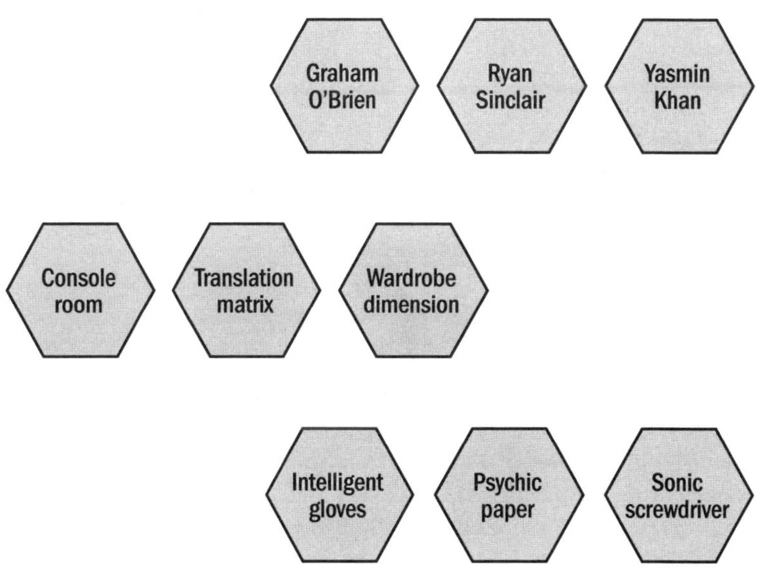

Kerblam!

Who was involved · Where they were · What they used:

Graham O'Brien: A retired bus-driver. He married Ryan's grandmother after they fell in love while she was helping treat his cancer. Ryan still hasn't entirely accepted that. Five foot eight inches tall, grey hair, blue eyes.
Ryan Sinclair: An electrical engineer in training. Ryan was raised by his grandmother, Grace, and he has some issues with physical coordination. Five foot eleven inches tall, black hair, brown eyes.
Yasmin Khan: A probationary police officer. She suffered from nightmares when she was younger, and vaguely knew Ryan at primary school. Five foot five inches tall, black hair, brown eyes.

Console room: TARDIS interior. The main control room. Lots of systems feed into the central console through the complex web of wiring beneath it.
Translation matrix: TARDIS interior. Makes sure all the TARDIS's residents get telepathic auto-translation of all language. Has an odd bias for British accents.
Wardrobe dimension: TARDIS interior. Outfits for every size and occasion, drawn from all of time and space. If you can imagine wearing it, it's in here – somewhere.

Intelligent gloves: Medium weight. A pair of very useful gloves that can hold much heavier weights than the wearer would normally be able to manage.
Psychic paper: Light weight. This handy sheet lets you imprint a psychic impression of a document onto its surface, and then convinces the reader that it's the real thing.
Sonic screwdriver: Light weight. The Doctor's most versatile tool, useful for everything from opening locked doors to fixing broken-down cars.

Puzzle 47: Easy

Fill in the grid below as you work through the clues.

	Graham	Ryan	Yaz	Intelligent gloves	Psychic paper	Sonic screwdriver
Console room						
Translation matrix						
Wardrobe dimension						
Intelligent gloves						
Psychic paper						
Sonic screwdriver						

Praxeus

Details:

The human evidence did not indicate that the bacterium was a possible weapon.

?

The disease that caused fading was associated with alien energy fields.

?

The survivor was aware, and the dead bird was not being turned to mush.

?

The signal was linked to blackmailing the human species.

?

Sample BETA did not cause coma, while sample DELTA did not gunk victims.

?

If Adam was showing signs of fault lines in his skin, which sample identifies the disease?

Puzzle 48: Medium

The Doctor and her companions are on Earth in the 2020s, and find themselves drawn into a mystery involving a strange disease, odd disappearances, birds behaving badly, alien energy readings, and more.

Adam Lang, working for the European Space Agency, vanishes after his spacecraft malfunctions, but he was clearly seriously ill before he was snatched. With the aid of his husband, Jake, two researchers and a vlogger, the Doctor and her companions need to get to the bottom of the disease. From the information given, can you see which potential bacterium is causing the disease?

Using the clues opposite and overleaf, fill in the grid on page 229 to work out who was causing what. Then draw lines below from box to box to show your answer. Finally, circle the box containing the name of the bacteria that's causing the disease.

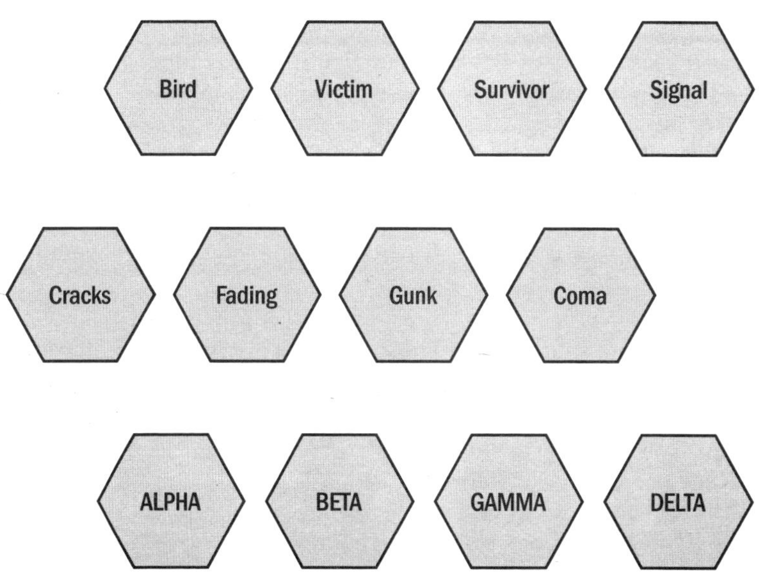

Praxeus

What evidence · List of symptoms · Sample number:

Bird: A dead bird that dropped right out of the sky, killed by the disease while it was mid-flight.
Victim: A human killed by the disease whose sad death was witnessed by note-taking researchers.
Survivor: A person who is suffering with the disease, but who has yet to succumb to its effects.
Signal: Anomalous energy readings that can only be the product of highly advanced alien technology.

Cracks: Sufferers develop pale cracks and spiky shards across their skin. Once the immune system is overwhelmed, the victim disintegrates into a cloud of dust.
Fading: People suffering from fading steadily get darker over a short period of time until they disappear entirely.
Gunk: Humans and other Earth life suffering with this symptom are slowly rendered down into a nasty organic slush.
Coma: This symptom can affect any multi-cellular form of life, rendering it completely non-responsive to all stimuli.

ALPHA: An omnivorous bacterium that came from Pluto on some space debris. It was used for waste disposal, but had the potential to eat the whole galaxy.
BETA: An alien bacterium that targets and consume microplastics. It's origins and source are unknown, but it's not impossible that it was originally designed to fight Autons.
GAMMA: A doomsday bacterium created to infect and kill all life on Earth after a year. It could be shut down, and its creators intended to use it as global blackmail.
DELTA: A bacterium produced by the Doctor during her studies at the Time Lord Academy. She was almost expelled for it. The Master wasn't involved – was he?

Fill in the grid below as you work through the clues.

	Bird	Victim	Survivor	Signal	ALPHA	BETA	GAMMA	DELTA
Cracks								
Fading								
Gunk								
Coma								
ALPHA								
BETA								
GAMMA								
DELTA								

The Timeless Children

Details:

Ryan's plan involved the death particle, but he didn't intend to set it off.

?

The Fugitive Doctor was not interested in the Cyber-suit.

?

Ashad could be found controlling the Cybercarrier.

?

Yaz planned to make use of the Matrix chamber, while Graham intended to attack the engine room.

?

The plan for the Tissue Compression Eliminator including turning it on the Master.

?

The Doctor intended to work on herself.

?

The plan for the cruiser involved disabling its power supply.

?

If the best plan included the use of a multitool, who came up with it?

Puzzle 49: Hard

In the far-distant future, the Master forces the Doctor to join him on Gallifrey. The planet is devastated, the Time Lords destroyed. With the Doctor caught in a paralysis field, the Master sends her mind into the simulated reality, the Matrix of Time.

Rescuing the Doctor is vital. However, despite the help of the Fugitive Doctor, it's not even clear who or what the group should be aiming to influence to save the day. There are many possible plans, but can you tell whose is best?

Using the clues opposite and overleaf, fill in the grid on page 233 to work out who came up with what. Then draw lines below from box to box to show your answer. Finally, circle the box containing the name of the person who came up with the best plan.

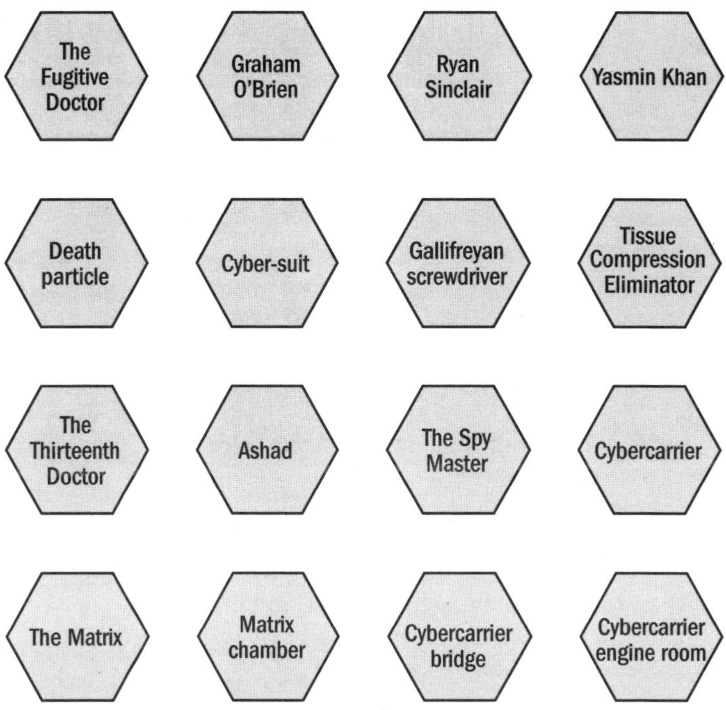

The Timeless Children

Who was involved · What equipment · Who influenced · Where it took place:

The Fugitive Doctor: An incarnation from earlier than the First Doctor, but somehow none of the next thirteen remember being her.
Graham O'Brien: A former bus driver from Essex, Graham was once passionately kissed by Captain Jack Harkness, who thought he was the Doctor at the time.
Ryan Sinclair: A good listener, and often lends an ear to other travellers aboard the TARDIS.
Yasmin Khan: As a trainee police officer, Yaz has a talent for spotting details, and she's great at effectively connecting the dots of disparate pieces of evidence.

Death particle: Designed by the Cyberium, the Cybermen's battle AI, which can be detonated to destroy all life in the Universe.
Cyber-suit: A Cyberman's armoured shell, with the previous occupant removed and the internal systems hook-ups and control mechanisms disabled.
Gallifreyan screwdriver: Sure, it's a tool designed by a Time Lord, but who built it, the Fugitive Doctor or the Master? Laser or sonic?
Tissue Compression Eliminator: One of the Master's weapons, the Doctor described it as 'killing by implosion'. The victim's remains can be as small as a dot.

The Thirteenth Doctor: Dynamic, curious and endlessly caring, but prone to unleashing her fury in short outbursts when stressed.
Ashad, the Lone Cyberman: A partially converted human in a damaged but functional Cyber-suit. He has no emotional inhibitor.
The Spy Master: This incarnation of the Master is particularly bitter and cruel, unable to handle the knowledge that he really is inferior to the Doctor.
Cybercarrier: A battle cruiser that is holding hundreds of thousands of Cybermen and an entire fleet of Cyber-fighter attack ships.

The Matrix: A simulated micro-universe inside a Gallifreyan supercomputer containing the sum total of all Time Lord experience, as the Doctor once put it.

Puzzle 49: Hard

Fill in the grid below as you work through the clues.

	The Fugutitve Doctor	Graham	Ryan	Yaz	Death particle	Cyber-suit	Gallifreyan screwdriver	T.C.E.	The Matrix	Matrix chamber	Cybercarrier bridge	Cybercarrier engine room
The Thirteenth Doctor												
Ashad												
The Spy Master												
Cybercarrier												
The Matrix												
Matrix chamber												
Cybercarrier bridge												
Cybercarrier engine room												
Death particle												
Cyber-suit												
Gallifreyan screwdriver												
T.C.E.												

Matrix chamber: The room in the council chambers from where high-ranking Time Lords access the Matrix – or they would if there were any of them left, anyway.
Cybercarrier bridge: A room filled with an enormous array of control panels and a large window, this is where the Cybercarrier is controlled from.
Cybercarrier engine room: Filled with imposing machinery, including vast power generation systems and colossal, faster-than-light engines.

Once, Upon Time

Details:

Of the five plans, one is hatched by Vinder, one involves the tunnels, one uses the Lupari vessel, one aims for reunion, and one calls on the Priest Triangle.

?

The plan involving the inner chamber aims at either reunion or restoration, but the latter of those goals does not require the Priest Triangle.

?

The Lupari ship is integral to the plan involving the platform.

?

Bel's plan requires the Mouri, but does not involve trying to hold the chokepoint. On the other hand, the plan involving the tunnels does not involve the Mouri, but it aims at abatement.

?

The plan involving the chokepoint uses medicine, but the Lupari are required to use the Gallifreyan rune.

?

Yaz's plan involves the inner chamber, but does not require the Priest Triangle, and the Doctor's plan does not involve the tunnels.

Puzzle 50: Extreme

The Division, the shadowy Gallifreyan special operations group responsible for Time Lord Black Ops, decides to sacrifice the Universe to kill the Doctor, and start over. It releases the Flux, a massively destructive antimatter force that disrupts spacetime itself.

Guided by Swarm and Azure, a pair of Ravagers, the Flux is attacking the Temple of Atropos on the planet Time, and so unravelling time itself. Who has the best plan to stop the fabric of time from completely unravelling and bringing the Universe to an end?

Using the clues opposite, below and on pages 238–239, fill in the grid on pages 240–241 to work out the solution. Then draw lines from box to box overleaf to show your answer. Finally, circle the box containing the name of the person who had the best plan.

?

The plan to restore the Temple does not involve either the chokepoint or the Temple approaches, and the plan to just survive requires the Visionary.

?

The Passenger form is not used in the plan that aims at warding, but the laser pistol is used in the reunion plan.

?

If the best plan requires a timely message, who comes up with it?

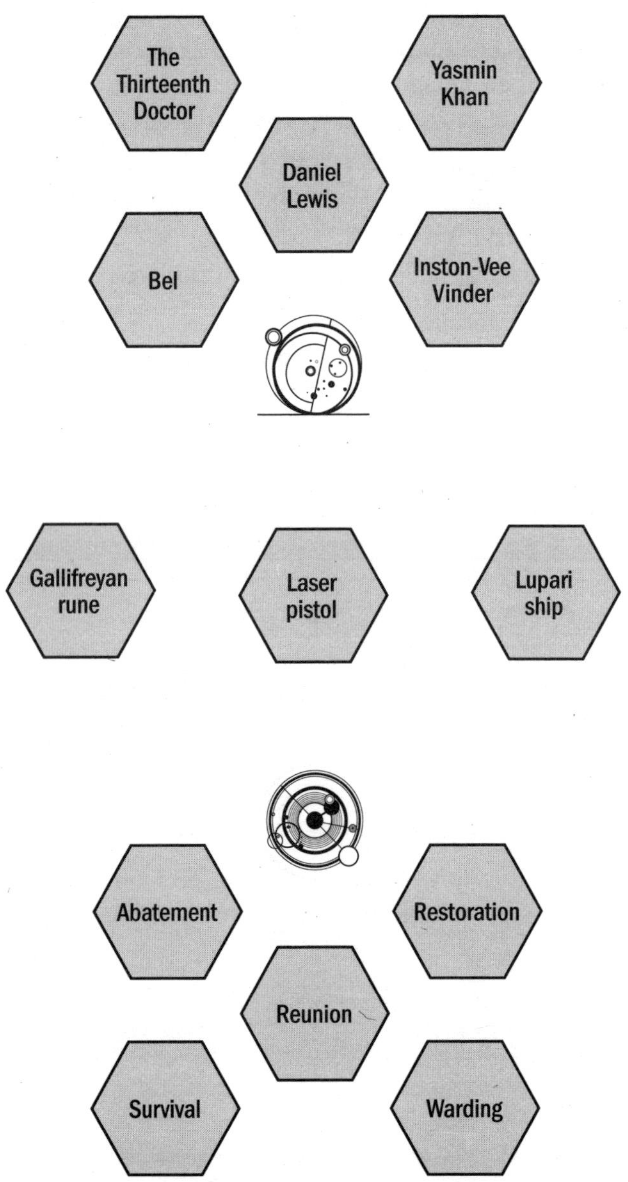
The Thirteenth Doctor
Yasmin Khan
Daniel Lewis
Bel
Inston-Vee Vinder
Gallifreyan rune
Laser pistol
Lupari ship
Abatement
Restoration
Reunion
Survival
Warding

Puzzle 50: Extreme

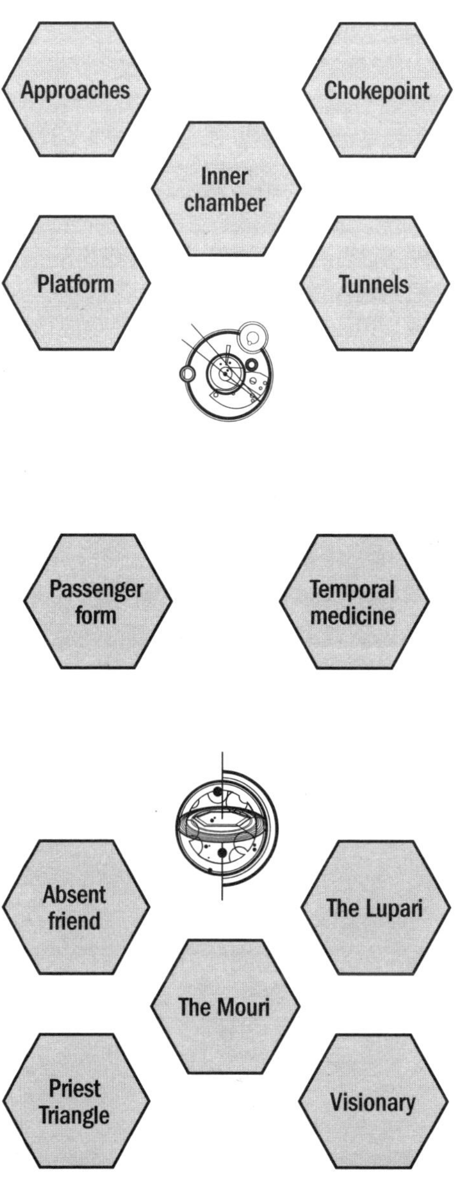

Once, Upon Time

Who was involved · Where it took place · What was used · Reason for action · Who helped:

The Thirteenth Doctor: The Doctor is a child at heart who cares about others, in part because of her last incarnation.
Yasmin Khan: Helpful and highly principled, Yaz does her best to keep the Doctor from being secretive with her friends.
Daniel Lewis: Dan is an insightful people-person. Born in Liverpool in 1980, he helped in a food bank before joining the Doctor.
Bel: A tenacious survivor, Bel has been on planets attacked, variously, by the Flux, Cybermen and Daleks.
Inston-Vee Vinder: A talented pilot brought low by corrupt politics and banished to a distant outpost, Vinder is Bel's husband.

Approaches: The area outside the Temple of Atropos, offering great lines of sight.
Chokepoint: A strategic corridor in the Temple, perfect for holding off strong foes.
Inner chamber: The heart of the Temple of Atropos, where time itself is stabilised.
Platform: A hexagonal platform within the Temple, used as a major access node.
Tunnels: Dim, wide-ranging subterranean passageways beneath an unknown location.

Gallifreyan rune: A deceptively simple-looking device with far-ranging abilities.
Laser pistol: A handheld laser weapon. This one fires red energy beams.
Lupari ship: A spacecraft stolen from the Lupari, an honourable race of warriors.

Passenger form: A living container capable of holding hundreds of thousands of people.
Temporal medicine: A drug to fix 'temporal hazing' and focus a mind in the present.

Abatement: Stop things from getting any worse until a permanent solution is available.
Restoration: Repair the Temple of Atropos, so that it can restore the flow of time.
Reunion: Find and retrieve a loved one lost in time, not least because they're needed.
Survival: Avoid death, don't get erased from the time stream, live to fight on.
Warding: Prevent a time jump from happening at a crucial moment and causing havoc.

Absent friend: A message, in lieu of presence. Like information, love is power.
The Lupari: Canine-like humanoids, including a sane former Division member.
The Mouri: Residents of the Temple of Atropos, capable of controlling time.
Priest Triangle: A small sentient pyramid, one of the Temple's maintenance workers.
Visionary: A Liverpool-based capitalist named Joseph who could see and work through time.

Once, Upon Time

	The Thirteenth Doctor	Yaz	Dan	Bel	Vinder	Approaches	Chokepoint	Inner chamber	Platform	Tunnels
Gallifreyan rune										
Laser pistol										
Lupari ship										
Passenger form										
Temporal medicine										
Absent friend										
The Lupari										
The Mouri										
Priest Triangle										
Visionary										
Abatement										
Restoration										
Reunion										
Survival										
Warding										
Approaches										
Chokepoint										
Inner chamber										
Platform										
Tunnels										

Puzzle 50: Extreme

Fill in the grid below as you work through the clues.

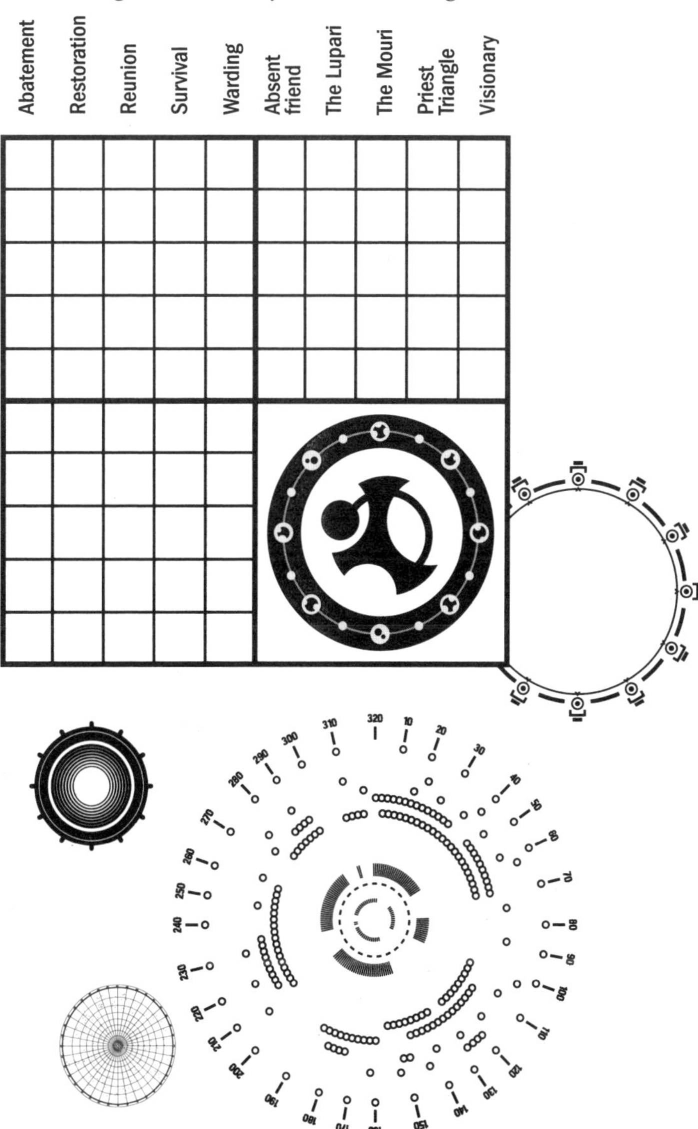

The Day of the Doctor

Details:

The Tenth Doctor's idea involved either the monarch or the aliens. The same is true of the idea involving the electronic tool.

?

The Queen's proponent was jumbled – Mel's sane.

?

The Zygon altimeter contained its own tool.

?

If the first five letters of the assistant for the best plan contained three letters that were all within two alphabetical positions of each other, who came up with the plan?

Puzzle 51: Easy

The War Doctor resolves to finally end the Time War by destroying both the Daleks and the Time Lords. His weapon is the Moment, a doomsday device so terrifying that even the Time Lords never dared use it. Before allowing him to activate it, the Moment forces him to confront his future self.

A series of time rifts bring the War Doctor, the Tenth Doctor and the Eleventh Doctor together in England in 1562 – where they are promptly captured by Queen Elizabeth I and her forces, and thrown into a cell. They immediately start bickering about how to get out. From the information given, can you say whose plan is the most successful?

Using the clues opposite and overleaf, fill in the grid on page 245 to work out who came up with what. Then draw lines below from box to box to show your answer. Finally, circle the box containing the name of the person whose plan was the best.

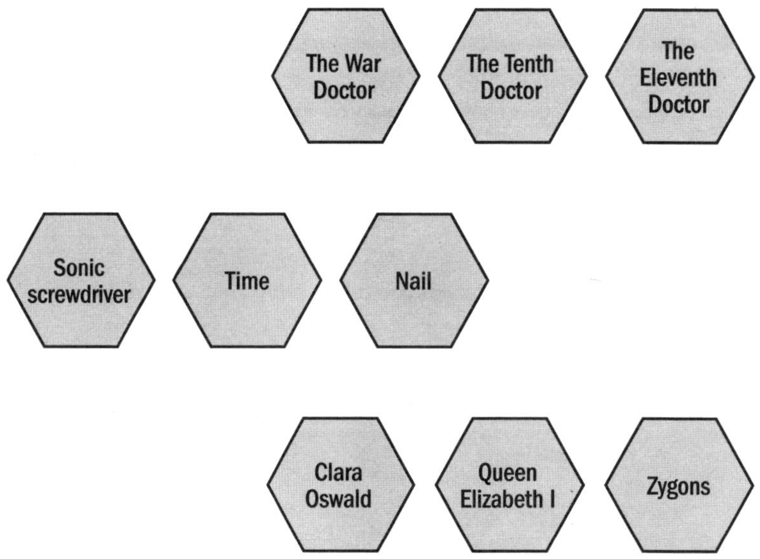

The Day of the Doctor

Who was involved · What they used · Who helped:

The War Doctor: Deeply depressed at what he has become, he doesn't believe that he is entitled to use the name 'Doctor', and prefers namelessness. Five foot nine inches tall, silver hair, blue eyes.
The Tenth Doctor: Habitually cheerful and enthusiastic, even inappropriately so at times, to distract himself from his deep, heavy regrets. Six foot one tall, brown hair, brown eyes.
The Eleventh Doctor: An eternal optimist who wants to believe in second chances, and puts far too much effort into suppressing his darker memories. Five foot eleven inches tall, brown hair, green eyes.

Sonic screwdriver: The Doctor's favourite tool. There are three of them here, and although they are all in different cases, they're still all the same software.
Time: A wibbly-wobbly sort of thing that imposes causality and a sense of linear order onto the great majority of mortals. We know better, eh?
Nail: A small iron bar sharpened at one end and flattened at the other, regularly used by humans and others to keep objects fastened to each other.

Clara Oswald: A companion to the Eleventh and Twelfth Doctors, Clara variously saved the lives of the first twelve of his incarnations.
Queen Elizabeth I: The shamefully neglected wife of the Tenth Doctor, Good Queen Bess ruled England from 1558 to 1603.
Zygons: A race of venomous, sucker-covered humanoids with conical heads, Zygons are shapechangers who can perfectly mimic specific people.

Puzzle 51: Easy

Fill in the grid below as you work through the clues.

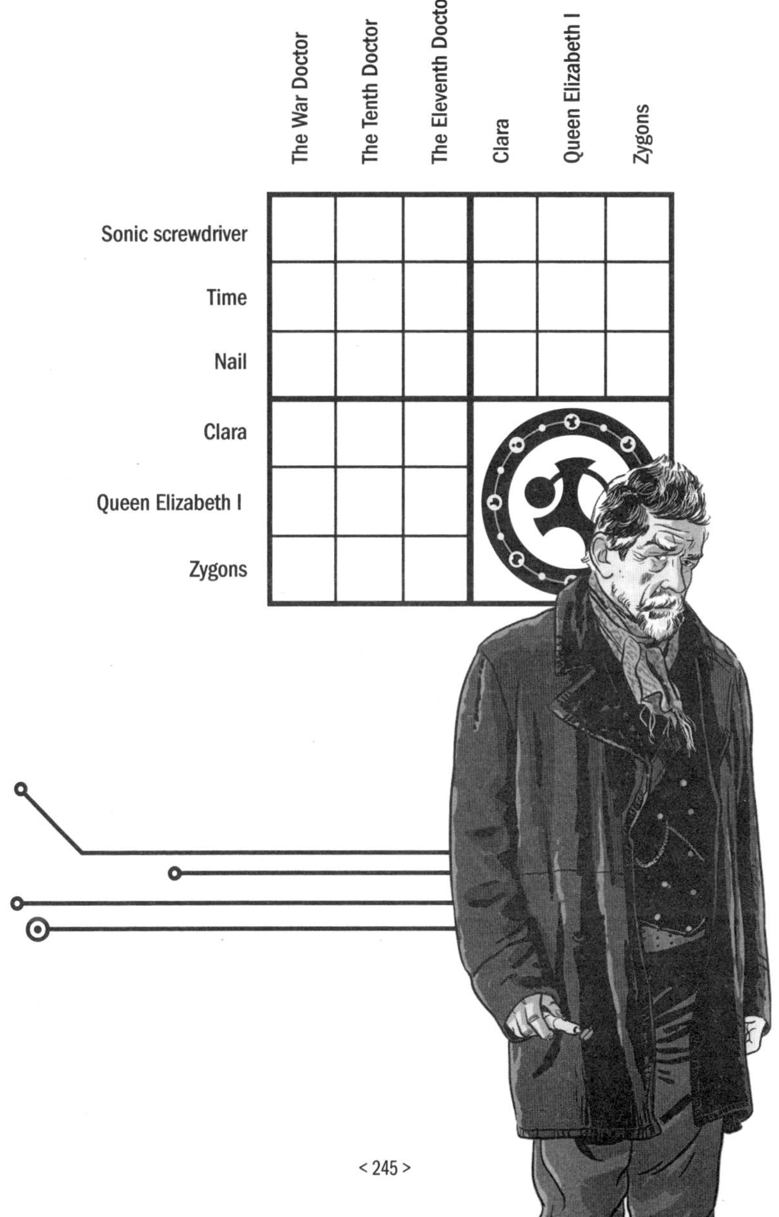

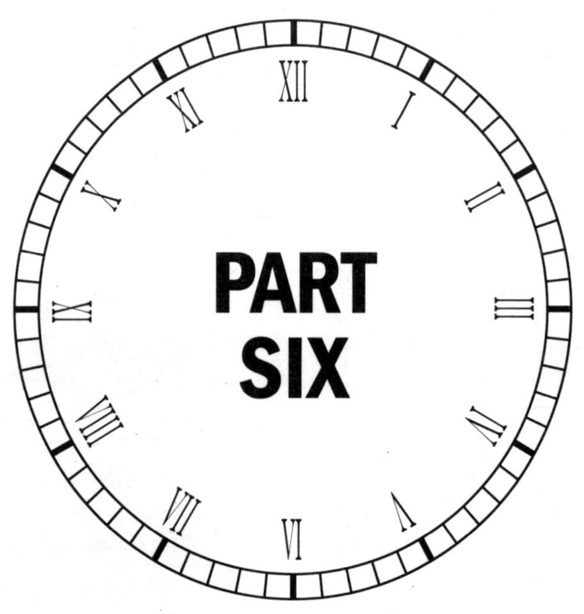

PART SIX

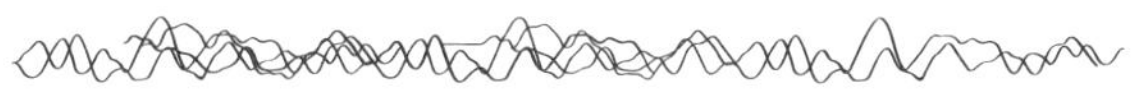

THE FOURTEENTH DOCTOR THE FIFTEENTH DOCTOR

The Star Beast

Details:

Neither Shirley nor Donna were swayed by the prismatic device.

?

The Doctor thought that the Meep was, at heart, a party animal.

?

Donna did not believe that the Meep was being tracked by furriers any more than Rose believed that it sought to impose its will on the galaxy.

?

The Doctor's evidence contains the name of a German city.

?

The person who thought that the Meep sought conquest was not impressed by the ship's engine, while the one who thought it just wanted to live was disinterested in the rainbow glow.

?

Given that the Meep actually had an issue with scrambling this LOGICAL, EPIC ACT, who identified its motivations?

Puzzle 52: Medium

After crash-landing in London in 2023, a cute, fluffy alien called the Meep seeks assistance from Donna Noble's family, and from the Doctor. It is being hunted by what it describes as monsters – sinister bug-like troops known as Wrarth Warriors. UNIT has sent a detachment of soldiers to investigate the crashed ship, but most of the UNIT soldiers have been mind-controlled, as evidenced by their glowing eyes.

Clearly something is wrong somewhere. From the information given, can you tell who first worked out what the Meep actually wanted, and what evidence clued them in?

Using the clues opposite and overleaf, fill in the grid on page 251 to work out who thought what, and with what evidence. Then draw lines below from box to box to show your answer. Finally, circle the box containing the name of the person who worked out what the Meep wanted.

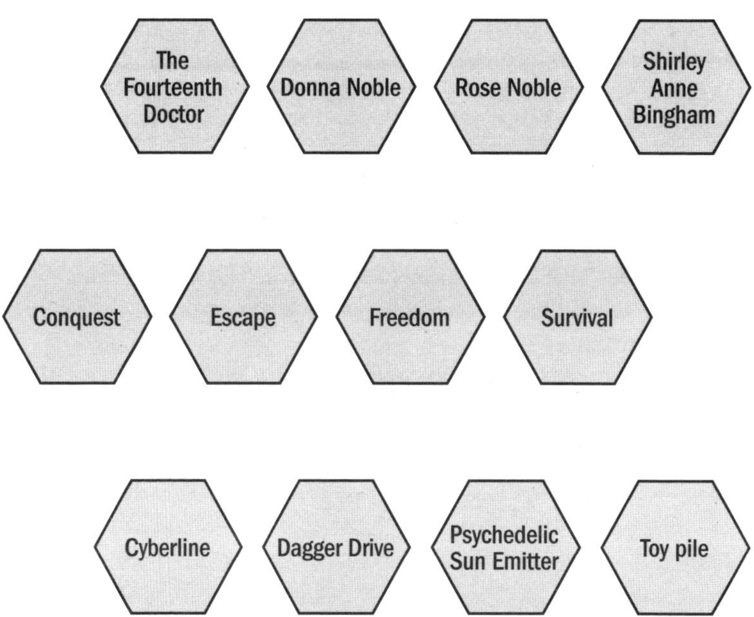

The Star Beast

Who was involved · What did the Meep want · What evidence:

The Fourteenth Doctor: Looks almost identical to his previous incarnation, the Tenth Doctor, a fact which confuses him no end.
Donna Noble: Donna managed to miss the 2005 Auton invasion of Earth completely, as she was sleeping off a really nasty hangover.
Rose Noble: Donna's thoughtful and considerate daughter, Rose is a talented artisan who sells home-made toys online.
Shirley Anne Bingham: UNIT's fifty-sixth Scientific Adviser is a distinguished neurosurgery researcher. She can walk a little, but generally uses her wheelchair for mobility.

Conquest: The Meep is actually a cute, fluffy demented megalomaniac whose only interest is in crushing the Milky Way beneath its adorable little footsies.
Escape: The Meep is in trouble with the law, and it wants to get out of here as quickly as possible to avoid being arrested.
Freedom: The Meep is a free spirit, and it just wants to be left alone in peace to roam the stars in its spaceship, hanging out and having a good time.
Survival: The Meep is terrified of the Wrarth for excellent reasons, and all it wants is to not be cruelly slain for its soft, glorious fur.

Cyberline: A key component of the Meep's spacecraft, the Cyberline needs to remain sufficiently unvindicated, or else the ship will be unable to take off.
Dagger Drive: This engine draws energy from the surrounding area using a pyramid 'blade', not entirely unlike a four-sided version of a Tibetan phurba.
Psychedelic Sun Emitter: Also called a Psychedelic Wave Emanator, this device emits a rainbow of hues.
Toy pile: Rose has a significant collection of finished toys waiting to go to a good home, including ones based on Ood, Lupari, Daleks, Cybermen, and the Face of Boe.

Puzzle 52: Medium

Fill in the grid below as you work through the clues.

	The Fourteenth Doctor	Donna	Rose	Shirley	Conquest	Escape	Freedom	Survival
Cyberline								
Dagger Drive								
Psychedelic Sun Emitter								
Toy pile								
Conquest								
Escape								
Freedom								
Survival								

The Giggle

Details:

Mel thinks that WiFi sent the Toymaker's plans into overdrive.

?

The person considering the voodoo dolls that used to be the Guardians of Time and Space feels that the signal is causing a derangement with a name that contains a square number of letters.

?

The person with the longest name does not think that a technology getting larger made any particular difference.

?

Donna thinks that the main effect of the signal is to stop everyone from caring about anything, while the Doctor thinks it is making people paranoid.

?

The person who was particularly struck by the Master thinks that 5G is the enabling breakthrough, while the person who considers the jack-in-the-box to be a clue thinks that the signal is causing a derangement with a name that starts with the sixteenth letter.

?

Kate is fascinated by the jigsaw that used to be the Doctor's timeline.

?

If the actual breakthrough is a step away from **B TBUFMMJUF MBVODI**, who correctly identified it?

Puzzle 53: Hard

The Toymaker is a mysterious, god-like force of chaos who exists to play cruel and destructive games. One of his plans is finally coming to fruition. It involves exposing humankind to a specific signal, with devastating consequences. The Doctor and Donna arrive in the 2020s to help UNIT stop the attack. A technological advance has led to the signal being greatly increased in recent weeks. As a result, humanity is becoming demented, and the Earth is sliding into chaos and violence.

Using the clues opposite and overleaf, fill in the grid on page 255 to work out who identified which hint, breakthrough, and the effect it's having. Then draw lines below from box to box to show your answer. Finally, circle the box containing the name of the person who worked it out correctly.

The Fourteenth Doctor	Donna Noble	Katherine Lethbridge-Stewart	Mel Bush
Gold tooth	Jack-in-the-box	Jigsaw	Voodoo dolls
LCD televisions	Mobile networks	Small satellites	Wireless internet
Apathy	Egotism	Paranoia	Solipsism

The Giggle

Who was involved · List of hints · The breakthrough · What delusion:

The Fourteenth Doctor: Exhausted and cynical, but retaining his compassion, he is suffering something of an identity crisis.
Donna Noble: Donna managed to miss the 2007 Battle of Canary Wharf with the Daleks and the Cybermen because she was in Spain.
Dr Katherine Sally Lethbridge-Stewart: Commander-in-Chief of UNIT, she has steered the organisation in a measured, scientific, direction.
Mel Bush: A brilliant programmer, Mel now works for UNIT. She remains cheerful, good natured and very capable.

Gold tooth: One of the Toymaker's teeth is solid gold. It used to be the Master, until he lost a game.
Jack-in-the-box: The Toymaker transformed God himself into an unsettling clown-on-a-spring toy.
Jigsaw: A jigsaw puzzle with thousands of pieces constructed by the Toymaker out of the fabric of the Doctor's past.
Voodoo dolls: A set of six dolls that the Toymaker fashioned out of the Guardians of Time and Space, aka the Sixfold God.

LCD televisions: With the advent of LCD screens, TVs were able to get much bigger than before, but could still fit into a normal home.
Mobile networks: Telephone networks keep getting more advanced. The latest generation of phone networks, 5G, is a favourite bugbear of conspiracy theorists everywhere.
Small satellites: The mass-deployment of small satellites – particularly CubeSats and MicroSats – has revolutionised a host of industries in the last twenty-five years.
Wireless internet: WiFi works on localised radio waves to provide a series of short-range internet connections at blistering speeds. Outside rural areas, it's everywhere.

Apathy: The delusion that nothing matters and whatever happens to anyone, it isn't worth considering.
Egotism: The delusion that everyone else is unimportant and their needs and opinions are irrelevant.

Puzzle 53: Hard

Fill in the grid below as you work through the clues.

	The Fourteenth Doctor	Donna	Katherine	Mel	Gold tooth	Jack-in-the-box	Jigsaw	Voodoo dolls	Apathy	Egotism	Paranoia	Solipsism
LCD televisions												
Mobile networks												
Small satellites												
Wireless internet												
Apathy												
Egotism												
Paranoia												
Solipsism												
Gold tooth												
Jack-in-the-box												
Jigsaw												
Voodoo dolls												

Paranoia: The delusion that random happenstance is malice towards you, and other people are plotting against you.
Solipsism: The delusion that while your own consciousness is real, everything else is just an illusion.

The Church on Ruby Road

Details:

The hour of Ruby's abandonment does not yield an integer when divided exactly by two.

?

One of the times is 9:42 pm.

?

The earliest hour does match with the earliest number of minutes.

?

The latest hour does not match up to the number of minutes whose individual digits sum to twice what its own digits sum to.

?

If you triple the number of the hour when Ruby's birth mother decided her plan and subtract two, you end up with a two-digit square number.

?

Ruby was not born at thirteen minutes past the hour, and she was not abandoned precisely on the hour.

?

If Ruby was attacked when her birth mother abandoned her, what time was that?

Puzzle 54: Medium

When orphan Ruby Sunday and TV personality Davina McCall begin suffering an inexplicable string of bad luck, the Doctor takes an interest. He and Ruby help rescue her new foster-sister from goblin-like aliens, and then Ruby disappears out of existence.

The Doctor realises that the goblins have attacked Ruby at the start of her timeline, Christmas Eve 2004, and that he needs to go back to that point to save her. But pinpointing the exact time is critical. From the information given, can you say exactly when Ruby is attacked by the goblins?

Using the clues opposite and overleaf, fill in the grid on page 259 to work out what happened at what time. Then draw lines below from box to box to show your answer. Finally, circle the boxes containing the time of the original goblin attack.

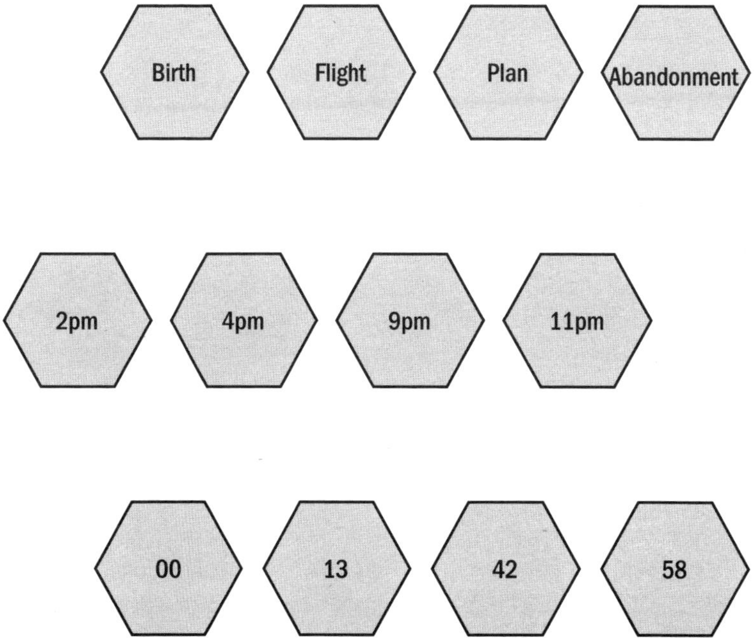

The Church on Ruby Road

What event · What hour · What minute:

Birth: When Ruby was born.
Flight: When Ruby's birth mother left the hospital in a panic.
Plan: When Ruby's birth mother decided what action to take.
Abandonment: When Ruby's birth mother left her outside the church.

2pm: Early afternoon. A typical time for rolling your sleeves up and getting some things done.
4pm: Mid-afternoon. The perfect opportunity for a jolly nice cup of tea, what? Ah, scrumptious.
9pm: Late evening. The sort of time when you're either winding down for the night, or gearing up for it.
11pm: Night. A liminal hour, when all sorts of things might happen – but usually, sleep is involved.

00: Spot on the hour. A nice, round number of minutes. Satisfying.
13: The most sinister number of minutes past the hour, if triskaidekaphobes are to be believed.
42: A number of minutes that comes with a deep sense of universal meaning attached.
58: Two minutes to the hour. Almost there, but not quite. Still time for. . . something, anyway.

Puzzle 54: Medium

Fill in the grid below as you work through the clues.

Space Babies

Details:

The frequency that is a prime number is not disorienting.

?

For 32 Hz, someone scribbled a jumbled note that read:
'R.I.P., Users'.

?

Jocelyn thought maybe she felt a twitching at the base of her brain.

?

Ruby did not select 17 Hz.

?

If adding the individual digits of the numeric value of the correct frequency gives you a cubic number, who identified the effect?

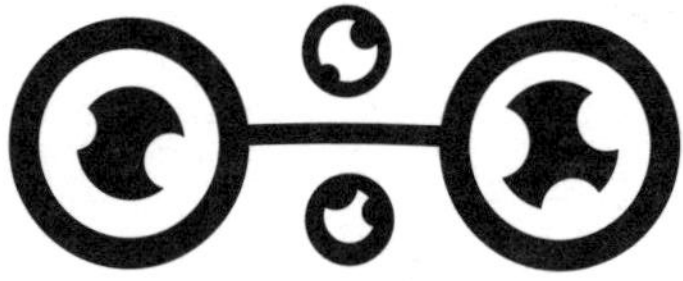

Puzzle 55: Easy

It is the year 21,506 and the Doctor and Ruby are on Baby Station Beta, a space station above the planet Pacifico Del Rio. Government budget cuts have led to the station being left in a sort of limbo, with the machinery still producing babies who are then allowed to grow intellectually but not physically.

The only caregiver on the station is an AI called Nan-E, but there is also a snot monster known as the Bogeyman roaming the lower decks and causing a great many problems for the babies. Trying to identify the creature, the Doctor analyses its howls. From the information given, can you tell what hertz level the Bogeyman roars at, what the effect is and who puts the pieces together?

Using the clues opposite and overleaf, fill in the grid on page 263 to work out who believes what. Then draw lines below from box to box to show your answer. Finally, circle the box containing the name of the person who identified the frequency.

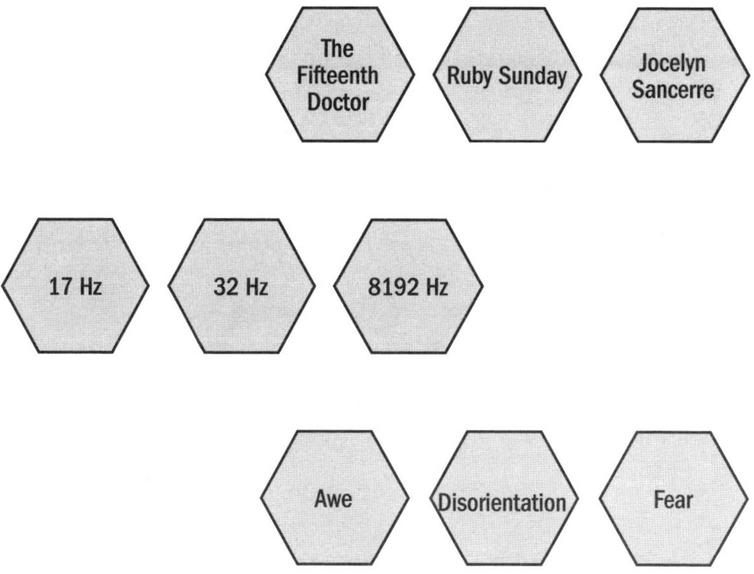

Space Babies

Who was involved · Frequency of sound · What was the effect:

The Fifteenth Doctor: The new Doctor has recently bi-regenerated and is ready for adventure, making him fun-loving, affectionate and open. Five foot eight inches tall, black hair, brown eyes.
Ruby Sunday: Named for the road she was left on, Ruby is a foundling who was adopted by Carla Sunday. Bubbly and energetic, she is a fiercely protective friend. Five foot two inches tall, blonde hair, blue eyes.
Jocelyn Sancerre: The human woman playing the Nan-E AI, Jocelyn was the accountant for the station, but stowed away to look after the babies rather than leave. Five foot seven inches tall, grey hair, brown eyes.

17 Hz: A whisker lower than many people can hear, this is very close to the lowest tone produced by a tuba.
32 Hz: A deep bass note, many instruments can play close to this, but it is difficult for audio players to reproduce well.
8192 Hz: Near the beginning of the ninth octave, this is a frequency sometimes associated with quartz watches.

Awe: Surprise without an accompanying sense of joy. This frequency is felt tangibly in the chest when the source is close and powerful.
Disorientation: This frequency has been alleged to decalcify the brain's pineal gland, which, to be quite honest, sounds like a reasonably serious threat.
Fear: This frequency is said to instil a sense of extraordinary unease – a sourceless, intuitive inkling that something supernatural is taking place.

Puzzle 55: Easy

Fill in the grid below as you work through the clues.

	The Fifteenth Doctor	Ruby	Jocelyn	17 Hz	32 Hz	8192 Hz
Awe						
Disorientation						
Fear						
17 Hz						
32 Hz						
8192 Hz						

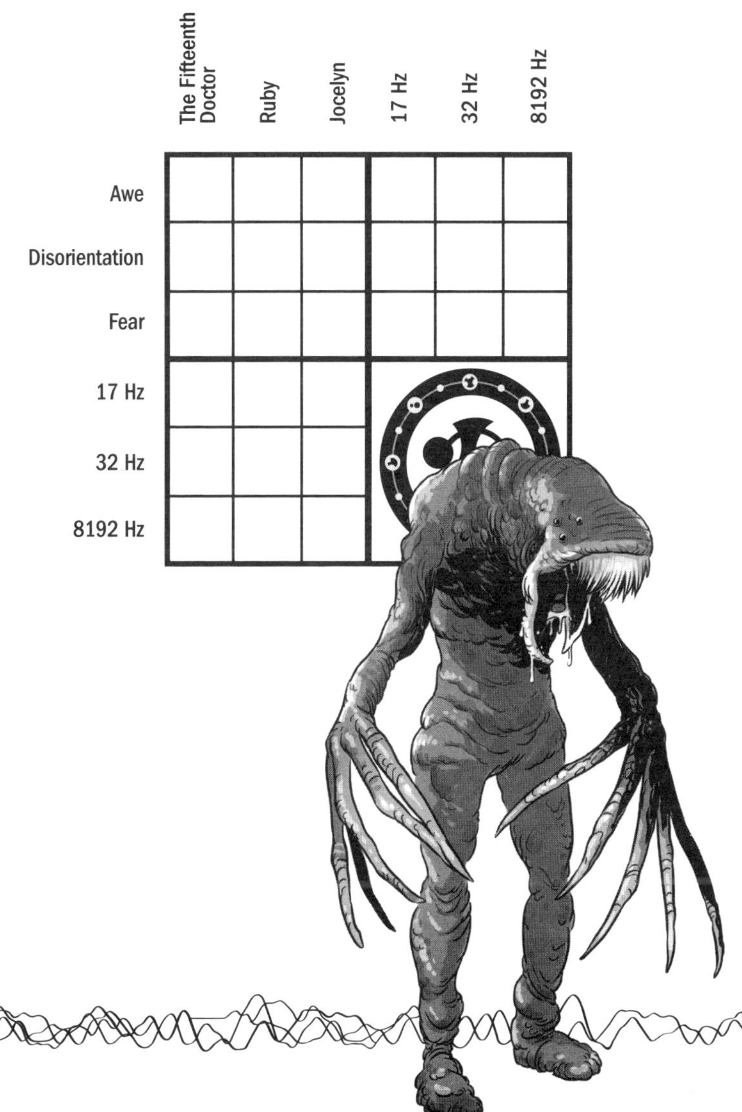

The Devil's Chord

Details:

The time travellers do not think the harbinger's name was Germanic.

?

John favours the theory that the chord had a comparatively minuscule interval.

?

Ruby does not think that the chord was a ditone, while Paul does not think that it was a meantone.

?

John feels that the harbinger's name is an expression of his most fundamental essence.

?

If the harbinger is called Hank, the chord was not a meantone, whereas if he is called Henry, it was not a ditone.

?

If the chord could be said to have '**pitied seamen**' when looked at oddly, who discovered the answer?

Puzzle 56: Medium

By manipulating a London musician in 1925, one of the harbingers of the Pantheon of Discord manages to open a pathway for his parent – the being known as Maestro, an evil elemental personification of the concept of music. Having come to Earth, Maestro devours the human musical spirit, setting the planet on a spiral of destruction.

With the aid of Ruby and the Beatles, the Doctor seeks to reverse the damage. To find the banishing notes, it is important to know who the harbinger is, and what type of chord summoned Maestro. Can you work out who discovered the correct answer?

Using the clues opposite and overleaf, fill in the grid on page 267 to work out who believes what. Then draw lines below from box to box to show your answer. Finally, circle the box containing the name of the person who found the right answer.

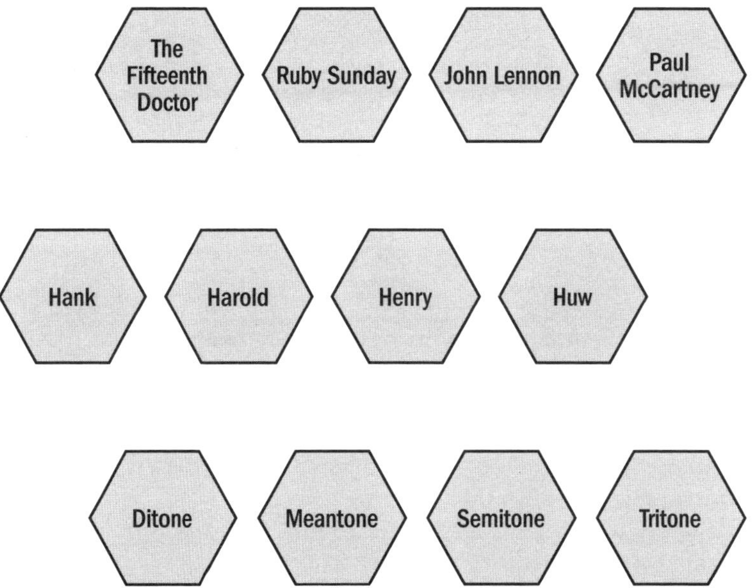

The Devil's Chord

Who was involved · Name of the harbinger · Name of the chord:

The Fifteenth Doctor: This incarnation of the Doctor is a talented singer and dancer, which often proves to be surprisingly handy. Five foot eight inches tall, black hair, brown eyes.
Ruby Sunday: A talented musician, keyboard player and songwriter with a good sense of rhythm and a talent for musical improvisation. Five foot two inches tall, blonde hair, blue eyes.
John Lennon: Before the Beatles, John built a reputation around Liverpool with the previous band he founded, the Quarrymen. Five foot ten inches tall, brown hair, brown eyes.
Paul McCartney: Paul joined the Quarrymen in 1957, and helped with the earlier skiffle band's storied transition to the Beatles. Five foot ten inches tall, brown hair, hazel eyes.

Hank: An Anglicised version of the Dutch name Henk, meaning 'groom'.
Harold: Harawald was a popular Viking name, meaning 'ruler of an army'.
Henry: An English take on the German Haimrich, meaning 'ruler of the home'.
Huw: A Welsh variant of the French name Hugo, meaning 'soul'.

Ditone: The largest example is the comma-redundant major third, or Pythagorean ditone.
Meantone: An uncommon musical temperament that is somewhat narrower than a perfect fifth.
Semitone: The minor second, or half-step, is the smallest of the Western musical intervals.
Tritone: Also known as augmented fourth, diminished fifth, semidiapente and semitritonus.

Puzzle 56: Medium

Fill in the grid below as you work through the clues.

	The Fifteenth Doctor	Ruby	John	Paul	Ditone	Meantone	Semitone	Tritone
Hank								
Harold								
Henry								
Huw								
Ditone								
Meantone								
Semitone								
Tritone								

Boom

Details:

Violence would be necessary to influence the ambulance directly.

?

Appealing to compassion would be quite dangerous.

?

A dead man is an additional layer of complexity all on his own.

?

Ruby feels it might be best to appeal to the system's avarice. She does not think that the battle computer is a good line of approach.

?

Using faith as a motivation force does not risk issues with either time or luck, but relying on luck is a risk of Splice's plan.

?

The Doctor is, understandably, focused on influencing the landmine.

?

If the retrograde solution is that '**TSIXE TONOD SNOIR ATSAK EHTTA HTDNA TSRED NUOTS DEENR ETUPM OCELT TABEHT**', who discovered the answer?

Puzzle 57: Hard

On the battlefield of Kastarion 3, Anglican Marines are in a war against the shadowy native Kastarions. Their force is supplied exclusively with material from the Villengard Corporation.

Ruby is severely injured and the Doctor steps on a deadly landmine. He can't help her without setting off the landmine and ravaging the planet. She needs treatment, but the ambulances are governed by the Villengard algorithm, which is only interested in the Corporation's profits. Who can persuade the ambulance to heal Ruby – and how?

Using the clues opposite and overleaf, fill in the grid on page 271 to work out who can do what. Then draw lines below from box to box to show your answer. Finally, circle the box containing the name of the person who successfully persuades the ambulance.

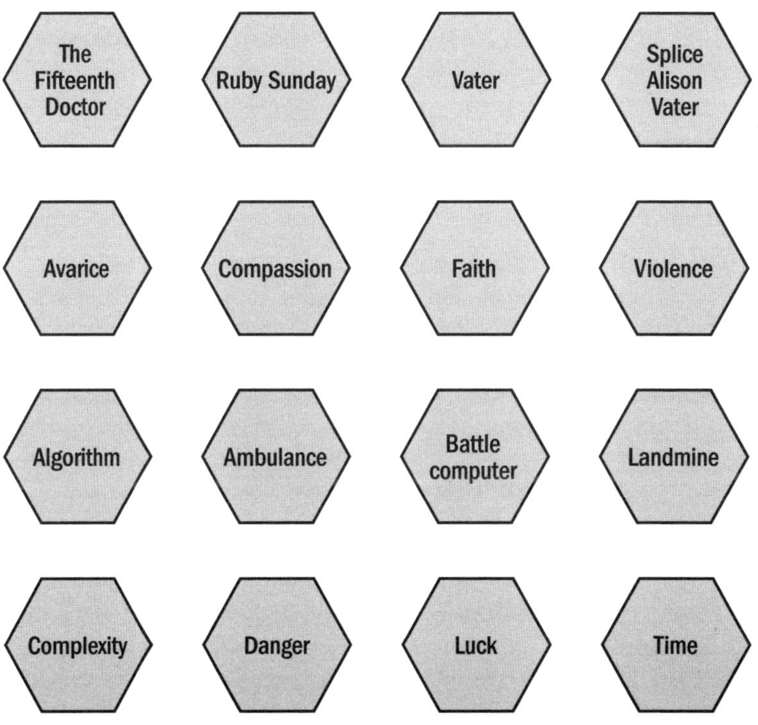

Boom

Who was involved · Reasons to help · How they help · What was the hurdle:

The Fifteenth Doctor: Charismatic and proud of his time traveller status, the Doctor sings to himself to remain calm when he finds himself getting nervous.
Ruby Sunday: Considerate and empathic, and quick to step in to help those in need. Consequently, Ruby often demonstrates little regard for her own safety.
Vater: A Villengard Corporation holographic AI of the deceased John Francis Vater, who was killed by an ambulance when temporarily blinded, to save money.
Splice Alison Vater: John's daughter. She is one of few children on Kastarion 3; her father had to bring her as he was her only relative.

Avarice: The Villengard algorithm that directs the actions of the Villengard Automated Ambulance Units serves profit above all.
Compassion: Most AIs are programmed with at least a basic sense of human morals and ethics, so some medical duty might be in there.
Faith: Ambulance Units are specifically programmed to heal the Anglican faithful, assuming it's cheaper than a new soldier.
Violence: While the Ambulance Units have no survival instinct, the algorithm understands that they're expensive to replace.

Algorithm: A precise set of mathematical instructions used by the Corporation to determine the optimal behaviour of its technology.
Ambulance: Robotic medical devices reminiscent of emergency vehicles, with a screen allowing the AI to interact with patients.
Battle computer: The central computer that monitors all activity on Kastarion 3. It issues behavioural directives to all military technology on Kastarion 3.
Landmine: A black and white disc that immolates its targets on a quantum level. If used on a Time Lord, the chain reaction would destroy half of the planet.

Complexity: The AI is extremely intelligent, but only in its own narrow field.
Danger: Threat can be a good motivator, but it can cause backlash.

Puzzle 57: Hard

Fill in the grid below as you work through the clues.

	The Fifteenth Doctor	Ruby	Vater	Splice Alison Vater	Avarice	Compassion	Faith	Violence	Algorithm	Ambulance	Battle computer	Landmine
Complexity												
Danger												
Luck												
Time												
Algorithm												
Ambulance												
Battle computer												
Landmine												
Avarice												
Compassion												
Faith												
Violence												

Luck: Sometimes, despite your best efforts, things just don't go the way you want.
Time: It can be quite difficult to persuade an AI, and time is of the essence.

73 Yards

Details:

The Grey King is not motivated by old hatreds.

?

Mad Jack initially roamed unhallowed lanes enchanting sacrifices.

?

The landlady was a bit of a witch.

?

Enid did not tell a story about the Brenin Llwyd.

?

If the closest story sounded like it could have been about a breakfast freezer, who was its teller?

Puzzle 58: Easy

While visiting Wales in 2024, the Doctor vanishes. Confused, Ruby attempts to enter the TARDIS, but it is locked, and the lights are off. She sees an old woman watching her from a distance, and asks if she's seen the Doctor. The woman doesn't answer, and as Ruby tries to get closer, the woman seems to glide back.

Heading towards a nearby village, Glyngatwg, Ruby meets a hiker who confirms that she too can see the woman. The hiker agrees to speak to the old woman, but when she does, she looks back at Ruby in terror, and runs screaming. In the pub, Y Pren Marw, each of the unsympathetic locals has an explanatory yarn to scare Ruby with. From the information given, can you say who is accidentally closest to the truth?

Using the clues opposite and overleaf, fill in the grid on page 275 to work out who told Ruby what, and why. Then draw lines below from box to box to show your answer. Finally, circle the box containing the name of the person who is closest to the truth.

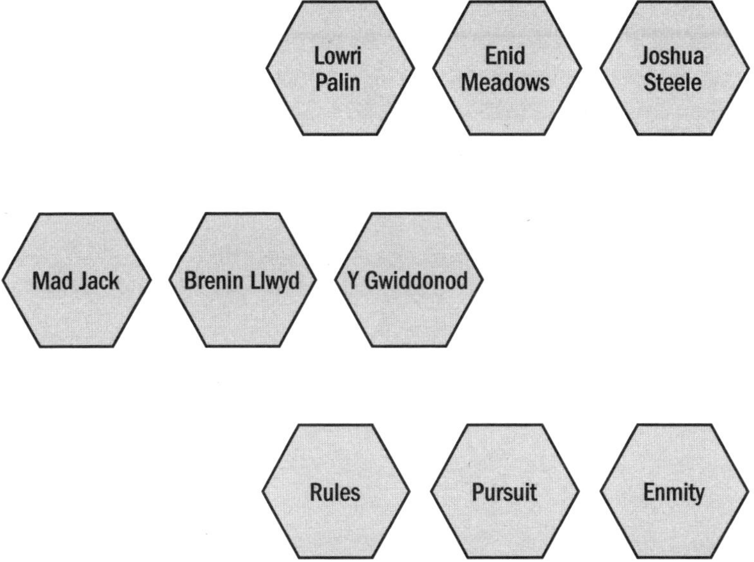

73 Yards

Who told the tale · What tale did they tell · Why they told the tale:

Lowri Palin: The dour landlady of the pub, the name of which means 'The Dead Wood', shamelessly overcharges Ruby for drinks.
Enid Meadows: An elderly woman with a mean streak. When Ruby arrives, she is writing notes about something at the bar.
Joshua Steele: The least unpleasant of the pub's drinkers, Josh is having a couple of pints before going back home to his wife.

Mad Jack: The ghost of an insane serial killer whose spirit was bound within a fairy circle, there to remain trapped through regular offerings.
Brenin Llwyd: The Grey King is a dark, silent, semi-corporeal wraith found across Wales, most often in the mountains, who preys on unwary travellers.
Y Gwiddonod: Traditional Welsh witches who can ride broomsticks, cause diseases, shape-shift, and cause all manner of supernatural evil.

Rules: Folk magic is bound around with chains of custom and behaviour. To break them is to declare yourself fair game, and offer yourself up as a victim.
Pursuit: Many of the forces of evil are hunters by nature, loving nothing more than to harry a lost traveller through strange and distant realms.
Enmity: The Wise Men, Y Dyn Hysbys, were learned folk-doctors who knew the future, and could drive off evil. Malign magic always sought to attack them.

Puzzle 58: Easy

Fill in the grid below as you work through the clues.

	Lowri	Enid	Joshua	Rules	Pursuit	Enmity
Mad Jack						
Brenin Llwyd						
Y Gwiddonod						
Rules						
Pursuit						
Enmity						

Dot and Bubble

Details:

Neither of the best friends would ever watch anything square.

?

Hoochy is following the herd, while Blake doesn't do anything that no one else is doing at the time.

?

Cooper is watching a feed with a little over six thousand other people.

?

Hoochy likes music.

?

The Doctor does not have the second-most number of viewers, while Gothic Paul does not have the least.

?

If the best channel has a unitary attendance, who is watching it?.

Puzzle 59: Medium

Finetime is a domed city on a dangerous planet covered in hostile forest. It was designed as a resort for the richest, whitest young citizens of Homeworld to party in. The residents of Finetime are aged seventeen to twenty-seven, and spend two hours a day on basic data processing. The rest of the time, they are glued to their social media channels, even when partying with other people in person. They are all functionally helpless without their Bubbles, augmented reality guidance provided by their Dots, personal AIs.

Spending all of your time in a reality generated by an artificial intelligence is perhaps not the safest way to live, so can you deduce what the best thing to watch this week is, and who is watching?

Using the clues opposite and overleaf, fill in the grid on page 279 to work out who is watching what. Then draw lines below from box to box to show your answer. Finally, circle the box containing the name of the best thing to watch.

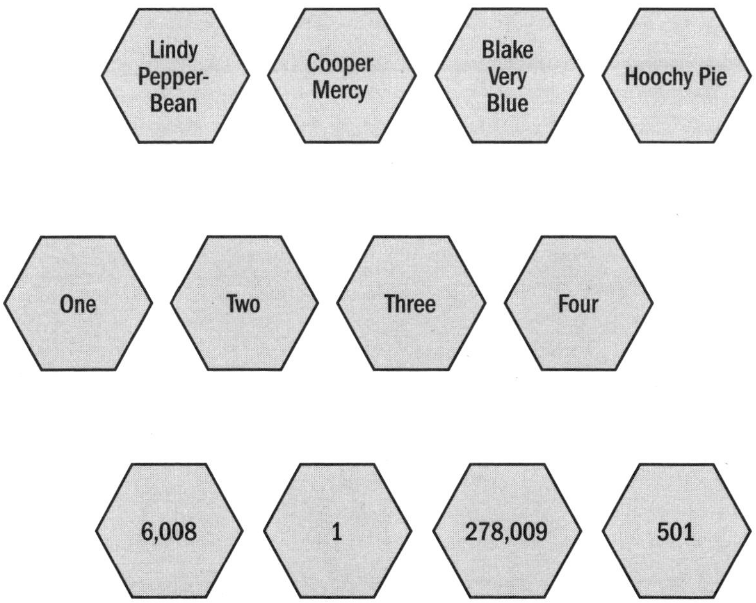

Dot and Bubble

Who is watching · What channel number · How many watching:

Lindy Pepper-Bean: Selfish, arrogant and cowardly, Lindy is too stupid to even walk without careful instructions from her Dot and Bubble.
Cooper Mercy: Nineteen-year-old Cooper is best friends with Lindy, who actually believes that she is kind, rather than horrible and self-obsessed.
Blake Very Blue: Blake has very blue eyes, and he is a close friend of Lindy's. He is a terrible person who doesn't understand how to hyphenate his own name.
Hoochy Pie: Unlike most of Finetime, Hoochy has ginger hair and freckles. She plays the trumpet, is ghastly, and believes that the TARDIS is powered by magic.

One: This is playing the most recent music video by Ricky September. Amazingly, Ricky spends most of his time with his Dot off, outside his Bubble, and likes reading.
Two: Weatherman Will and the weather forecast. Since Finetime has a powerful protective dome, the weather is rarely of interest to the residents.
Three: The Doctor's feed. When a time-travelling alien genius pops up to give you advice, it is generally wise to pay at least a degree of attention.
Four: Gothic, the personal feed of Gothic Paul. He's got a few things to say about demographics. His first name was originally 'Alexander', not 'Gothic'.

6,008: Good figures, but not as impressive as Dr Pee's channel that explains when and how to use the bathroom.
1: Oh, that's just sad. This is the sort of figure that makes you really have to wonder why you're bothering.
278,009: Now we're talking. Most of Finetime has a window open to this feed, and for an excellent reason too.
501: Pretty respectable for a lower-tier feed. It's not enough to really call yourself influential, but it's a solid start.

Puzzle 59: Medium

Fill in the grid below as you work through the clues.

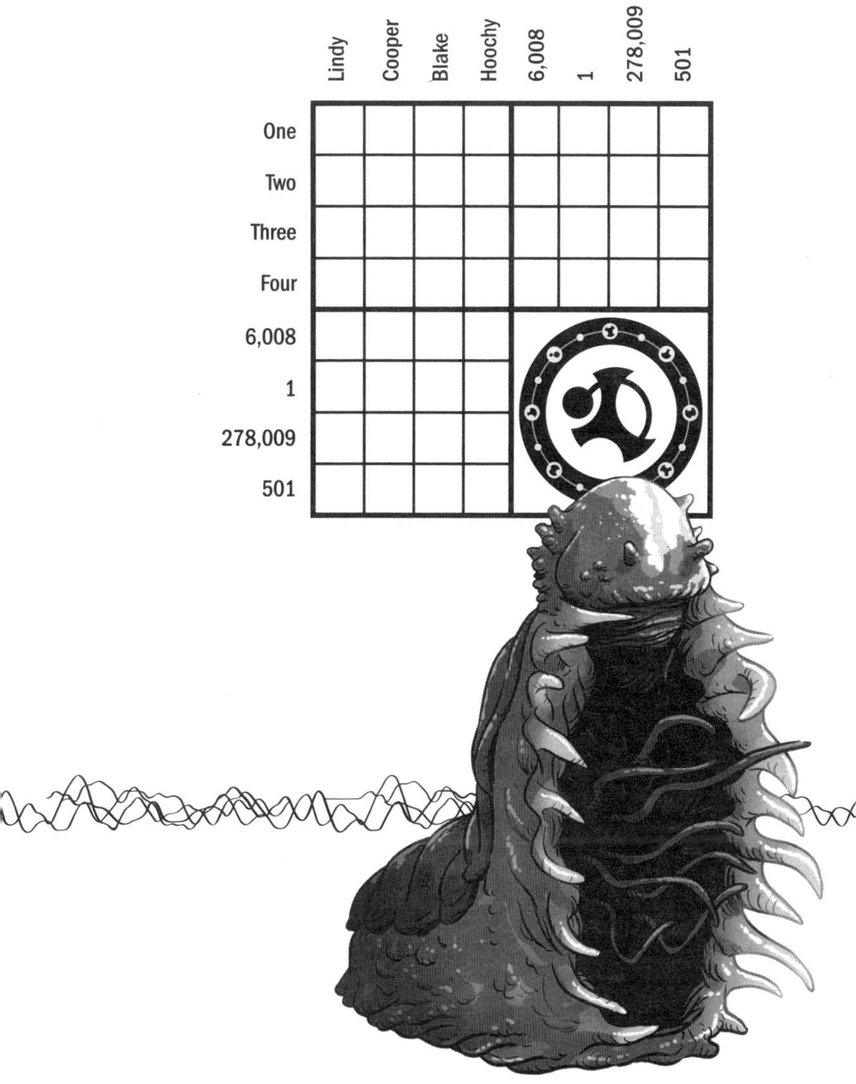

Rogue

Details:

Emily is very taken with the dress.

?

Miss Talbot expects something like attention from her onlookers.

?

Ruby believes that the right person could wear a cloth sack and still look the best.

?

The Doctor feels that footwear should facilitate dance.

?

The most expensive outfit feels the most prestigious to the gamer.

?

Lord Barton does look very good in charcoal.

?

It is perhaps unsurprising that the professor impresses the Doctor.

?

Lady Corrin is, when all is said and done, exceedingly rich.

?

If the best outfit could be characterised as possessing tenebrity, who correctly picked it?

Puzzle 60: Hard

It is 1813, and the Duchess of Pemberton is throwing a ball at her stately home in Bath. The Doctor and Ruby are in attendance. Indulging in the Regency high-life in full, both Ruby and the Doctor impress the Duchess with their dancing.

Of course, one question is on everyone's lips – who is the best-dressed person at the ball this evening? It leads to some spirited debate among the Doctor, Ruby and the guests they have connected with. Can you work out who is the best-dressed guest?

Using the clues opposite and overleaf, fill in the grid on page 283 to work out who wore what, and why. Then draw lines below from box to box to show your answer. Finally, circle the box containing the name of the person who was best dressed.

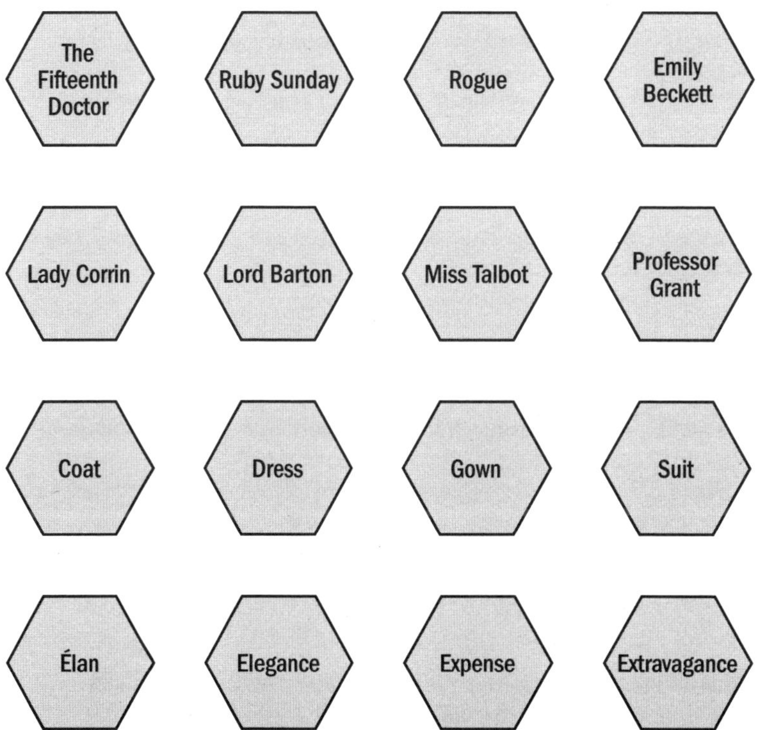

Rogue

Who is judging · Guest involved · Which outfit · What distinction:

The Fifteenth Doctor: The magnetic and surprisingly flirtatious Doctor possesses razor-sharp reasoning and a clean pair of heels.
Ruby Sunday: Bubbly and vivacious, Ruby finds a deep sense of joy in music and dancing, and among many styles has a fondness for the music of the Regency era.
Rogue: A humanoid alien bounty hunter, he picked his alias from the game *Dungeons & Dragons*. On Earth hunting a shape-shifter.
Emily Beckett: Of a lower status than many at the ball, Emily hopes to ascend in the social hierarchy by marrying someone of note.

Lady Corrin: She seeks female companionship at the ball, subtly, to avoid a scandalous scene. She has long red hair and green eyes.
Lord Barton: An aristocratic dilettante, known as a rakish and immoral libertine, he's attending to pursue women. He has dark brown hair and brown eyes.
Miss Talbot: One of the more delightful guests at the ball, Miss Talbot is largely present to dance and to gossip. She has blonde hair and blue eyes.
Professor Grant: A dapper man of science, the professor is primarily at the ball this evening because he was too polite to say no. Long silver-grey hair and blue eyes.

Coat: A dark grey felted wool frock coat with matching trousers, a ruffled white shirt, a crimson waistcoat and dress shoes.
Dress: Cream-coloured, with gold embroidery, matching gloves, and a necklace bearing several cameo pendants. Flat and minimalist footwear.
Gown: Forest green velvet, accented with Celtic-inspired designs of silver and gold. Impractically heeled shoes.
Suit: A suit of deepest black, with black waistcoat, shirt, shoes, socks and cloak. Broken up by a silver amulet with a small ruby, and a matching signet ring.

Élan: True style comes from within. These outfits aren't being judged as worn by shop-window display Autons, after all.

Puzzle 60: Hard

Fill in the grid below as you work through the clues.

Elegance: This outfit was created by the very finest tailors, with an absolutely perfect fit and superlative materials. A masterwork.
Expense: A powerful statement of wealth, this outfit is made from the most expensive materials available.
Extravagance: The most effective garments are those that most confidently demand the eye. This outfit is easily the most striking.

The Legend of Ruby Sunday/Empire of Death

Details:

Of the five possible projects, one is Rose's suspicion, one has a logo of an eye, one is VoIP, one comes in a deep blue capsule and one uses the slogan, 'Let us do it for you'.

?

The jumbled **TELL PEARLED PUP** logo represents the connections between all people.

?

The burnishd chrome-wrapped tech does not want to take actions for you, and the barrelled ogre contains the logo that is either deep blue or burnished chrome.

?

Kate is concerned about Slogan One, but does not think the bird logo is relevant, while Mel thinks the dog logo is key, but is not bothered by Slogan Three.

?

The tri-lobed eye is on a fluorescent red background, but its slogan does not claim knowledge and the medical implant uses a bird logo.

?

Ominously, the post-death technology says it'll make contact in the near future.

Puzzle 61: Extreme

Arriving on Earth in 2024, the Doctor and Ruby discover that the woman they've been encountering throughout time is now leading a global IT giant called Triad Technology. She is its deeply mysterious founder, Susan Triad.

Triad is about to speak at the UN and release a secret, super-advanced piece of technology, codenamed Iris, to everyone, worldwide, for free. UNIT is understandably concerned. From the information given, can you say what new tech Triad is about to unleash, how it is being marketed, what it actually does and who puts the pieces together?

Using the clues opposite, below and on pages 288–289, fill in the grid on pages 290–291 to work out the solution. Then draw lines from box to box overleaf to show your answer. Finally, circle the box containing the name of the person who was correct.

The soothing green package presents a product that is always monitoring what you say, while the burnished chrome package does not have a logo of either a rainbow or a bird, and Ultra-Search is represented by deep blue colours.

?

Iris is not held in an Acid Yellow box, and the Doctor is not concerned by the eye logo.

?

Mj xli jsyvxl wpsker mw xli sri xs fi ywih mr xli Xvmeh tvshygx peyrgl, als mhirxmjmih mx?

The Legend of Ruby Sunday/Empire of Death

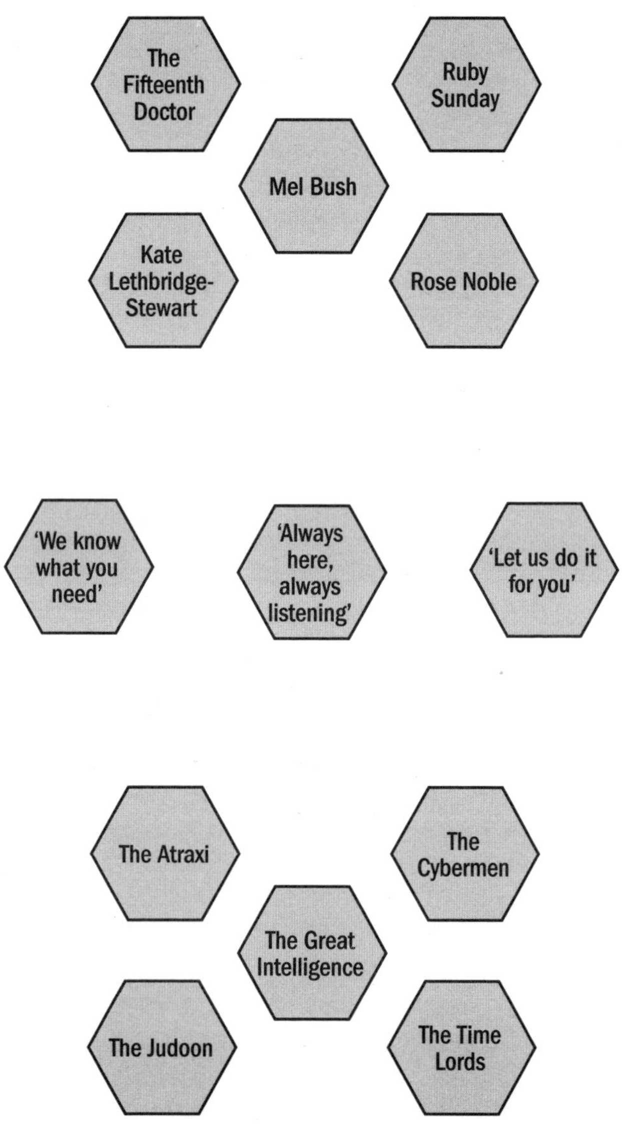

Puzzle 61: Extreme

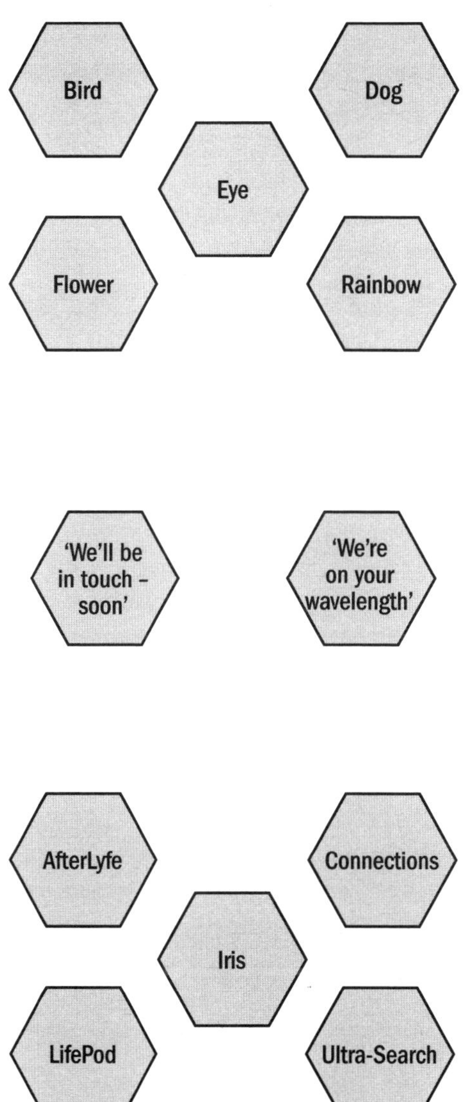

The Legend of Ruby Sunday/Empire of Death

Who was involved · Logo list · Slogans involved · Main colour · Which technology:

The Fifteenth Doctor: The Doctor takes great pride in the TARDIS and his role as a time traveller, and disapproves of UNIT's rudimentary Time Window.
Ruby Sunday: Ruby may be sweet-natured, but she isn't afraid of confronting people who need to be told off, particularly to defend a friend.
Mel Bush: Working undercover for UNIT as a consultant in Susan Triad's PR team. Surprised that Susan seems to be genuinely nice.
Kate Lethbridge-Stewart: Sharp-witted and resourceful, Kate is doing an excellent job leading UNIT, and was already investigating Susan Triad.
Rose Noble: Rose is employed at UNIT in an unspecified capacity. As someone with familiarity with the Doctor, Kate is keeping her on hand.

Bird: Silhouette of a bird with a single amethyst eye on the side of its head.
Dog: A stylised golden retriever of an unnatural hue.
Eye: A friendly looking eyeball with a three-lobed iris.
Flower: Line art of a flower with three purple petals sitting above a green stem.
Rainbow: A glittering rainbow braided into a swirly 'plus' sign.

Slogan One: 'We know what you need'.
Slogan Two: 'Always here, always listening'.
Slogan Three: 'Let us do it for you'.
Slogan Four: 'We'll be in touch – soon'.
Slogan Five: 'We're on your wavelength'.

Puzzle 61: Extreme

Soothing Green: This box is carefully designed to be relaxing and natural-feeling.
Burnished Chrome: A high-tech colour dominates this exciting package.
Fluorescent Red: Streaks of vibrant colour churn on an ash background to build hype.
Deep Blue: This capsule-shaped pack reminds the customer of oceans.
Acid Yellow: Sharply attention-grabbing packaging for an attention-grabbing product.

AfterLyfe: Records everything you do on- and off-line so when you die, your loved ones can interact with an AI mimicking your personality, tastes and feelings.
Connections: Instant Voice over IP telephony to anyone in the world by name, for free, at any time. Now you will always be connected to everyone.
Iris: A new generation of virtual assistant capable of true creative thinking. She will organise everything for you, from the cradle to the grave.
LifePod: A medical device that constantly monitors dozens of biometric data points, tracking your health needs and mortality factors.
Ultra-Search: This device can find almost anything – a face from CCTV footage, the page you need on the internet, your keys, where you are hiding, etc.

The Legend of Ruby Sunday/Empire of Death

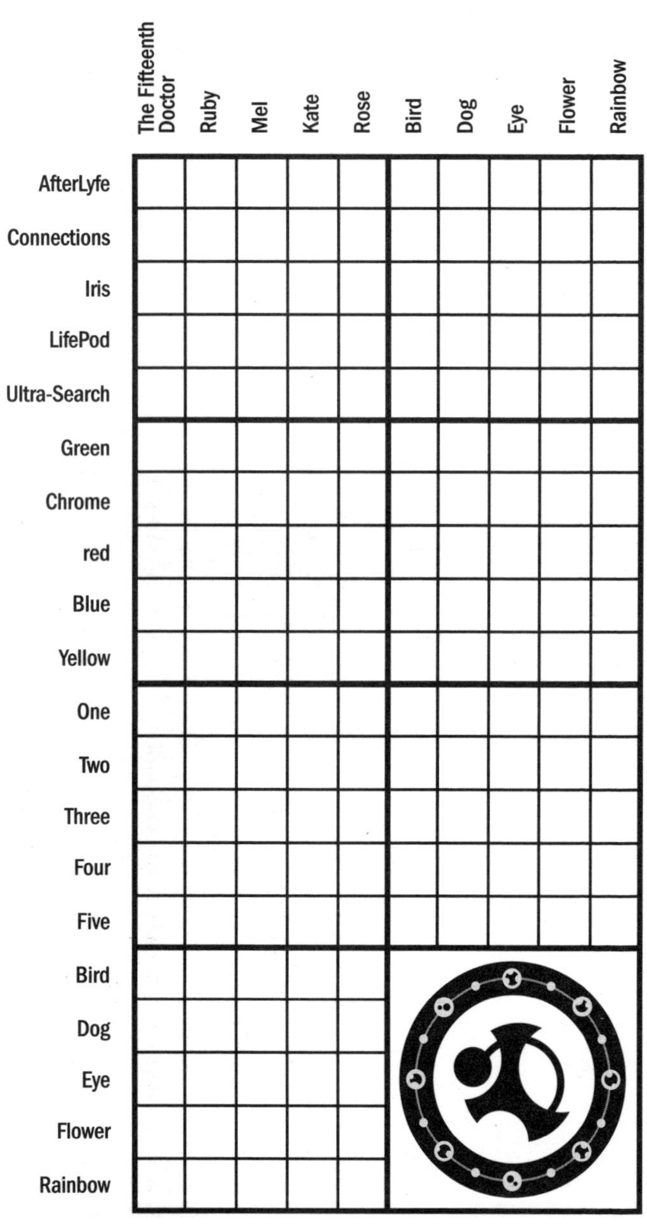

	The Fifteenth Doctor	Ruby	Mel	Kate	Rose	Bird	Dog	Eye	Flower	Rainbow
AfterLyfe										
Connections										
Iris										
LifePod										
Ultra-Search										
Green										
Chrome										
red										
Blue										
Yellow										
One										
Two										
Three										
Four										
Five										
Bird										
Dog										
Eye										
Flower										
Rainbow										

Puzzle 61: Extreme

Fill in the grid below as you work through the clues.

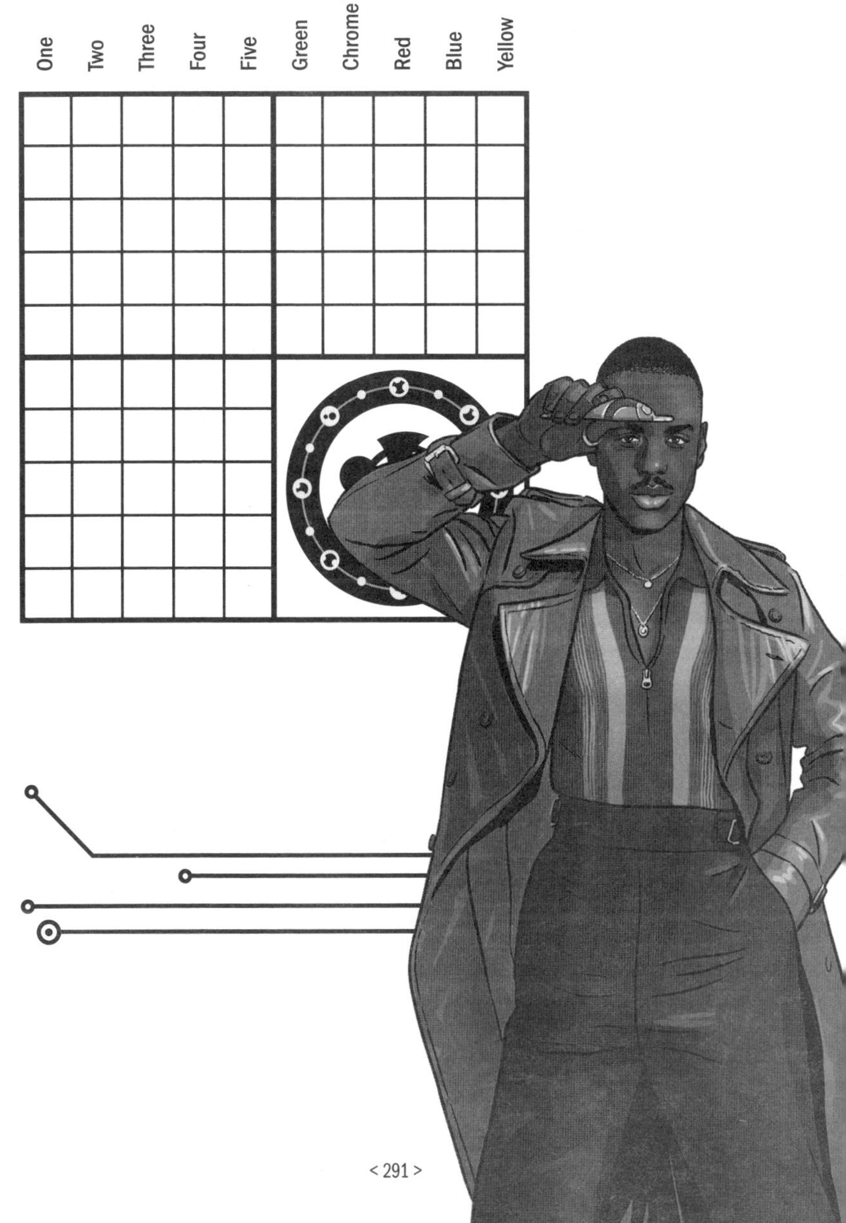

Solutions

Puzzle 1: The Daleks

Answer: **Susan**

Ian	Neutron bomb	Dalek City
Susan	Anti-radiation drugs	Thal camp
Barbara	Mercury	Petrified jungle

Puzzle 2: The Myth-Makers

Answer: **The First Doctor**

Katarina	Dardanian Gate	Subterfuge
Steven	Lower City	Boldness
The First Doctor	Palace of King Priam	Opportunism
Vicki	Temple of Athena	Stealth

Puzzle 3: The War Machines

Answer: **Noon tomorrow**

The First Doctor	Console Room	Deduction	Dawn tomorrow
Polly	Royal Scientific Club	Observation	Noon tomorrow
Dodo	Inferno nightclub	Educated guesswork	Sunset tonight
Ben	Professor's Offices	Elimination	Midnight tonight

Puzzle 4: The Abominable Snowmen

Answer: **Locus**

The Second Doctor	Abbot's chambers	Holy Ghanta
Jamie	Yeti cave	Control sphere
Victoria	High Lama's throne	Locus

Puzzle 5: The Invasion

Answer: **The Moon**

The Second Doctor	Big Ben	Paralysis
Jamie	The sewers	Amnesia
Zoe	The Moon	Hypnosis
Alistair	The TARDIS	Blindness

Clue: When the letters in the note are joined together, the following sentence can be made: **THEY WILL MAKE EVERYONE BLIND ACK** [NOWLEDGE].

Puzzle 6: The War Games

Answer: **Jamie**

Jamie	The barracks	Lockpick	Fire
Jennifer	The gate	Crowbar	Sabotage
Jeremy	The mess	Axe	Incoming attack
Zoe	The ward	Pistol	Medical emergency

Puzzle 7: Spearhead from Space

Answer: **Alistair**

Liz Shaw	Bestsellers	Kipper tie
Alistair	Central display	Red hat
The Third Doctor	New This Month	Flared jeans

Puzzle 8: The Dæmons

Answer: **Jo**

The Third Doctor	The Cloven Hoof	Science
John	The church graveyard	Witchcraft
Jo	The cavern	Sacrifice
Mike	The Devil's Hump	Explosives

Puzzle 9: The Time Warrior

Answer: **Alistair**

The Third Doctor	Eccentric	Desperation	Miniaturised prison
Alistair	Alien	Curiosity	Parallel dimension
Sarah Jane	Criminal	Profit	Deep space
Joseph	Spy	Boredom	Hideout

Puzzle 10: Planet of the Spiders

Answer: **Sarah Jane**

Alistair	Great Intelligence	TARDIS	Blackmail	Destroy UNIT
Mike	Ice Warriors	Buck. Palace	Replacement	Blow up Earth
Sarah Jane	Eight Legs	Off-world	Mind control	Rule Universe
Third Doctor	Daleks	Third century	Bribery	Enslave humanity
John	Cybermen	Mariana Tr.	Spite	Eliminate the Doctor

Solutions

Puzzle 11: Genesis of the Daleks

Answer: **Harry**

The Doctor	Proving ground	Eyestalk
Sarah Jane	Lab	Chassis
Harry	Davros's office	Gunstick

Puzzle 12: The Robots of Death

Answer: **Poul**

The Doctor	Borg	Mess
Leela	Uvanov	Workshop
Poul	Dask	Control deck
D84	Zilda	Storage bay

Puzzle 13: Shada

Answer: **Chris Parsons**

The Doctor	*Origins...*	Brown	The fireplace
Chris Parsons	*The Worshipful...*	Red	The desk
Romana	*The History...*	Burgundy	East shelf
K9	*The Hitchhiker's...*	Leather	West shelf

Puzzle 14: Earthshock

Answer: **Nyssa**

Tegan	Tool closet	Sonic screwdriver
Nyssa	Storage Room 4	Laser rifle
Adric	Control console	Toolkit

Puzzle 15: Terminus

Answer: **The Doctor**

The Doctor	Heart	Time travel
Nyssa	Resource	Transmission
Tegan	Crater	Space travel
Turlough	Nexus	Confinement

Clue: The cryptic note, when read backwards, spells out '**I leap through time itself**'.

Puzzle 16: Planet of Fire

Answer: **Turlough**

Turlough	Procurement	Master's TARDIS	T.C.E.
The Doctor	Catastrophe	Doctor's TARDIS	Telepathic booster
Peri	Random chance	Great Hall	Sonic umbrella
Kamelion	Contacts	Cave of Fire	Laser screwdriver

Puzzle 17: The Five Doctors

Answer: **The Fifth Doctor**

Fifth Doctor	Brigadier	The Master	Ring	Become immortal
First Doctor	Tegan	Dalek	Black Scrolls	Restart Game
Second Doctor	Susan	Warrior Robot	Coronet	Revive Rassilon
Third Doctor	Sarah Jane	Cyberman	Harp	Purge the Council
Fourth Doctor	Turlough	Yeti	Sash	Control the Universe

Puzzle 18: The Twin Dilemma

Answer: **Peri**

The Doctor	Transmat	Azmael
Peri	Tractor beam	Mestor
Hugo	Revitalising Modulator	The twins

Puzzle 19: The Two Doctors

Answer: **The Second Doctor**

Second Doctor	Deception	Sonic screwdriver
Sixth Doctor	Sleight of hand	Stattenheim remote control
Jamie	Intimidation	Surveillance system
Peri	Persuasion	Kartz-Reimer module

Puzzle 20: The Mysterious Planet

Answer: **Glitz**

Glitz	Marble Arch	Terminal M	Logic
The Doctor	Oxford Circus	Maintenance Corridor 159	Instinct
Peri	Bond Street	Service Area 28	Accessibility
Dibber	Lancaster Gate	Tunnel B	Safety

Solutions

Puzzle 21: Delta and the Bannermen

Answer: **Goronwy**

Goronwy	The TARDIS	Sonic cone
The Doctor	Beehive	Sonic modulator
Mel Bush	Motorbike	Sonic mine

Puzzle 22: Remembrance of the Daleks

Answer: **Cellar**

Ace	Cellar	Blinking lights
The Doctor	Class C4	Burn marks
Gilmore	Headmaster's office	Unusual smell
Mike	Class C3	Humming

Puzzle 23: Battlefield

Answer: **Lake Vortigern**

The Doctor	Spaceship	Lake Vortigern	Ancelyn
Ace	Scabbard	Carbury Quarry	Arthur
Shou Yuing	Another dimension	Dig site	Morgaine
The Brigadier	Sarcophagus	Gore Crow Hotel	Mordred

Puzzle 24: Doctor Who: The Movie

Answer: **Suspect Two**

Suspect One	Displacement	The TARDIS
Suspect Two	Motion	Ambulance
Suspect Three	Truancy	ITAR

Puzzle 25: The Eight Doctors

Answer: **Tegan**

Tegan	The Time Lords	Caution
The Fifth Doctor	The Master	Vengeance
The Eighth Doctor	Omega	Greed
Turlough	Davros	Malice

Clue: **YOUR ARCANE TIP** is an anagram of **PRECAUTIONARY**.

Puzzle 26: Placebo Effect

Answer: **22nd Century**

Sam	Twenty-second century	Arcturus	Codename 'Crocus'
The Doctor	Seventy-eighth century	Earth	Codename 'Rose'
Stacy	Twenty-sixth century	Betelguse V	Codename 'Carnation'
Ssard	Fifty-first century	Alpha Centauri	Codename 'Tulip'

Puzzle 27: The End of the World

Answer: **Jabe**

Jabe	Maintenance Duct J	Motivation
The Face of Boe	Manchester Suite	Location
The Moxx	Steward's office	Knowledge

Puzzle 28: The Long Game

Answer: **The Doctor**

The Doctor	Superphone	Keylogger
Rose	Type II port	Trojan
Adam	Sonic screwdriver	Worm
Cathica	Credit stick	Virus

Puzzle 29: The Unquiet Dead

Answer: **Rose**

Rose	Invasion	The Rift	Convenience
The Doctor	Sanctuary	Meteorite	Efficiency
Gwyneth	Message	Disrespect	Impact
Dickens	Vengeance	A person	Haste

Puzzle 30: Rose

Answer: **Article 374**

Article 57	Purple	Dismissed	Terse	Five species
Article 374	Blue	Accepted	Dull	Four species
Article 6	Yellow	Acclaimed	Tangled	Three species
Article 1327	Red	Debated	Bureaucratic	Two species
Article 829	Green	Shunned	Wordy	Six species

Solutions

Puzzle 31: The Christmas Invasion

Answer: **Teapot**

Leaves	Teapot	Warm cup
Bags	Cup	Room temperature cup
Pyramids	Kettle	Cold cup

Puzzle 32: Rise of the Cybermen

Answer: **Rose**

The Doctor	Jackie	Décor
Mrs Moore	Ricky	Whisper
Mickey	Rita-Anne	Email
Rose	Pete	Tattoo

Puzzle 33: The Shakespeare Code

Answer: **Burbage**

Burbage	The Globe	Tetrameter	Akkadian
The Doctor	Borough Market	Hexameter	Sumerian
Martha	Southwark Church	Pentameter	Ancient Greek
Shakespeare	Bedlam	Hendecasyllabic	Old High German

Puzzle 34: Blink

Answer: **Living room**

1969	Useful	Scratches	Living room	Fifth
1908	Obvious	Charcoal	Hall	Third
1920	Worrying	Chalk	Dining room	Fourth
1989	Scary	Spray paint	Stairwell	First
2001	Great	Ballpoint pen	Porch	Second

Puzzle 35: Planet of the Ood

Answer: **Donna**

Donna	Pylons	Ood Sigma
The Doctor	Gas canisters	Lambda Three
Dr Ryder	Warehouse Fifteen	Zeta Seven

Puzzle 36: Cold Blood

Answer: **The Doctor**

The Doctor	Machinery	Laboratory
Rory	Aim	Village green
Amy	Power supply	TARDIS
Nasreen	Software	Mine entry

Puzzle 37: A Good Man Goes to War

Answer: **Strax**

Vastra	3:38	Ood Sigma	Helped grow
Strax	3:42	Captain Jack	Saved after stranded
Henry	3:44	Liz Ten	Fought the Lux
Dorium	3:40	Cyber-soldiers	Returning the favour

Puzzle 38: The Snowmen

Answer: **Vastra**

Vastra	TARDIS	Pond
Strax	Darkover House	Who
Clara	The coach	Run

Puzzle 39: Hide

Answer: **Emma**

Emma	Metebelis crystal	Portal
The Doctor	The Eye of Harmony	Transmat
Clara	Vortex manipulator	Block Transfer
Alec	TARDIS	Time Vortex

Puzzle 40: The Impossible Astronaut

Answer: **17:02 on 22 April 2011**

The Doctor	One	07:00, red/lilac	Cafe
River	Two	16:30, black/green	Bus stop
Amy and Rory	Three	16:30, black/blue	Meeting point
Canton	Four	17:00, blue/white	Lake

Solutions

Puzzle 41: Robot of Sherwood

Answer: **The Doctor**

The Doctor	Western wing	AI core
Clara	Northern wing	Carved tablet
Robin, Earl of Loxley	Eastern wing	Vellum scroll

Puzzle 42: Time Heist

Answer: **Psi**

Psi	ORG 339	Blood control matrix
The Doctor	HEX 106	Neophyte circuit
Clara	TECH 251	Gene suppressant
Saibra	CHEM 078	Atomic shredder

Puzzle 43: Heaven Sent

Answer: **Interrogation chamber**

Stars	Time	Interrogation chamber	Reinforcement
Sand	Gravity	Science lab	Speed
Clothes	Age	Conundrum	Grasp
Teleporter	Scale	Prison cell	Stealth

Puzzle 44: The Pilot

Answer: **Service yard**

Service yard	Sound	Rotation
Medical centre	Movement	Shifting
Bike sheds	Source	Delay

Puzzle 45: Extremis

Answer: **Bill**

Bill	The Haereticum	Candle
The Doctor	The Goetic Vault	Tile
Angelo	The Maleficarum	Plaque
Nardole	The Sepulchre Venefica	Whistle

Puzzle 46: The Ghost Monument

Answer: **Graham**

Graham	Acetylene fields	Althusian cigar	Remnants
The Doctor	Ruins	Laser rifle	Epzo
Yaz	Underground	Sonic screwdriver	SniperBots
Ryan	Swamps	EMP	Angstrom

Puzzle 47: Kerblam!

Answer: **Ryan**

Ryan	Psychic paper	Console room
Graham	Translation matrix	Sonic screwdriver
Yaz	Wardrobe dimension	Intelligent gloves

Puzzle 48: Praxeus

Answer: **BETA**

Bird	Cracks	BETA
Victim	Coma	DELTA
Survivor	Gunk	ALPHA
Signal	Fading	GAMMA

Puzzle 49: The Timeless Children

Answer: **The Fugitive Doctor**

The Fugitive Doctor	Screwdriver	The Thirteenth Doctor	The Matrix
Graham	Cyber-suit	Cybercarrier	Engine room
Ryan	Death particle	Ashad	Bridge
Yaz	T.C.E.	The Spy Master	Matrix chamber

Puzzle 50: Once, Upon Time

Answer: **Yaz**

Vinder	Approaches	Passenger form	Survival	Visionary
Dan	Tunnels	Gallifreyan rune	Abatement	The Lupari
Bel	Platform	Lupari ship	Restoration	The Mouri
Yaz	Inner chamber	Laser pistol	Reunion	Absent friend
The Doctor	Chokepoint	Temporal medicine	Warding	Priest Triangle

Puzzle 51: The Day of the Doctor

Answer: **The Eleventh Doctor**

The War Doctor	Queen Elizabeth I	Sonic screwdriver
The Eleventh Doctor	Clara	Nail
The Tenth Doctor	Zygons	Time

Clue: '**Mel's sane**' is an anagram of '**Nameless**' and **Clara has three letters within A–C.**

Solutions

Puzzle 52: The Star Beast

Answer: **Rose**

Rose	Escape	Sun Emitter
The Doctor	Freedom	Cyberline
Donna	Conquest	Toy pile
Shirley	Survival	Dagger Drive

Clues: **'Cyberline'** contains the name **'Berlin'** and **'LOGICAL EPIC ACT'** is an anagram of **'GALACTIC POLICE'**.

Puzzle 53: The Giggle

Answer: **Katherine**

Katherine	Small satellites	Jigsaw	Egotism
The Doctor	LCD televisions	Jack-in-the-box	Paranoia
Donna	Mobile networks	Gold tooth	Apathy
Mel	WiFi	Voodoo dolls	Solipsism

Clue: **'B TBUFMMJUF MBVODI' = 'A SATELLITE LAUNCH'** with each letter replaced with the next in the alphabet.

Puzzle 54: The Church on Ruby Road

Answer: **11:58pm**

11pm	58	Abandonment
2pm	00	Birth
4pm	13	Flight
9pm	42	Plan

Puzzle 55: Space Babies

Answer: **The Doctor**

The Doctor	17 Hz	Fear
Jocelyn	8192 Hz	Disorientation
Ruby	32 Hz	Awe

Clues: **'R.I.P., Users'** is an anagram of **'Surprise'**, and **1+7=8,** which is 2 cubed.

Puzzle 56: The Devil's Chord

Answer: **Paul**

Paul	Tritone	Henry
The Doctor	Ditone	Hank
Ruby	Meantone	Harold
John	Semitone	Huw

Clue: **'pitied seamen'** is an anagram of **'semidiapente'**.

Puzzle 57: Boom

Answer: **Vater**

Vater	Battle computer	Faith	Complexity
The Doctor	Landmine	Compassion	Danger
Ruby	Algorithm	Avarice	Time
Splice	Ambulance	Violence	Luck

Clue: The text reads **'THE BATTLE COMPUTER NEEDS TO UNDERSTAND THAT THE KASTARIONS DO NOT EXIST'** backwards, with the word spacing changed.

Puzzle 58: 73 Yards

Answer: **Enid**

Enid	Mad Jack	Rules
Lowri	Y Gwiddonod	Enmity
Josh	Brenin Llwyd	Pursuit

Clue: Serial sounds like cereal, or a breakfast; killer sounds like chiller, or a freezer.

Puzzle 59: Dot and Bubble

Answer: **Lindy**

Lindy	1	Three
Cooper	6,008	Two
Blake	501	Four
Hoochy	278,009	One

Puzzle 60: Rogue

Answer: **The Doctor**

The Doctor	Suit	Prof. Grant	Elegance
Ruby	Coat	Lord Barton	Élan
Rogue	Gown	Lady Corrin	Expense
Emily	Dress	Miss Talbot	Extravagance

Clue: **Tenebrity** is the quality of being dark.

Solutions

Puzzle 61: The Legend of Ruby Sunday/Empire of Death

Answer: **Ruby**

Ruby	Eye	AfterLyfe	Flourescent red	Four
The Doctor	Bird	LifePod	Acid yellow	Three
Mel	Dog	Ultra-Search	Deep blue	Five
Kate	Flower	Connections	Burnished chrome	One
Rose	Rainbow	Iris	Soothing green	Two

Clues: **'TELL PEARLED PUP'** is an anagram of **'PURPLE PETALLED'** and **'Mj xli jsyvxl wpsker mw xli sri xs fi ywih mr xli Xvmeh tvshygx peyrgl, als mhirxmjmih mx?'** = 'If the fourth slogan is the one to be used in the Triad product launch, who identified it?', with each letter shifted four places forwards alphabetically.